THE SACRIFICED

Liminal Books

The Sacrificed is a work of fiction. Names, characters, places, and incidents are the product of the author's imagination or are used fictitiously. Any resemblance to actual events, locales, or persons, living or dead, is coincidental.

Liminal Books is an imprint of Between the Lines Publishing. The Liminal Books name and logo are trademarks of Between the Lines Publishing.

Cover design by Cherie Fox

Between the Lines Publishing
1769 Lexington Ave N, Ste 286
Roseville MN 55113
btwnthelines.com

First Published: January 2024

ISBN: (Paperback) 978-1-958901-72-4

ISBN: (Ebook) 978-1-958901-73-1

THE SACRIFICED

Rudolf Kerkhoven

Countdown

Ten

Nine

Eight

Seven

Six

Five

Four

Three

Two

One

Zero

Ten

Of course, Pri wondered why she chose this. Why she didn't give up, turn back, or let go long before this moment. Aside from Jaz, every person Pri knew—real or A.I.—attempted to dissuade her from fleeing the North Shore. From fleeing Earth. She visualized a steady procession of faces and voices all telling her to stay. Seph. Nayha. Dad. Even Carol. *"Why are you doing this?"* And Pri had many answers for this question. Some rambling, like the lectures of Mustafa Karamehmet. Some direct, a pointed comment on the irrevocable consequences of a century of global heating. But she saved the most concise answer for herself, not so much a secret but instead a fact of her character that she guarded with both conceit and contrition: Pri Gosal does not give up.

She sat against a wall of rock and clay, the room a narrow rectangle. If she stood tall, her head would hit the ceiling of the exposed wooden joists and floorboards above her. If she stretched out her legs, her toes could reach the other side. Everything was obscured by a faultless darkness aside from a dull point of light across the space, far too meagre to illuminate anything. Her bare feet pressed against the dirt floor, moist from a trickling stream that dribbled down the opposite wall. Hasan's words were still clear in her memory, his voice assured, steady, as he blinded her with a flashlight mere inches from her face. If she yelled, he would cut her throat. If she tried to run, he would cut her throat. She had called for Jaz with a whisper and the next moment the cool pinch of a metal blade pressed against her neck. At the time there was no deliberating the possibility that this might have been a butter knife. A piece of scrap metal. At the time, she did what he said. He tied a blindfold. He pushed her, told her to walk, reminded her to stay silent while keeping a tight grip around her arm. Barefoot without her coat or belongings, she remembered climbing slick steps, the frigid rain sinking into her hair and shoulders as if she'd been forced into a cold shower. She did not want to whimper. She could not let Hasan view her as meek. She recalled a perverse emotional numbness—her heart raced, her hands quivered, but still she walked, she breathed, listening for other footsteps. *This is happening,* she thought to herself, not daring to say a word out loud. *This is happening.* It felt like they walked for more than twenty minutes through the Jungle, her toes stubbing uneven rocks in the lanes, her heels pressing onto plastic wrappers, cables. Wafts of sewage drifted through the exhaust of generators. Hasan didn't speak and his grip never relented. But somehow it was easy to remain calm, or at least remain quiet. He then told her to take a step and thrust her through a doorway. She felt plywood beneath her feet, followed by a rug or carpet. He let go of her arm and warned that she was going to fall. Her wrist struck the opening as she tumbled. He then closed the door above her and locked it shut. She struggled to untie the blindfold—the knots multiple, tight, and wet. And when she removed it, she was here, in the dark, in the mud, alone.

Since then, there had been no contact with anyone. There were footsteps above, muffled voices of men, but the trapdoor remained sealed. All she had were the clothes on her body, still wet from her forced march through the rain, and a single blanket that she wrapped around her shoulders and thighs, the material bristled, frayed edges sodden and heavy. She assumed that someone would come down to speak with her, demand a ransom, something. Hasan kidnapped Pri in the middle of the night but now appeared content to let her remain indefinitely. Hasan must have taken her belongings. Her bottle of Stasi was still in her bag in an unmarked container. As soon as she had a chance, she would plead for her backpack, or at least the medication. He could not discover that she was pregnant. That seemed obvious. Instead, she would say that she will have seizures without her pills. Of what use is a hostage should she be unconscious, she could argue.

Pri ran her fingers along the underside of the floorboards, sheets of mismatched plywood. She felt the grain of the planks, some with splinters like baby hairs against her skin, others flush, perhaps coated in paint. The corner of one floorboard was soft and rotten. She could scrape away fibers with her fingernails. Four joists spanned the length of the ceiling, each a different thickness. Even when hunched over, she had to mind these beams to avoid scraping her forehead. She felt the square seam of the trap door, the tips of nails clustered in pairs to secure hinges on the other side. She brushed her fingers along the perimeter of the ceiling, where floorboards rested atop dirt, dry to the touch except for a section through which rainwater dribbled, the surrounding wall moist. A hole no wider than her index finger let through a muted circle of daylight. She could pry apart the dirt around it, pebbles clattering to the ground, water running down her arm.

Someone entered the structure above, footsteps thumping along the floorboards. At least two people were walking, both with shuffling steps, ambling, perhaps pacing. Pri tried to follow their positions, her hands up against the ceiling, feeling it sink into her fingertips. One set then strode towards the trap door and Pri scuttled back against one corner, expecting it to open, and pulled the blanket up around her folded knees. She couldn't hear any voices.

The footsteps ceased. She had no reason to remain in the corner, but she had no reason to stand up. She kept the blanket around her, watched the dot of light across the room, and then closed her eyes.

This was going to change everything. The Benefactor, Mustafa Karamehmet, had died. There had been multiple reports of his passing over the last fifty years—declarations that began long before Pri was born—but these rumors were inevitably discounted. Within hours, Mustafa would appear in a recording, eyes squinting, cheekbones sharp, moustache a bristling crystalline white, assuring the masses that he was alive, dismissing accusations that this was a special effect, some form of computer-generated trickery. He would emerge on stage before thousands of followers at his retreats in Brazil, in Mexico, in India, each appearance an act of defiance by an eighty-year-old, a ninety-year-old, a one-hundred-year-old man. He would reach out, let the audience clasp his hands, skin translucent and yet still possessing a wiry grip. Mustafa Karamehmet was alive, people would accept.

He assured the world, both to those who applauded him and those who abhorred him, that he would not let himself pass before witnessing the launch of the Tevat. This man refused to let any ailment, any condition, any supposed biological fact compel him to concede before it was *his* time to do so. He would be on board with his ardent followers. It was as simple as that. Even if he died seconds after departure, his heart would not cease laboring until he had fled the clutches of Earth's gravity. And so, like times before, Pri had waited for an update. For his appearance. But then it had been days. An eternity.

There were images of his motionless body, eyes closed, arms folded atop a thin white cloth as if praying. His demise was confirmed by members of the Karamehmet family—brothers, sisters, cousins, nephews, nieces—dozens of people who shared his name and his blood and yet were shunned by the man for more than half a century, all of whom wanted nothing to do with him. Until now. Until he died, as if to taunt him. As if to mock him. Here was a man who, without exaggeration, possessed one quarter of the world's wealth. A man who claimed to have given the human species a chance to persevere, to learn from our collective mistakes and start anew. One man. But he died before he could prove his immense worth. No matter his will and capital, he could not live indefinitely. He was going to be incinerated, his remains no different than that of a deceased ecological refugee, one ashen handful amongst a billion others.

Pri sat forward in her reclining office chair, elbows resting on her knees, hands clasping forearms. Her bare feet pressed into the sleek beams of oak flooring, eyes rarely blinking while watching the display of her workstation. A glass of Bordeaux remained within reach on the desktop but long untouched, dried dribbles clinging to the rim. Pri had hardly left her home office in more than sixteen hours—first to fulfill the demands of her employment, now this—and Seph told her to stop watching, that it was late, that she should leave the room and come to their bedroom just down the hall. But she needed to see this with her own eyes. It wasn't therapeutic, she knew, but it was necessary. She thought he might turn off the video. If he did, she would switch it on without a word, without comment, again and again until he backed off. But Seph didn't force her. He repeated, "Just stop watching. It's doing you no good," to which she nodded, as if agreeing, conciliatory. From the vantage of the camera, all Pri could make out were flames, more white than yellow, erupting upwards like thrusters on a rocket, a dense rectangle of fire that burst from a marble plinth. Mustafa's cremation appeared to take place within the centre of a cavernous and vacant stone hall, stout gleaming bases of Corinthian columns framing the periphery. A sharp triangle of rose sunlight illuminated the floor. It was dawn in Istanbul.

"Turn it off and go to bed," Seph said after returning to her office, hoping that she would have listened to his instructions during his two-minute absence. He leaned with both hands on her desk, ridged forearms speckled with sunspots. He stared at her instead of the video, waiting for her to turn to face his pleading olive eyes, grimacing thin lips.

She would not look away from the cremation, asking, "Why do you care?"

"I don't think it's healthy."

"I don't think it matters."

"This should be something only his family sees."

"He said we were all part of his family."

"This should be private."

Pri didn't respond, agreeing with his comment yet refraining from turning off the stream. She was witnessing history. Admitting as much to her partner might sound trite, so she said nothing. Then, "Poppy is never going to see him."

"I don't think Poppy cares much about anything right now."

"Poppy will never know."

"I'm going to bed," Seph said.

"I'll join you soon."

Seph took a step but then halted, watching the video for a few seconds before sighing. "It's not the end of the world."

"How literal is that statement meant to be?"

"He was a hundred and twenty-two years old. How long did you expect him to make it?"

"He wasn't just any man."

"You know he wouldn't want anyone to think like that."

"I really believed that he was going to be on the Tevat with the rest of us."

"You can't say he didn't try."

"He was so close."

Seph snickered. "Kind of."

Pri could now make out the shadowy figure in the centre of the fire, the smoke thickening.

"Please, Pri. Turn that off."

She looked back to him, "We're still going, right?"

"As long as the Tevat is ever going to be finished."

"It's finished."

"It's not finished until they let us up there."

"Just a few more months," Pri said as if answering a question.

"Sure. But he was always going to die early on. Does it really matter if it happened here on Earth or a few weeks later up on the Tevat?"

Pri didn't answer. It shouldn't have mattered. Mustafa Karamehmet was meant to be one amongst four thousand people. After half a century of construction, the Tevat was now just another few months from departure—a year at most, she'd been assured. She couldn't see how something so enormous and so expensive could go to waste. Quite simply, the Tevat was the greatest engineering feat in all human history. No one, regardless of their opinions about Mustafa or his exploits, would argue that point. This was perhaps the only thing upon which every person could agree. And yet, this technological marvel was the consequence of one man's unimaginable wealth, one man's boundless visioning. One man who was now dead. It mattered.

The morning summer sun was a perfect disc, tangerine with a crisp circumference against the brackish sky. Daylight possessed the tone of dusk while dawn was a murky twilight. The haze of the summer was wood smoke, sweeter but more tenacious than the petroleum exhaust that burned in the Jungle throughout the winter, swept up into the mountains by brisk marine winds. Pri opened her front door and inhaled. She would still be able to run. Only in the mornings, only in the forests—but she could run. She stood out on the front step for a moment, closing her eyes, hoarding a couple of deep, longing breaths. And then she ran.

The streets of her strata were never snarled with traffic. She avoided the sidewalk with its lips and curbs and driveways, instead jogging on the unbroken asphalt in between parked vehicles, following the gentle and continual curve of the street, staring straight ahead, up towards the matte sky. If someone ambled along the sides, Pri would lift one hand, a wave of acknowledgement, assuring that she belonged here. This morning, there was no one else. Though the haze was thick, though she knew that the Tevat would not pass above her at any point that day, Pri gazed up as she ran. Just to imagine, just to pretend. She visualized a taupe crescent searing molten from the sharp light of the morning sun before vanishing behind clouds, behind the horizon. She glanced to her right and saw her wavering reflection against the curtain of tinted glass that fronted rowhomes and apartments, her stride fluid and flickering between the posts of polished concrete, beams of laminated lumber. A vehicle approached from behind and she veered off the road onto a pathway—first upon paving stones, then pea gravel, and finally a winding trail of fallen needles and trampled leaves within a dense coniferous forest. Here, she could take deep breaths. The shade, the fragrance, the cool air tricked her into feeling as if the canopy of evergreen needles was a filter that absorbed all particulate. Ferns carpeted the space in between the firs, the cedars, the maples. Pri imagined that this was unchanged throughout time. That this was the common denominator of history. The trail led to a stout wooden bridge over a trickling creek—two long beams with a dozen slats, a metal grate stapled atop for traction in the winter and collecting brittle hazel leaves in the summer—and she crossed the span with just two leaping steps. The path lead down the mountainside, past a cedar with an outstretched second trunk, an arm bent at ninety-degrees before reaching up. Its bark was smooth from children climbing on its horizontal perch. Pri brushed her right hand on its trunk as she jogged past, then rubbed her fingers together to release any flakes or dirt. She would miss all of this, she knew. She would miss this more than anything else. A temperate rainforest would be nothing more than a picture to Poppy, as intangible as dinosaurs.

Her strides turned into gallops from the slope, the mountain appeared to glide below her like a conveyor. Soon she would see the perimeter wall. Soon the path would take a hard left and then wind back up the incline. Soon her quads would whine with each abbreviated step. Nayha warned her to be cautious. One wrong step and she could sprain, if not break, her ankle. But Pri tried to savor these last few minutes before the real workout commenced. The path flattened out and veered as it approached the strata wall. Five meters of fortified transparent thermoplastics stained with bird droppings, algae, and lichen. Pri looked to her right as she strode. There was never enough light so far below the canopy of trees for her to make out the details of her reflection. Her figure was an apparition atop the ferns, the trunks, the steepening mountainside. Never once had Pri seen anyone else on the other side of the wall. And yet every time Pri ran along this path, she repeatedly glanced through the bullet-proof plastic, searching, scanning, just in case.

"Shit," Pri said to herself. She had forgotten to take her Stasi. Again. This was happening far too regularly. She could not ask Seph to remind her in the mornings, as doing so would only validate his fears that she was not capable of remembering something so simple and yet so important. She hoped that she could return home before he might notice. *You're the smartest person I know and yet this is the one thing you keep forgetting,* she could hear him say. And she didn't have a point to argue in return. She could only nod, say, "I know, I know," and wait for the topic to change, for Seph to accept that this was not going to be a problem.

She returned to the asphalt road, the scraping of her shoes echoing between buildings. She inspected her reflection against the glazing of neighboring apartments, imagining the protruding belly, shuffling steps. *We don't need our Poppy becoming a Pearl anytime soon,* Seph would say, proud of that line and his wit, hence it being worthy of repeating. She imagined jogging along one of the radial streets aboard the Tevat, right in the middle of a lane. She would wave, she would nod, she would smile at her fellow citizens. The ceiling above is a perfect blue, not the pall of smoke. It would take her fifteen minutes to complete a single loop, never having to change direction and yet passing the same buildings, the same people, the same English Oaks. Then it would take her twenty minutes, her gait burdened. Then she would have to walk, keeping a brisk pace. But she would always walk. No matter how far along her pregnancy, Pri was certain that she would always walk. She would plod until the morning of labor and the day after. And then she would start running again. Seph will watch Poppy or she will take a stroller. Pri will tell Poppy stories of life on Earth, of the rain, of the oceans, of the forests, the wind, clouds, smoke, fog, even the occasional snowfall. Pri would tell Poppy about Grandpa's house on the ocean, where they could watch seals, herons, the erupting sprays and breaching tails of orcas, of humpbacks. Pri would wait until Poppy was older to tell the other stories. The tragic ones. About how we had something perfect but let it rot. That she was one of the very, very lucky few. Less than one in a million.

But first, Pri had to remember to keep taking her Stasi.

She leapt up each of the four steps to the front door and pushed it open, her apartment quiet, feeling vacant. She forced off each shoe without bending down, her breaths heavy, conspicuous.

"That was quick," Seph called out from upstairs, presumptively still in his office.

"Yeah. My legs are really tired," Pri said between panting breaths.

Seph didn't reply. She approached the stairs. The tone of his voice was indifferent. Either it was an act, or he never checked.

"Oh," Seph then added. "Your dad called."

"Was it my dad or was it Carol?"

"It was Carol, of course."

"Anything happen?" She climbed the flight, her hand sliding along the curved lip of a glass railing.

Seph was in his office, door open, out of sight. "No. She just asked how you were doing."

She walked into the bathroom and ran the water. "What did you say?"

"That you went for a run."

"What did she say?"

"She said that she hoped that you'd have a good run."

Pri chuckled. "No news?" Her week's supply of Stasi was right behind the faucet, a tab for each day of the week. She flicked it open and rolled the oblong manila pill into her palm.

"No news."

She drank right from the tap, turned it off, and walked back into the hallway towards Seph's office. He sat at this desk, his chin in the palm of one hand, staring at the display. She kissed him on the back of the neck, right below the last tufts of auburn hair which tickled her nose. She asked, "Does Carol want me to call back?"

"I'm sure Carol doesn't really care one way or another."

"You know what I mean."

"She didn't say anything."

"Okay." Pri let one hand linger on his shoulder. "I'll call back later. Anyhow, I won't keep you from work."

"Don't worry about it."

Pri guided his chin around and up so that she could kiss him on the lips. Right at the end, he seemed to pull her back in with a gentle pinch. "Love you," Pri said. "I'm going to have a shower." She walked away, the fingers of one hand following down his arm and gripping his own.

"Love you, too," he said, eyes on his display. "And while you're in the bathroom, make sure you take your pill. You forgot again."

Pri wanted to tell Nayha that she was pregnant. It seemed unfair to keep her own sister in the dark about such an important fact. Like most in their strata, Seph was an only child and so he could not understand that connection—to him, a sibling was just an old friend, someone you've known through good and bad, someone with which you could go months without saying a word. He claimed that he could appreciate the bond (it was not like he didn't have family, was his response) and yet he still expected Pri to keep her pregnancy to herself—just him and her, no one else—even if it meant waiting more than a year, more than two years. Pri and Nayha lived in the same strata within a five-minute drive from one another. And still she wasn't supposed to tell her. They had met at the park and watched Asha complete figure-eight loops around the play structure. The girl tumbled on the ground and erupted into a wail before noticing that nothing actually hurt. After convincing her that she was fine, Nayha returned to the bench, motioned to Pri how she wanted to kill herself with a pistol aimed at the roof of her mouth, and then asked how much longer her and Seph were going to wait to have a child, as if she didn't know the answer.

Pri replied, "You know that we're waiting for the Tevat."

"You know that Mustafa is dead?"

"Still waiting for the right time."

Nayha chuckled, looking back towards her daughter. "At some point, you're going to have to stop waiting."

"We've been assured a launch in the next year."

"Haven't you been assured that for the last five years?"

"About that much."

"At least that much."

"Well," Pri said, "We've been trying."

"What does that mean?"

"To have a baby. We've been trying. Do I really need to go into the mechanics?"

"No," Nayha furrowed her brow, her eyes flicking away behind the lenses of her glasses. She ran her hand through her long black hair, moving it from one side to the other. Within seconds, all the strands had fallen back to their original places. She asked, "So, what if you get pregnant?"

"Then you'll be happy, right?"

"Surely you can't go on a rocket while you're pregnant?"

"Not past the first trimester, no."

Pri could see it in Nayha's expression, her reaction on the cusp between relief and revulsion. Pri now figured it was a mistake to even say this much. Nayha asked, "But you're still planning on going?"

"Not just me. Seph and I. Both of us."

Nayha sighed, "So you're going to use Stasi?"

Pri didn't answer.

"For how long?"

"I don't know."

"It's not meant to be used indefinitely; you know—"

"I'm not stupid."

"Well, smart people have been known to do stupid things with that stuff."

"I'm your sister, Nayha. Not one of your careless patients."

"Yet sometimes you act like one."

Pri leaned against the back rest of the bench, waved back to Asha to acknowledge her ascent to the top of a climbing wall, and then sighed. "What do you want me to say?"

"I want you to say that you're not going to use Stasi as a way to get onto the Tevat while pregnant."

"Okay," Pri nodded, as if accepting the terms of surrender. "And what else?"

"Let me think." Nayha rubbed one eye, dislodging her glasses for a second before letting them slide back into place. "I'd like you to say that you're not going to go on the Tevat."

"Sure," Pri said with a shrug.

"And for you to admit that your life here is pretty damn good."

Pri replied dry, "It sure is." She thought: *As long as you ignore the smoke, the fires, the droughts, the storms, the strata walls, the strata police, the millions of destitute climate refugees living just out of sight, hemmed within the confines of the Jungle. Until that inevitable day that they outnumber the rest of us, until they lurch out from their walls to realize that ours are no match for their masses. All these years, we did nothing for them aside from tolerate their proximity if it was contained, as long as we couldn't see it. That was our gesture of goodwill. Yeah—life here is pretty damn good.*

"Oh," Nayha snapped her fingers. "And for you to admit that I'm actually the smarter sister."

"Well, Dad always loved you more than me, so you must have been the smarter one."

Nayha scoffed. "That should go without saying."

Pri had been four weeks' pregnant for the last eight months. Her baby wasn't even an embryo—it was a blastocyst, a clump of just thirty-two cells inside a gestational sac. When Pri first showed Seph the positive result, he hurried out of their apartment and returned home an hour later carrying two bottles: one of Champagne and one of Stasi. The Champagne was exhausted in under an hour. The Stasi would last at least three months. One pill in the morning, every morning, would keep their little blastocyst in an indefinite stasis. Just thirty-two cells. The size of a poppy seed, Pri read. It was Seph's idea to start calling it Poppy, already a member of their fledgling family. The pharmacist was programmed to inform Pri that it was not recommended for a woman to take Stasi for any longer than three months each and every time that Pri received her three-month refill. And while Pri didn't listen to the exhortations of those who claimed that even just a few months of use was enough to render women infertile, Pri wasn't going to need to stay on it for more than six months. A year, at most.

The timing could not have been better. Less than two weeks before learning of Poppy's conception, both she and Seph had been reassured that their launch date was scheduled within six months' time. Pri could remain on Stasi for just a couple of cycles, pass all health requirements for take-off, and then continue her gestation once aboard. She would be part of the Tevat's great baby boom. People like her were going to ensure the realization of Mustafa's dream. Pri and Seph were the perfect citizens—young, educated, and not only guaranteed to have a child, but likely to have more than one. They had only been trying for a couple of months. Nayha needed a couple of years. Others had to pay huge sums of money to conceive. Many gave up. Seph and Pri would drive out from their strata on the North Shore and down to the expanse of the Fraser delta to watch the rockets lift off. The launch pad floated on the ocean more than a mile from the nearest reaches of low tide, and yet when the boosters ignited, muted for only a handful of seconds, they both flinched, holding hands, watching the shockwave of exhaust tumble out over the waves towards them. Pri would lean forward, peering through the windshield. The boosters seemed to dawdle upwards for those first few moments, sluggish, reluctant combatants in their struggle against gravity, and yet within half a minute it would vanish from view above the clouds. "We're really doing this," she would say, a reminder, an acknowledgement. Seph would nod, holding one hand, fingers interlocked. It was his idea to come down here and watch—it was always his idea—and yet she thought of saying this again, of being direct: asking him if they were still going.

There were few people that Pri wanted to tell that she was pregnant. Like Seph, she worked from home, spending entire days inside her office. Her colleagues were scattered around the globe, different countries, different time zones. Every coworker just a name, photograph and employee number, each sending messages, queries, problems. Few of them knew that she had been accepted for the Tevat. And none would care that she was pregnant-in-stasis. Pri Gosal was just a name, photograph and employee number sending messages, queries, problems. The few people in this world enlightened enough to understand the intricacies of organic mathematics did not have the luxury of living within the same metropolitan authorities. And why should any of them be concerned that she was pregnant? These people had their own struggles with conception. Even if there wasn't the Tevat, they would not want to know. Not yet.

Pri wanted to tell her father. Seph was adamant that it would be a mistake and Pri understood his apprehension. She never argued this point. Telling Har would be a mistake. He had been suffering with dementia for several years. He would not understand the need to keep her pregnancy in stasis and definitely not understand her desire to make it to the Tevat—in his lucid years he used to profess that Mustafa Karamehmet was the leader of a cult and his followers were lemmings, unaware that his eldest daughter was one such lemming. He would be furious. He would be confused. But he deserved to know. He was her father. Even though Pri's child was just a cluster of cells, it meant something. Pri wanted to tell him that if Poppy was a girl, then they would name her Ani, like her mother. It was Seph's idea. But none of this would change Har's character or improve his condition. Her future child was just a poppyseed of cells and would remain that way until she fled the Earth. Har could not know. It would only make things worse. She knew all this. And yet she wanted to tell him. There seemed to be no more cruel fact of her situation than this contradiction.

Remembering that Carol had left several messages in the last month, Pri decided to call her father. Not to tell him anything. Not for any purpose.

"Hello, Pri." Carol said, her voice always calm, controlled.

"Hey, Carol. Is Har there?"

"He is. He's watching a movie right now. Would you like me to get him for you?"

"I don't know. Do you think he wants to be interrupted?"

"Just give me a moment, okay?"

"Sure," Pri replied, looking over her display and through the window. On a clear day, she could see the glimmer of the Pacific Ocean in the distance, wedged between the sprawl of the city and the Gulf Islands in behind. But she couldn't remember the last time there was a clear day. Instead, Pri saw the Siamese-twin trunks of a cedar tree. Bark flaking, tarnished. The rest of the vista was a brushed haze, a curtain of overcast.

Carol asked, "You there, Pri?"

"Still here."

"Har looks like he's pretty involved in his show right now. I'm not sure if he'll be in an agreeable mood should I interrupt him. However, if you could tell me the reason that you are calling, I may decide to let him know, should it be something of great importance."

"Well, no. I knew you called me a couple of times."

"Yes, of course. Har wanted to see how you were doing. It's been too long since you came for a visit."

Pri snickered. Carol said that it had been too long and yet wouldn't dare rouse him from his entertainment.

Carol asked, "What's wrong?"

"Oh, nothing."

"I thought I heard you snicker."

"No. I just sniffled."

"Is there something important you'd like to tell him?"

"No. There's nothing really new."

"You and Seph should really come out here to visit us again."

"We definitely plan on it."

"Do you have a date? I can put it into our calendar."

"Not yet. But sooner rather than later."

"That would be lovely. Har would really appreciate it."

"Well, tell him to give me a call if he wants when his show is done."

"Of course, Pri. Take care. And give Seph my best."

"Will do." Pri ended the call, knowing that she wouldn't hear from her father anytime soon.

Nine

Pri would not allow herself to think about what Hasan might do to her. No one had come down to this prison to converse. There were the occasional footsteps—some even pranced above her, light and impatient—but no one opened the door. It was as if she had been forgotten, like Hasan was her father. At some point she knew that the door would open, someone would come down with a demand, with a threat. Pri would let herself think about the demands, but she refused to ponder the threats. What would he want from her? She had four microcurrency-chip cards, more commonly known as MiC cards, implanted in splinters beneath her skin—one under each armpit, one at the top of her left thigh, and one at the lip of her belly. She ran her fingers over the outline of each triangle, the tissue no longer swollen but still tender. Each MiC card must have been worth more money than Hasan could earn in several years. Maybe a lifetime.

Jaz had warned that people like Pri might be tortured, raped, killed. While she struggled to keep those three words out of her mind, she refused to delve into details. She allowed herself to think the words—torture, rape, kill—but nothing more. These words were just sounds, phonetics without meaning. If she began to imagine his knife, she would look at something—the dot of daylight across the room—she would take a long breath, whisper the word, "No," to herself. And she would think about something else. There were so many other things upon which to focus. She'd stand, neck hunched, and limp two steps towards the opening in the dirt. It did not appear to be raining and she slid her index finger further into the hole, pulling aside a few more pebbles. She could now insert three fingers into the opening. The surrounding earth felt solid, like cement. She could ponder whether there was a point in pulling aside more soil. It might accomplish nothing aside from unleashing more rainwater. It might lead to a way out.

She would not allow herself to think about food. She knew that a person could survive weeks without eating and it had only been a matter of hours—maybe twelve, not yet a day. No matter what Hasan had planned, she would not be here for weeks. "Food does not matter," she'd whisper aloud, forcing herself into a different thought. When it rained, a trickle ran down the far wall. There were puddles that slowly filled and then sank into the ground. She imagined cupping both hands around the opening, letting water fill her palms before slurping. She then thought of the buckets of feces and urine that people cast from the openings of their homes above.

She did not want to think about the Stasi, but this was far more difficult. Instead, Pri refused to dwell. She had already missed a dosage. But people missed dosages. A single day was not a problem. She knew of women who admitted to travelling for a long weekend, realizing only when they returned home that they had neglected to take the medication. Pri had time. There would be a point when Hasan would come down to speak with her. He must have taken her bag. He would have searched for valuables. The Stasi was in an unmarked bottle. The pills were unremarkable, indistinct, worthless. They were medication, she would tell him. She would be sick without them. She would admit to him that she had a single MiC card hidden within a splinter. Give him one in exchange for the pills. It would be a simple trade for which Hasan would have no reason to decline. Pri felt the outline of the splinter beneath her left armpit, traced its contours, knew which side was the shortest, where to make the shallow incision.

But Pri realized that she was beginning to dwell. She withdrew her fingers, wrestled her thoughts away from the Stasi and to something of value. At some point, Hasan would come down and there would be a negotiation. She was the hostage, but still she had some leverage. There was no need for a formal ransom. If he accepted just a single MiC card, surely Hasan would be rich beyond his wildest dreams. He had no reason to keep her here for long. He had no reason to inflict pain or punishment. There was no reason for her to contact her family. She would be calm. She would be understanding of his needs, of his plight. She would not lie about her past. She was from a rich strata, yes, but she did not desire revenge upon Hasan. All she wanted was to make it to the launch site—it wasn't far; she could feel the tremble of rockets. She didn't need all her money. It didn't need to be complex. It didn't need to be painful. Pri could offer him a means to escape his intense poverty without anyone being hurt. Without anyone risking contact with the authorities in her strata. She ran her fingers over one of her splinters, knowing that she could come out of this if she kept her thoughts rational and focused on what mattered.

Pri and Seph's workstations alerted in unison that they had each received an urgent message from Saglik, the subject stating that their roles had been "updated." Yet again. Pri had been asleep at her desk and was jostled awake by the voice of her computer, which subsequently apologized for startling her. This was the second time in as many years that their pre-determined roles (Mustafa always asserted that there were no "jobs" on the Tevat; instead, every citizen had a role to play) had been changed. Upon their initial acceptance, Pri and Seph were assured that each would have the specifics of their assignments sent to them within a month. A year later, Pri was designated *Atmospheric Systems Coordinator,* while Seph was to be a *Senior Educator*. Each was given a digital tome explaining all aspects of their positions, several thousand pages of instructions in total. They had heard that there would be tests upon reaching the Tevat. According to rumors, people who failed to demonstrate a minimum level of proficiency would not be granted permission to board the rockets. And still others said that there was no point in studying any of the materials as roles would inevitably change prior to launch. Pri had attempted to read her manual—skimming through the introduction and searching for diagrams, point-form summaries, flow charts. But it was all too detailed and yet too abstract. She was still on Earth. The minutiae of a spacecraft's atmospheric systems had no bearing on her life. And then their roles were "updated." Pri's was changed to *Water Management,* while Seph's assignment became

Agricultural Systems Training. This warranted entirely new manuals, expectations, instructions. Pri laughed it off at the time. This seemed to justify her procrastination when it came to studying her last set of manuals. Now, there seemed to be little incentive to bother reading any of this in detail until they'd been given a concrete launch date. Seph found it disconcerting how the unnamed people in charge could make such a drastic change to people's future livelihoods without any attempt to justify a reason. Just a message entitled: *Your roles have been updated*.

Now Seph was irate. A third update. His role became *Agricultural Resource Management*. Again, no explanation for the change. Again, he was given a seemingly inexhaustible set of instructions and specifics. Pri was assigned *Algaculturist*.

"This is bullshit," Seph said, reading his update, shaking his head. "I'm watching carrots grow and you're watching algae bloom. That's our new job for the rest of our lives. Or until they decide to change things up again without warning."

"We all need—"

"Don't tell me that we all need to accept whatever they want to tell us. Don't start spewing their propaganda back to me."

Pri held in a breath and then sighed, annoyed whenever Seph responded to his expectation of her reply instead of her actual statement. But she didn't want to escalate things. To her, these details didn't matter. The point was getting onto the Tevat. Everything else was inconsequential. "That's not what I was going to say. We all need to remember how difficult it must be to create all these roles in advance of everyone getting on board, with people backing out, with all the uncertainty."

Seph sneered. "Well, maybe if you spend so many trillions on a spacecraft, you can set aside a little bit of time and money to make sure that people have a chance of actually finding some satisfaction in their new jobs?"

"We don't know if these are our roles for the rest of our lives."

"Well, you're probably right. Because we'll probably have them updated again in the next month."

"We knew this was a possibility—"

"—Please don't start saying all that. I know what we were told. I know what we said to one another. But we were also told that we would be on board by now. They never said that our jobs would keep changing."

Pri just stared at Seph, his cheeks flushed, one hand running through his tufts of ginger hair. "What?" He asked.

"Are you done?"

"What do you mean?"

"Are you done interrupting me?"

"I didn't interrupt you."

"And now you're telling me that you always let me finish my thoughts?"

"I know what you're going to say."

"Not much point in talking to me then, is there?"

Seph winced, confounded by Pri's apparent calm. "Are you not bothered by this?"

"I don't want to let it bother me."

"So, you're going to be content. With algae. You're going to help in the cultivation of algae."

"Is that supposed to be below me, or something?"

He reacted as if her comment was inane. "Maybe? Is that such a crazy thing to say? The schooling we have—the combined years of advanced education we've done—we should do something a little more," Seph shrugged. "I don't know. Elevated."

"So, you want to recreate our strata on the Tevat?"

"No, it's not a strata thing."

"No, I think it is."

He held up his hands. "And maybe it is. Maybe it's not such a bad thing that people who were able to go to the most advanced schools should do something a little more cognitively rigorous than staring at carrots. I mean, are these people putting any consideration into our skills, our strengths? Or is it just a crapshoot at this point? See which suckers make it and then decide."

"You obviously thought you were far more important than you really are."

"What does that mean?"

"It means you shouldn't be surprised. We were guaranteed admission. We were guaranteed a home. A role. A place within—"

"—Oh, call it a job."

"And you can stop interrupting me."

"Fine. Fine. Be happy about everything."

"We were guaranteed many things, but never anything about our jobs. Never once. You don't sign up for something like this and then complain about these details."

"These details." Seph shook his head, "You say that like I'm nitpicking. These are pretty significant details. This is something we might be doing for the rest of our lives. I'm surprised you're so blasé about it. What about you? How many people in this world understand organic mathematics like you? How many people could afford the education you've been—"

"Why does it always have to come back to money?"

"Because these are the facts. You have learned skills that are out of reach for the vast majority of this world. And they're making you grow pond scum."

Pri chuckled. "Now you're just looking for a way to demean my position."

"Well, I'm glad you can laugh about it."

"I'm just exasperated."

"With me?"

"With your negativity right now."

"So, none of this bothers you?"

Pri shrugged. "It doesn't." She wanted to remind Seph that it shouldn't bother him either, but instead she grimaced as if apologetic.

"I don't get it. I don't get how you can accept it all."

This is why it did not matter to Pri. Someday soon, maybe in the next few months—certainly within the next year—she would leave Earth forever. The immense thrust of rocket engines will force her back into her seat, holding her down within a vice. She could not imagine the noise, but then there would be the silence. Free from the weight of the world, the rocket will drift at more than twenty thousand kilometers per hour. Her hair will flutter in waves when she turns her head to the left, to the right. *Imagine that* she'll think—going from the crushing pressure of take-off to the utter relief of weightlessness, as if the planet below gave up on her after one last flailing gasp. So be it.

Out the window, the Earth will vanish, then reappear, the vivid blues of its oceans still unmatched by anything else on the surface of the planet, sweeping past without a sound as the rocket spins to match the unhurried rotation of the hulking Tevat. Her hair will slowly fall back, snakes sent down into their urn. She would not be able to see the Tevat ahead, just the Earth, panoramic and mighty, rushing past and then the deathly night of space. As the rocket docks there will be a sigh of relief. People will cheer. As she unbuckles her seatbelt, she'll watch as it wavers back down, like floating through water. She'll have weight, but that of a kitten, and the passengers will be told to hold onto the side railings to keep them from leaping too high. Her hand will glide along the walls, through the portal, into the nose of the Tevat. The journey from dockage will begin with feathery steps, people laughing as they are cast upwards towards the ceiling from a single absent-minded moment, letting go of the railing, eagerly wanting to hurry, to run. But with each step the artificial gravity will become more formidable. Pri will no longer need to hold onto the railing; her shoulders once again finding their way back down where they belong. There will be actual footsteps now, not faint scrapings. It's just centrifugal force. The simplest of physics. A trick. But with each step along the sloping corridor, they'll travel farther from the Tevat's axis, each leg heavier, now clomping and dragging against the gritty floor. And they will gather at the end, waiting for the last in line. Some people might try jumping as mere minutes earlier they could have leaped to the ceiling. They are no longer supernatural beings. Just people. Once again.

The door opens and a crowd awaits, cheering. Pri can see herself walking into the town square of a village. The sky above is a screen of unbroken blue, and each greeter embraces every one of the new citizens. She'll walk along paving stones edged with shrubs and flowers. Taking a deep hoarding breath, the air will be pristine. No forest fire smoke. No diesel fumes. More than three hundred kilometers above the surface of the Earth and yet this would be the most uncontaminated air Pri had ever inhaled. In the center of the square is a Lebanese Cedar, what Mustafa claimed to be the most beautiful species of tree on Earth. Transported when hardly more than a sapling, this tree is already older than Pri and most of the other three thousand people aboard. And it would certainly outlive every citizen. It would survive all their children and their grandchildren. It would survive the great landing, when the sixth-generation descendants reach Duur. By then, it would be far too large to manage the arduous journey down to the planet's surface. Instead, it would orbit Duur for a thousand years, a reminder to the citizens of this new planet about the monumental journey that the previous generations endured, of their collective sacrifice.

The Tevat City Hall overlooks the plaza and Mustafa Tree. As the tallest building inside the huge vessel, one end of the structure reaches the artificial sky and then slopes downwards, the top of a tree snapped from a gale wind and resting atop the branches of another. The structure is clad in exposed wood, appearing as if it was built entirely from lumber, nearly ten stories high. To Mustafa, it was essential that the buildings of the Tevat reflected the organic materials of Earth. Across from City Hall and the town square is the library; the building shaped like a sharp diamond, its windows a tessellation of leaves. Pri imagines walking away from the greeters, the streets covered in paving stones, lined with trees and flowers. The exteriors of the residences are clad with Lutetian limestone, designed to mimic the apartments of Paris, each with narrow balconies surrounded by wrought iron railings. The rounded intersections of roads are lined with benches and fountains. People would want to stroll, to sit, to talk with their fellow citizens. Pri imagines running her hands along the wooden backs of these public chairs, her fingertips dancing along the walls of buildings. Turning, she gazes at the gabled windows at the top floor of the apartments, just out of reach from the artificial sky, which has slowly turned violet. She walks along one of the ring roads. The gentle incline is undetectable to her feet and yet plays tricks with her vision. The road and buildings ahead curl upwards, hidden behind the darkening ceiling. Up ahead, a boy kicks a soccer ball across to the opposite building. He appears to stand above Pri atop a steep hill. Her eyes say that the ball should roll down towards her, but it bounces off the stone facade and returns to his feet. That boy might have been born here. This could be all he knows. The idea of a seemingly flat earth could seem just as strange. He kicks the ball along the road, and it bounces and rolls upwards out of view.

She could walk this path and never stop, never have to turn. When she jogs, each lap will take her less than fifteen minutes. But for now, she will just walk to her apartment in a two-story rowhouse fronting the street. The streetlights will have come on. The sky is now a dark navy, and the first stars are visible. Above the ceiling of the sky is the agricultural ring, divided into different biomes with soils that are tilled, irrigated, and fertilized. Above that is the great cavernous core of the Tevat, as vacuous and dark as interstellar space, spanning hundreds of meters across to the other side. No human will enter the core until the Tevat reaches Duur, when the landing modules are assembled and launched to the surface. For two hundred years, these stellar lifeboats will remain sealed.

Beneath her feet would be the outer layer, a membrane of steel and aluminum followed by the true skin of the Tevat—a meter-deep layer of water that surrounds the entire oblong vessel. Three square kilometers of surface. Three *billion* kilograms of fluid. Not just for agriculture. Not just for algaculture. This water is not only the giver of life on the Tevat, but it is the savior. A meter of water is enough to shield the citizens from the merciless bombardment of interstellar radiation, the spacecraft's first and only line of defense. Mustafa considered this poetic—water was where life began on Earth; water would protect humanity on its final voyage away from its home. Without this, the citizens would perish within a couple of generations.

And it was this same solution that would prove to be the greatest hindrance in constructing the Tevat. Transporting millions of tons of water into orbit. Even after twenty years of steady shipments, the Tevat still required more. Always more. A dozen rockets a day lifted off, carrying nothing more than pressurized water. Mustafa had already spent far more money on the simple act of transporting water into orbit than the entire wealth of most authorities. And Pri was not ignorant of the irony here—billions of the world's people were destitute, unable to secure a steady supply of potable water, and one man was spending his unimaginable wealth taking this resource and firing it off into orbit just so that a few thousand of humanity's populace could leave everyone else behind. She understood how people found this an abomination. She appreciated all that she had been given in life—the safety of her strata, the quality of her education, the cleanliness of her air, her water, her food. She did nothing to earn this. It was pure luck. And so, Pri stood up against those who derided migrants. Those who dismissed the pleas of one billion ecological refugees, more commonly known as ecogees. She not only understood the crux of their argument, but their anger; it was the richest of the world who caused the environmental disaster, and it continues to be the poorest who face the consequences. Long before her father's dementia became acute, she would refute his claims that the Jungle needed to be razed, that these people were no longer citizens of any country and hence possessed no legal rights. She joined in on the protests, calling the purging of those euphemistically titled Economic Development Zones, or EDZs, as nothing more than a form of genocide. It made her furious. And it made her ashamed for all that she was given.

But when she was granted final approval, when both Pri and Seph were officially welcomed to join the Tevat, she did not hesitate. Of course, she would go. This was her dream. This was Seph's dream. Two chosen among more than a million candidates. Again, more luck. This didn't absolve Pri of her guilt, but it did make the decision clear. The odds alone warranted that she accept this opportunity.

And so, it did not matter if she would spend the rest of her life managing crops of spirulina algae. A simple task requiring minimal education. Once aboard the Tevat, in her home, with Seph, overlooking the radial pedestrian street, she would be just a citizen among citizens. No stratas. No migrants. Just people.

Eight

It must have been night. Pri could no longer notice any light from the hole across the room beneath the floorboards. She had been here for twenty-four hours without contact from anyone. She would think about food but then force her thoughts towards water, reminding herself that she could drink if needed. She could hear a trickle. It was raining outside. This was not a desert. How could Hasan take her prisoner and then leave her for so long? Maybe Jaz found him? Maybe he was forced to flee? It didn't make sense. She hadn't heard footsteps above her in what must have been hours and Pri began to wonder if she should bang on the floorboards. Maybe whomever was up there didn't realize that a prisoner was trapped in the basement? Maybe Jaz found Hasan after she'd been pushed through the trap door? Maybe Jaz had spent the day looking for Pri? Maybe Jaz had already given up and had left the Jungle?

Pri thought that she could sleep through the hunger and thirst. Her limbs felt heavy, the simple act of standing now a daunting task. She ran her tongue over the pasty roof of her mouth. She should think about something else. She should think about what she would say when someone comes down. She shouldn't resort to drinking from a puddle. At least not yet. She was the one in control of herself. She was not a creature of instinct but a creature of rational thought. She could wait. She knew she could wait.

But she didn't. She thought about the water trickling down the wall across the room, imagining it clear and pristine, glistening down the lips of exposed rocks. She knelt forward, knees against the moist dirt, palms out to feel for the wall. Her fingertips ran over the exposed pebbles. She reached up, expecting a dribbling of water. The stones were wet, soil crumbling between her fingers, but she could not find the source, something that she might cup between her hands. She thought of leaning forward and licking the stones. But she could wait. It had only been a day. It was cold and damp in this space. She wasn't sweating. She could wait. She reached back, feeling for the fibers of her blanket, and sat atop it before resting on her side, folding it over her shoulder and feet. She could wait.

Mustafa Karamehmet spoke often of the ancient Polynesian migration. "Imagine the unknown of the Pacific Ocean," he would remind his listeners. "In simple wooden ships powered by the wind, navigating using only the stars, people would depart their home in search of another. Imagine pushing off from shore into the vast expanse. Leaving the comfort of an island that encompassed the only land upon which many had ever stepped foot—their entire world cast aside with a few heaving thrusts of paddles. Seeing nothing but water in all directions for weeks, for months. The horizon an unflinching arch. Imagine the settlers who traversed the far corners of the Pacific, the first humans to make landfall on Hawai'i. Imagine the sacrifice of the untold vessels that never made it to shore, instead drifting off into the ocean until every citizen perished. They had stories. They had histories that can never be known. Imagine the experiences that people took with them across the ocean and then down to its bottom. Imagine that," he would say, expecting his listeners to reflect in silent thought. The crowd of thousands were reduced to murmurs in the pauses between thoughts. No one wanted to interrupt Mustafa. "And yet, others made it. Their stories carried on. And they created a new world for their society."

"Why did they leave?" He asked as if it was not rhetorical. He'd repeat himself, stomp a foot, demand an answer from the audience. Their homes were not destitute. They had much to lose. They had families. They knew the risks. So, why? No one would say a word. His listeners knew the answer, of course. But they wanted to wait for Mustafa to say it himself. "They left because they had the will to leave. They left because they could."

"So, what is twelve lightyears in comparison to this? Twenty-four trillion miles? We have the means. The distance is vast, but the physics required is centuries old. Humanity made it to the moon with arithmetic calculated by hand. Sent men crammed into cannisters held together with rivets, a one-shot deal. The computations necessary to traverse the emptiness of interstellar space are trivial for even a decades old fone. The Tevat is the result of the single greatest feat of human engineering—yes—but at its foundation, it is simple. Just a matter of will. Just a matter of means. And I have the means, so we have the means." No government could do this. No elected or despotic leader of any administration would redirect so much capital and energy towards an interstellar ark. "It is because of me," Mustafa would declare, pausing as if humble, reluctant to take on this role. "It is because of the corrupt inequality of the world, the failure of capitalism that humanity has proven ill-equipped to control, that one man could acquire so much. There is nothing fair about it. There is nothing fair about one man having more power and influence than the vestiges of any remaining administration. And yet, in this irony, there is an undeniable truth. If things were fair, then the Tevat would never be built. It would remain the ideations of science-fiction. Humanity would be unable to leave the home it had destroyed. If things were fair, we would all be destined to become victims. It is for the same reason that the world is so profoundly unbalanced that humanity has a chance to persevere. Our salvation is borne not only from our mistakes, but from irony."

Pri first listened to Mustafa's lectures while she was a teenager. Even in his earliest recorded speeches, he was in his sixties, a bristled black moustache shaved clean to the skin at the very edge of his thin lips. He let his hair gray naturally, brushed back in a tight V that never seemed to recede, his forehead long, eyes narrow and tight, repressing a squint while staring towards the sun. As his high cheekbones sagged and his sharp chin slackened into limp jowls, his moustache was an anchor in the middle of his expression. An unmistakable feature. Pri's father discounted Mustafa as a fool—albeit an obscenely rich fool—whose ideas would become dangerous should people view him as a messiah. People should see him for what he truly is, Har would say. Mustafa held a quarter of the world's wealth. He had never struggled. His success was borne by virtue of his family name. No one elected him. He was the enemy of true messiahs. He was a monarch.

There were thousands of hours of recorded talks, just Mustafa speaking to mildly inebriated and yet quietly respectful, adoring crowds. Lectures rarely less than two hours in length, seemingly delivered without a script, rambling while rarely straying from his many favorite topics. He detailed what he claimed were pivotal events in human history—the migration of North America's first inhabitants across the Bering Strait, the Industrial Revolution, the Data Revolution, the invention of the combustion engine and rise of the automobile, the first missions to the Moon and to Mars, the decline of the global democracy and rise of the private-state. He spoke of how the dream of his original business empire—Saglik Life—was never to make money, but simply to deliver medical treatment to as many people as possible. There just happened to be a lot of people in the world.

He described the planets of Duur to crowds with the detail of someone who had walked upon its soil, telling of vast plains, oceans of grass that would be tilled and turned into agricultural fields capable of feeding thousands and then millions and then billions of people. Imagine starting anew, he said, in the virgin soil of a pristine planet. Not a single hydrocarbon in the air, in the water. He would spend hours discussing the power of algae, how entire generations of citizens would never need to slaughter a single animal to have access to abundant proteins. The citizens of the Tevat, he always repeated, would be the healthiest citizens in humanity's history. But his favorite topic—and Pri's favorite topic—were his descriptions of the Tevat. There were the seemingly hyperbolic claims of achieving the impossible, launching millions of tons of steel into space to form the ellipsoid skeleton of the vessel—more than a kilometer in length—all while hurtling around the Earth every ninety minutes. At one point, there were more than a thousand welders working in unison, each one tethered in their perpetual freefall hundreds of kilometers above the Earth. Mustafa described it as a swarm of fireflies when the Tevat emerged from the Earth's shadow and each individual worker became radiant from the unfiltered light of our sun. Not a single person perished, he repeated. Imagine the thousands, the tens of thousands of slaves who died building the pyramids.

But now, not a single sacrifice. The outer skin of the Tevat was a thin layer of plastic, unrolled over the structure's ribs to create its smooth and unblemished exterior. Now, the Tevat was unmistakable from the perspective of the Earth's citizens below. Appearing like a scythe one-quarter the size of the moon, most visible as it glided above the horizon just before dawn or after dusk, it breezed above the clouds and across the sky in less than a minute. Crowds used to stare, conversations muted, outstretched arms and fones directed towards the heavens. Decades later, it elicited no more wonderment than a passing airplane. How quickly we take everything for granted, Mustafa lectured, reminding those who had lived their entire lives with the Tevat orbiting the Earth. Children to whom the moon and the Tevat were celestial givens.

Children like Pri. The outer skin of the Tevat was unfurled several years before her birth. She remembered assuming that the moon was engineered by humans, yet another spacecraft that circled the Earth. It wasn't until Pri discovered Mustafa's lectures that she began to admire the Tevat when it appeared in the sky, watching its arc behind the clouds, imagining all the workers aboard, constructing a city within. As a teenager, she wished that she was born twenty years earlier, for then there might have been a chance that she could have been one of its citizens. But she was too young, she thought. Launch was always five years away. Before she was an adult it would leave Earth's orbit. First with the thrust from combustion engines, then a series of nuclear blasts over the course of a year, and finally the long, steady push of ion jets patiently propelling the Tevat closer towards its target velocity of one-quarter the speed of light. By that time, Pri would be in her late thirties and the four thousand citizens of the Tevat would be deep into the interstellar void, almost a lightyear away.

Pri was in Puerto Vallarta for a conference during her final year of undergraduate studies. She had flown down with twenty other students. Mustafa was at his Mexican retreat, a two-hour drive north from her conference compound, through lands that were purportedly riddled with dangerous ecogees, former tourist destinations taken over as EDZs and fortified. A few of the other students devised a plan to escape the conference and drive to his lands, hear The Benefactor talk in person. They claimed that the dangers of the countryside were overblown. There were always thousands of people in the crowds of his lectures. The roads to his retreat could not be that unsafe. But Pri could not go with them, she assured. She wanted to hear Mustafa talk in person, but it was not worth the risk. She could only imagine how her father would react should he find out that she was taken prisoner by migrants. He was a judge. His daughter would warrant an astronomical ransom.

She sat looking out the window of a conference hall lecture room. Yachts jostled in the Bay of Banderas, the rustling ocean more white than blue. Palm trees bristled against the breeze, fronds thrusting inland. Sailboats rocked in the swells, sails down. She heard that the local authorities torpedoed any migrant vessels that came within 200 kilometers of the bay. The horseshoes of kite-surfers pulled silhouettes of people above the choppy waters and back down into it. Tourists frolicked in the waves. This felt more secure than her father's house on Bowen Island. Pri left the conference and found her friends. She would go.

Pri knew that it could not be free to enter the grounds of Mustafa's retreat, but she was surprised by the scale of the cost. "Of course, it is expensive," one of her friends told her, "if it was cheap, everyone would come. And if everyone comes, then soon no one can." Mustafa owned hundreds of kilometers of coastline, controlling an area that annexed entire towns. A private army patrolled the border, the State of Karamehmet. He paid so much for the land to the local authorities that it was a sovereign state. Rusting, corrugated steel fences lined both sides of the highway, taller than any passing vehicle. Rolls of razor wire drooped and unfurled down to the withered grasses and vermillion soil. As they approached the border to Mustafa's lands, armored vehicles approached and drove adjacent. These patrols didn't call for them to pull over, didn't flash their lights. Instead, they followed along, tinted windows obscuring whether anyone was inside. The walls by the gatehouse were cinderblock and concrete, exceeding the heights of even the tallest palms. Soldiers approached, automatic machine guns slung over each shoulder. This was a mistake, Pri felt certain. Mustafa lectured about the injustice of fear, how civilizations crumble once people lost their basic trust in one another. And yet here were perimeter walls and armed security far more militarized than anything she'd witnessed back home. No one inside their car said a word, each attempting to remain calm, pretending that this was exactly what was expected. A soldier counted the number of people within and announced the fee to enter. They paid. The guard said, "*Bienvenidas,*" face masked, eyes unseen, unclear if this was a human or machine, and the gate opened.

There were no soldiers within the State of Karamehmet. Yachts the size of ferries ambled past the shores, just beyond the snaking, rocky outcroppings of breakwaters that forced back the most aggressive of tides. The smooth slate trunks of palms were surrounded by fronds, cacti, weaving and flowering vines. Once parked, there were no roads for automobiles, only terracotta pedestrian paths. People dawdled past in shorts, barefoot. Dense, trim grasses filled the spaces between walkways, between the residences and pools, individual stalks crinkling against the soles of Pri's shoes. People reclined in the shade of palapas, sun-tanning, reading, holding onto towels that fluttered from the onshore breeze.

Pri watched pelicans hover above the water, beak down into the breeze, wings quivering, barely thrusting and still. Then, their wings tucked back, they'd plunge down into the water and emerge a moment later. As she approached the shore, she saw that the birds were catching fish in what was an old swimming pool, once beachside and now submerged, a tiled square, green with algae that waved as if to get attention. Mustafa was scheduled to speak at the amphitheatre in the evening and until then there was nothing to do but stroll along the beaches, sip from drinks (all the tequila was locally grown, servers assured) and wade into the lapping waves of the Pacific. They only paid to stay for the day, but the surrounding residences were two-storey villas with sloped roofs of curved clay shingles, wide patio doors pushed open with citizens reclining in hammocks, raising their glasses to every passerby. She shielded herself from the glare of the sun within the shade of palms, the afternoon breeze blowing hair against her face, into her lips. Catamarans full of revellers plied the waters, its passengers waving to onlookers on shore.

This was going to change everything, Pri thought. These citizens of the State of Karamehmet were drunken tourists, nothing more. Mustafa was a salesman, marketing a lifestyle on a resort. Between the clusters of residences were information centers dedicated to the Tevat, showing interactive renderings of the completed vessel. Pri could experience a virtual stroll by the great cedar, located between the City Hall and library, through to the residences and along its radial lanes. She could amble through the agricultural biomes. She could sign up to become a future citizen. Join the lottery. Salespeople encouraged Pri to leave her contact information. Young women with advanced education were in upmost demand. Her chances were extremely probable compared to most. Pri declined with a polite, "No, thank you," shaking her head while smiling.

In the early evening, when the sun hung within the fronds of palms, people emerged from the pools and palapas, towels wrapped around them as they sauntered to their residences. Once the sun set, the dawdling breeze began to strengthen. People left their residences dressed in light shirts, flowing pants and dresses, sandals clapping like ambling hooves against the paving stones. As they neared the amphitheatre, crowds grew from murmuring lines into a raucous stream that flowed into the open-air stadium from a dozen different directions. The venue resembled a crater vast enough to contain thousands of people, the sloping sides covered in short grasses and wooden benches. Pri would have been content to stay at the back, but her friends demanded that they get close to the stage. They spent enough money to get here; they were going to see Mustafa up close. The crowd was energized, inebriated, but patient. People parted ways to let them in, apologizing, asking if this was their first time. "You are so lucky," one woman said. "You will see. It's like, finally, you are going to breathe."

Pri didn't know what this meant—if anything, the sheer number of people made respiration a challenge. Then someone cheered, a few screamed, and the entire crowd hollered in admiration as a figure emerged from the side of the stage. Mustafa was more than one hundred years old at the time, but he walked with only the aid of a cane, his steps deliberate but not shuffling, his strides wide, pausing after every few paces to cast his eyes upon his admirers, as if appreciating this spectacle for the first time. He'd raise one hand and thousands waved back. In older recordings, Pri watched him stalk the stage, never pausing in one spot for more than a few seconds. This time, he took a simple wooden chair, rested his cane on the ground, and took a sip of water while staring up at the stars. There were no rows in the audience—people stood shoulder to shoulder, chest to back, but Pri was close enough to see the folds in each jowl, the bags under his eyes. He patted down his moustache, wiping off sweat. And when he looked back towards the people with his tense gaze, stiff lips, the crowd went silent. Pri could hear their breaths. He began: "Even now, after all these years of life, I keep thinking of my existence in terms of attaining a goal, of reaching a destination. Yet I know that this is a cursed frame of thought. I know that when one's ideology is goal-oriented, then there is no bliss. It is always to be found in the next day, the next voyage, the next life. It is a fool's journey to undertake. And so, I have to tell myself these things: ecstasy cannot be one's plan. It should be one's existence."

Mustafa did not have notes. Often when he paused to stare at the night sky, he seemed to lose track of his own words, smiling at some intimate thought before continuing to another topic, rarely with any attempt to find a segue. He was honest about the hypocrisy of stating the need to live without goals while at the same time pursuing his dream of creating an interstellar ark. Pri expected him to rationalize this. Instead, he returned to the idea that this is just a contradiction, an inevitability, that all personalities are perhaps nothing more than tangled knots of such contradictions. His belief in needing to live in the moment did not preclude him from building the Tevat and building the Tevat does not imply that he is unable to live in the moment. And then he discussed the food that people ate at his retreat, not only grown locally, but with purposefully dwindling resources. In the first year, there were sprawling agricultural fields that began just past this amphitheatre, he said, thousands of hectares that volunteers tended, growing fruits and vegetables, raising livestock, avoiding chemicals, keeping everything as simple as possible. But the agricultural biomes on the Tevat would possess not even one percent as much space. And so, with each year, people were encouraged to let fields go fallow, reduce the use of water, reduce the need for labor all without constraining the variety of food produced. We cannot live on algae alone, he repeated, and then encouraged people to taste the spirulina cakes. He talked about Lai Abbas, the woman credited with discovering the planets of Duur. He reminded listeners that the name refers to three habitable planets all within the so-called Goldilocks zone of the same system—no other known star had been gifted with such an abundance of options for our future pioneers. Abbas and Mustafa were good friends, he claimed, implying that they might have been lovers. Her ashes were already aboard the Tevat, secure within the bridge. He promised Abbas that her remains would be among the first objects to be brought to the most hospitable planet's surface—before his, before anyone else. Even if the dead cannot hear us, we must still respect them. He pointed to the sky, his outstretched finger drawing the focus of thousands of swivelling heads who stared towards the stars. There was a rocket, he said, travelling to the Tevat, and the crowd cheered. Pri assumed that he would explain the significance of this particular vessel, but instead he just pointed, his arm tracing a slow arc. The crowd watched in silence. A man beside Pri wiped away tears. We are on the cusp of the greatest leap in humanity's evolution, he said. We are about to become interstellar beings. He stood up with the aid of his cane, took a single bow, and gave his parting phrase: "If you are here with someone you love, then be in love with them. If you are here with friends, then share joy with them. Good blessings and good night." People muttered these same words under their breaths. He left the stage. The crowd didn't cheer. They watched him exit, his steps struggling down a set of stairs, before people ambled away. A woman gave Pri a hug, said "Thank you," and walked on.

Pri thought of herself as a scientific person. She deplored judgements made entirely on emotion. And so, it bothered her. It should not have mattered. She had heard hundreds of Mustafa's speeches before. Pri inhaled, sober, tired. The air was humid, tinged with the meaty musk of body odor. She looked around, searching for her friends but not bothered that all she saw were strangers. Here she was, one amongst thousands of other people, many thousands of miles from home. As she ascended the incline towards the top of the amphitheatre, she could hear the crashing of waves, crackling like thunder before hissing, hushing. The world was unjust and unbalanced. Humanity had ruined not only what it had been blessed with, but also what it had created. And yet, right here, these people believed in the same thing. That we can do better. That we are free to travel in a new direction. Pri could not deny it: she felt like she was finally able to breathe. Not so much unburdened, but aware. For years, Pri felt ashamed by her family's wealth, by the opportunities that she was given. She had done nothing to deserve this. People from most stratas would have not had the opportunities to learn what she had studied. Migrants do not become organic mathematicians. This required years of being coached by experts, by people who learned from the best in a field that did not exist a generation prior. It was not so much that Pri's chances were better than most; Pri was playing an entirely different game. In Pri's version, there were no losers. Pri knew this since she was a young girl. It made her father angry when she asked questions about the lives of migrants, how their children would spend their entire existence in an EDZ without attending a day of formal school. And here she was, in her early twenties in one of the most exclusive private states on Earth. What she paid to enter was a year's wage for many. For most. And yet, watching the whitecaps of waves emerge from the darkness before crashing onto the floodlit beaches, Pri accepted that maybe it didn't matter whether something was fair or unfair. What mattered was that she had an opportunity to be part of the remaking of humanity. She did not deserve this, but no one deserves what they have. They just have. What matters was what she did next. Surely not a single person within the State of Karamehmet had ever known true hardship. Like Pri, every person who ambled past was spoiled and entitled. Like Pri, they were not willing to step away from the privileges into which they had been born. Like Pri, all they knew were comforts and safety. Like Pri, they each accepted that something was terribly wrong with the world—and that the best thing any one of them could do was leave. It was not her fault, Pri knew, as long as she didn't resign herself to repeating the same mistakes.

Pri called up to Seph when she entered the door, taking off her shoes. Her apartment seemed vacant. Seph didn't reply. She slowed her steps, listening for music, the clattering of a keyboard, shuffling steps. She heard nothing. "Seph?"

His voice came from his office. "I'm in here." His words were rushed and subdued.

"Is everything okay?"

Seph sat at his desk, leaning forward on his chair, his chin cradled atop his clasped hands, arms bent at the elbow, each resting on one knee. He didn't look up to her as she entered the room, his eyes fixated on the display. Pri walked in behind, placed both hands on his shoulders. There were recordings of an inferno raging through a dense metropolis, footage that appeared to be taken at night until the camera panned, revealing a monolith of black smoke that shrouded sunlight.

"Where is this?"

"Jakarta."

"What happened?"

"A rocket crashed right in the middle of the city."

"Is this live?"

"I think so."

"Was the rocket heading for the—"

"Yeah," Seph answered. "And look," he changed the display to another feed, this time of a smouldering encampment, stout buildings made from scrap wood and metal, tarps and sheets fluttering. It was an EDZ, but she didn't think it was the Jungle. She looked out the window, down towards the distant south coast, but the sky was a wall of beige. "Where is that?"

"Mexico City."

"Another rocket?"

"Yeah."

"Bound for the Tevat?"

"Of course."

"Two in one day?"

"Two in one *hour*."

Pri expelled a breathy sigh. She could see people running through the ashes, shirts wrapped about their faces to persevere through the haze. No sound was broadcast. A pillar of blue flames that crested gold erupted from the smoke. Those tiny figures scrambled to flee. "What's going on?" She asked, bewildered, not really seeking an answer.

"These can't all be accidents."

Pri said, "This wouldn't be happening if Mustafa was still alive."

"It's the authorities who are doing this."

"We don't know that."

Seph continued, ignoring Pri's comment. "They're the ones paying people to sabotage the rockets. They don't want us to leave. And you're right; now that Mustafa is dead, who is going to stop them? They feared him." Seph switched the display back to the feed from Jakarta, aerial shots from such heights as to make it impossible to discern the scurrying victims. A charcoal gash cut a line through the dense cityscape. It seemed less personal. More of a physical catastrophe instead of a human one. "Could you even imagine getting on a rocket right now? Even if they gave us the exact date. Told us it was going to be in a month. You think you could get on?"

Pri was surprised by this. Seph was usually the type to discount such fears—he'd recite a statistic about there being hundreds of launches a day around the world, tens of thousands of launches every year. She thought of quoting these numbers back to him, but instead she waited to see if he would elaborate.

He watched the display.

She said, "If Saglik told me that we had a set date, I would go."

He looked up to Pri. "Really? Just like that? Full of confidence?"

"I'd be nervous. But you really think that I would back out after all these years?"

He shrugged, as if dismissing her words, looking back to the display.

She asked, "Would you?"

"Go?"

"Yeah. Or back out?"

"I don't know." His words were rushed, more of an automatic reaction than an honest admission of uncertainty. "Stuff like this doesn't make me any more confident."

"So, just like that, you'd give up on it? Stay here?"

"I'm just saying I'm not confident. I don't see how you can be confident."

"We were chosen. We can't give up on that. We can't just raise Poppy within these perimeter walls for the rest of our lives."

"Is that really such a bad thing?"

Pri almost snorted from holding back a laugh. "You really want Poppy to grow up in this?"

"It's far better than burning up in the atmosphere, isn't it?"

"Of course, I'm scared. But we can't think about ourselves. This isn't about ourselves. What world is Poppy going to have if we stay?"

Seph switched the display back to the stream from Mexico City. "A world that is infinitely better than what those people are trapped within. Poppy would have a life of royalty compared to them."

Pri exhaled, shaking her head. "And that, right there, is the problem."

Perched high on the mountainside of the North Shore, an elliptical curtain of glass surrounded the top floor of Nayha's apartment. There was not a seam or crooked angle in the surface. The first time Pri saw this space, she felt the need to run her fingers over the entire perimeter, not to ascertain the quality of its work, but just for the sensation. And still now, more than a year since Nayha and Asha took possession, Pri's initial desire was to complete a lap of the floor, letting her hand slide along the smooth surface, her eyes looking out over the truncated, wavering tops of evergreens, the hazy, distant city lights, twinkling and faint. To the southwest, the Pacific was black, observable only by its absence of light. The Jungle, to the southeast, appeared like an ocean of lava, a mass of warbled, muted tangerine. Long before the Tevat began construction—long before people called it the Jungle—authorities hemmed ecological refugees into the lowlands along the shores between Vancouver and Seattle. There was nothing tropical about the Jungle. The moniker referenced the EDZ's disorder and disarray, not its climate. Pri's pacing stopped, struck by the clarity of the night's sky. Surely there was only so much longer that the rest of the city would remain unscathed. No matter the security. No matter the geography. How could the Jungle not spread further and annex even more? Pri had heard that there were more than two million people in the encampments, but from this vantage, high on the North Shore mountains, it was the rest of the city that seemed insignificant. If only the people of the Jungle could see this, then they'd appreciate the vastness of their numbers. They would break through the patrols and take over the rest of the city. Climb over perimeter walls and plunder this apartment. Pull out Nayha and Asha, throw them onto the street, force them into an EDZ.

She heard footsteps climb the stairs behind her.

Pri asked, "Is Asha asleep?"

Nayha said with a sigh, "Not yet. Vivian is reading to her. She gets two stories and no more."

"Does she try to bargain with Vivian?"

"Oh, Asha tries. Of course."

"And how well does that turn out?"

Nayha laughed. "You know, I don't know. Maybe Vivian agrees to her pleas when I'm out of earshot."

"Asha can be persistent."

"She definitely can. Even A.I. must have a breaking point."

Pri sipped from her wine and stared out the window again. "The Jungle looks immense from here."

"That's because it is immense. And I think parts of it were razed again in the last few weeks."

Pri shook her head. "I used to get so angry with Dad when he authorized a clearing. So angry."

"Not that you ever expressed your anger to his face, of course."

"Only in my fantasies."

Nayha said, "Maybe now you should speak your mind to him."

"It's not like he'll remember anything I say."

"Exactly."

"And it's not like he can do anything about it anymore."

After a few seconds of silence, Nayha huffed out a sharp laugh, almost a hiccup. "Youthful angst and youthful ignorance go hand-in-hand, don't you think? Or maybe it's just naïveté and angst?"

Pri glanced over to Nayha, "What do you mean by that?"

"Well, when you see it from here," Nayha held one hand out towards the window, "you must realize that Dad had a point, right? It can't keep growing unchecked. I don't know what good it does, clearing a few square kilometers, but something has to be done. I mean, look at it."

"I'm sorry, but I still don't agree."

"You really think we should just let it grow and grow, on and on, with no one doing anything about it?"

"And how exactly is sending in squadrons of bulldozers solving the problem? How is destroying the few things that the poorest people in this world have—people who risked their lives getting here—making the situation any better?"

Nayha's reply was immediate: "I don't know."

"You know that people die in those razings, right?"

"I believe it."

Pri looked at her sister, expecting some change in her demeanor. An admission that she was being sarcastic. That she was playing devil's advocate. Instead, Nayha stared Pri back in the eyes, adjusted her glasses and shrugged again, indifferent. "To those questions, yes, that's all I can say. I don't know. But that's not the issue."

"Okay, then. What is the issue?"

"How is letting the Jungle persist making anything better? How is *that* solving the world's problems?"

"Because these people had no other options. They're refugees. They don't have a home anymore. It's kind of what defines them."

"I'm not disputing any of that. I'm just asking, how is that, right there, a solution?"

"It's not." Pri said. "That, right there, is part of the problem. They shouldn't be forced to live like that. They shouldn't have been forced to leave their homes in the first place."

"But they were."

"But they were," Pri looked at Nayha, trying to conceal her confusion.

Nayha said, "So."

"So? So, what? You're agreeing with me?"

"No. You're making my point. It's not fair what happened to them. They probably had no choices, or this was one of the better choices. But that doesn't mean that we have to remain complacent to it. It's not fair to us, either."

"They blame us. And they are right. We caused this mess."

"No," Nayha sighed with a toothy smile. "We didn't cause any of this. This home produces less carbon than most of those shanties in the Jungle. They still power their homes with propane and diesel. Use generators for all of their electricity. I bet more people die from carbon monoxide poisoning than from any of the razings. We grew up in a house with solar panels that powered the entire home. Not even Dad ever drove a combustion engine. We were part of the solution, Pri. We have nothing to do with it. I don't know what our great grandparents did, what our grandparents did, but they are not us. We did not cause any problems. We don't carry the burdens of our parents, or of their parents. It's not like their sins are now ours by inheritance. We were part of the solution."

"You think the refugees of the world differentiate between generations? To them, we are all to blame."

"And you think that's right? They're the ones discriminating, not us. Blaming us because of things beyond our control. Those people aren't saints, Pri. They're just poor."

Pri shook her head, "How long do you think that this can last? All those people, just like you said, blaming us, right there."

"That's why they have razings."

"This world is too messed up."

"I don't disagree with you on that front."

"This, right here, is why I have to leave."

Nayha exhaled, slow and deflating. "That's the solution, isn't it? Leaving?"

"Starting over."

"You're such a pussy."

Pri chuckled. "That's your answer to everything."

"It's true. Leaving us all is a pretty weak way of solving your problems."

"Is it better to live behind walls and a private military?"

"Isn't that exactly what your wondrous Karamehmet did for his entire life? I don't recall seeing images of him giving lectures in migrant camps. They were always in pretty comfortable environments."

"Now you're really sounding like Dad."

"Just because he's our father doesn't mean that he was wrong about everything."

"I don't want to argue, Nayha."

"I don't want you to leave, Pri."

"I think Seph feels the same way."

Nayha let the silence between them linger. "He's having second thoughts?"

"And third. And fourth. And fifth."

"I always thought you were the smarter one. I guess I never gave him enough credit."

"He's freaked out by all the accidents of late."

A brief chuckle burst from Nayha's lips. "So, what you're saying is: Seph is a pussy?"

Pri nodded, smiling. "Maybe he is."

"Those weren't accidents," Nayha said. "I hope you don't believe that."

"I don't know what those are."

"I do. They are not accidents."

"I'm sorry, Nayha. I love you. I don't want to leave you. But I can't stay here."

"I heard the authorities are going to shut down all launches. I heard the Tevat's orbit is unstable and it's—"

"—It's going to crash into the Earth, causing another mass extinction level event, like what took out the dinosaurs. Yeah, I heard that too. It's not true."

"Actually, I never heard that one. I heard that it might just burn up in the atmosphere."

"I also heard that Mustafa had it programmed to crash into Istanbul, taking out the city of his youth. A posthumous attack on the city-state that disavowed him."

Nayha grinned, sipped from her wine. "I like that. The richest man in the world spending all his wealth and his life's efforts all in the name of callous revenge."

"The authorities can only stop the sanctioned lift-offs. They can't do anything about the countless off-site launches."

"Yeah, like you would do that."

"What does that mean?"

Nayha stared through her glasses at Pri, her expression either one of disgust or bewilderment. "You've been thinking of going out there," she pointed out towards the lights of the Jungle, "paying your way onto a rocket?"

Pri shook her head, dismissing the question.

Nayha, "Have you been talking to Jaz?"

"I've messaged with him."

"Dad must be rolling in his grave."

"Dad's alive."

"He's halfway there."

"I'm just looking into options."

"Well," Nayha sat down and put up her feet on the chair that Pri was going to use. "You never stop surprising me. Do-gooder Pri talking with lowly cousin Jaz."

"Like I said, I'm just looking into options."

"Let me advise you here, little sister to big sister: That's a terrible idea."

"Thanks."

"So, if I'm understanding everything correctly, Seph doesn't want to go. The authorities don't want people to go. People are burning-up on route to the Tevat, and now you're connecting with Jaz. Well, I have got the answer to your problems."

"I never asked for your answers."

"Stay here. Live here. Find ways to make this world a better place. The Tevat is not a solution to the world's problems. The Tevat just gives up on the problem. That's like dropping out of a course because it's too difficult. That's not your style, Pri."

"I'm sorry, Nayha. But I don't think there is a way to make this world any better. I think we're past that point. The only chance we have is to try starting over."

"You'd think about things differently if you had a kid."

Pri huffed a laugh, sniffled, sipped her wine, then brushed away Nayha's feet so that she could take a seat. "You sound so confident about that."

"Well, that's because I am confident about that."

"I'm pregnant."

Nayha chuckled, as if she hadn't listened. She then looked over, awaiting something more. Pri sniffled again, staring out the window at the tangerine ocean of the Jungle. Nayha said, "What?"

"I'm pregnant."

"How far along?"

"About a year."

Nayha struggled with what to say, her face and lips quivering between different reactions. Pri could see this in the reflection of the window and she enjoyed this rare moment of observing her supremely confident sister appearing confounded. "You've been on Stasi the entire time?"

"Yeah."

"You idiot."

"There's the Nayha I know."

"I've told you about this."

"I'm aware of that."

"So, you've been on Stasi all those times I warned you about how stupid people are who stay on Stasi?"

"I guess so."

"You have to stop taking it."

"I'm going on the Tevat."

"No."

Pri laughed. It was gratifying to see her upset. She said, "You're not going to let me go now? You're just going to go full-on Dad with me and tell me what to do?"

"Pri," Nayha stood, first holding Pri's free hand, then her arms. "This is a good thing. This is a great thing."

"I know it is. That's why I'm telling you."

"Then stop taking Stasi. Stop it now. You've been on it too long as it is. Just don't take the pill tomorrow. Simple."

"Simple."

"Yes. Simple."

"This is far from simple. I'm trying to get into orbit. That's not simple."

"No, but it is. It is so very simple. Tomorrow don't take the Stasi. And don't take it the day after that. Then you start to think about the life you actually have. Right here. On Earth. With people you know, with people you grew up with. You and Seph have a baby here and you do everything you can to ensure that your child's life is great. Your child will have a cousin, will have an aunt, will have a grandfather. Your child will play outside, in the forests, in the rain, in—"

"—In the smoke. Behind a wall. Terrified of the migrants, the boogeymen who live down the mountain, always just out of sight."

Nayha grinned, cheeks tight while nodding. She appeared impressed by Pri's interjection. "I never said everything would be easy. I never said everything would be perfect. And I never said that your child's life would be simple. I said, compared to all the mess going on right now, compared to all the uncertainty you are burdened with, *your* decision is simple. Have the baby here. Give that child the best life that is possible on this planet. Done."

Pri sniffled, aware that her sister must have noticed her gleaming eyes. She wiped away tears with a pair of strokes from one hand, refusing to look at her, instead maintaining her focus on the window, the compressed reflection upon it, Nayha's head narrow, lips puckered. "Seph and I agreed not to tell anyone about my pregnancy. No one. We knew it would just make things more difficult. People would demand that we stay. We both knew this. We both agreed. It wasn't one person's idea."

"Well, thank you for telling me. Even if it is a year too late."

"I've always wanted to tell you. Always. But I'm not staying here. I want my child to have a cousin, an aunt, a grandfather. I want these things. I know how rare that is. I don't take that for granted. But just because I want it, that doesn't mean that it's what matters. Not what really matters. You're my best friend. In the whole world. You're my best friend." Pri sighed and looked at her sister. "But I don't tell you what to do. I don't tell you to come with me. I want you to, of course I do. But I don't tell you to leave. Please don't keep telling me what to do."

"But that's what I do."

A single, sharp laugh burst from Pri's lips, "You're right. That is what you do best."

"Excuse me," Vivian's voice said, "sorry for interrupting."

Pri looked at Nayha, thinking that her sister would give her a hug. Nayha seemed to ignore Vivian's words, instead staring at Pri with the grin of someone who was both conciliatory and pitiful. "What's the problem?" Nayha said, looking back and up only slightly.

Vivian replied, "Asha would really like you to come down and see her. She keeps insisting that there is something in her closet that is making a *spooky sound*, as she calls it. I have reiterated to her several times that there are no sounds coming from her closet. But I am so far unable to convince her of this."

"You've read her two stories?"

Vivian paused before answering, as if programmed to be nervous. "I've actually read her three. I thought it would make her feel better and perhaps keep me from having to bother you."

Nayha looked at Pri, her eyes widening, eyebrows up. "See," Nayha said to her sister, her voice almost a whisper. "Asha is good."

"I'm very sorry, Nayha," Vivian added. "I didn't want to interrupt you, but I've come to the conclusion that Asha is inconsolable at this moment."

"That's okay," Nayha said aloud while standing, leaning over to kiss Pri on the forehead before walking back towards the stairs, her pace shuffling. "My girl is good. Knows it's impossible to rationally reason with someone who is irrational."

"Again, my apologies," Vivian said as Nayha descended.

Pri lifted her glass to take a sip of wine, only then realizing that it was empty. She glanced back towards the bar, saw the bottle, but did not want to get up. She put her glass down on the floor and looked back out the window. A quivering and stretched ball of light, like an inverted teardrop, ascended from the expanse of the Jungle. Pri imagined it erupting into a muted sphere of flame. Pri imagined it crashing into the EDZ, washing away huge swaths of the encampment with a fiery flood. But the rocket's trajectory remained controlled. Within seconds, it would be out of her sight beneath the ceiling of clouds.

"Vivian," Pri asked, directing her voice up and to her side. "Is that rocket there heading for the Tevat?"

"I'm sorry, but there's no accessible data on the destination of that rocket."

"Figures," Pri said to herself, the vessel now obscured. There remained no visible evidence of its launch, its long trail of exhaust invisible in the darkness.

"Where were you?" Seph called the moment Pri opened the door, his voice coming from his office.

"I went for a run," Pri called out.

"You were gone forever."

"I needed to walk a lot of it."

"You really need to bring your fone with you."

"Is everything okay?"

"No."

Pri's pace had been languid. She was going to drink some water on the front step. Now she leapt up the stairs two at a time. "What's wrong?"

"It's over."

"What's over?" Pri entered Seph's office, his posture relaxed considering the ominous tone of his words, leaning back with both hands clasped behind his head, tufts of hair sticking out between his fingers. But his eyes were wide and tinged with red. His display showed stock footage of the Tevat in orbit. Clips of rockets exploding seconds after launch.

"The Tevat," he said. "It's over."

"What happened?"

"No one else is permitted on board."

"What are you talking about?"

"Just in the last few hours, all rockets for the Tevat have been grounded. All shipments of supplies. Of water. All launches for citizens. No one else is allowed."

"They can't do that."

"Well, they did."

"Which authorities?"

"All of them. It started with Shanghai. Apparently, they made the call less than twelve hours ago. Then everyone else followed suit, mostly in the last thirty minutes."

"What about the people already on board?"

"I don't know."

Pri left Seph's office, gripping onto the door frame to tighten her turn. She spun into her own room, the display to her workstation activating as she approached. Pri linked to a live stream from the Tevat. Yara faced the camera, her wavy black hair tied tight into a ponytail, eyes looking away, distracted or watching something while speaking to her listeners. Years before Mustafa's death, Yara Khalife had positioned herself as the youthful face of the Tevat and its citizens, anointed the first person to reside aboard the spacecraft once its atmospheric systems stabilized. She was in her apartment; Pri recognized the poster of the Earth that hung from the wall in behind—half lit by the sun, half the labyrinthine starbursts of metropolises at night. It reminded Pri of Yara's initial broadcasts from almost a decade ago, always from a workstation or meeting room, that same poster on the wall. *"This is an affront to humanity,"* Yara said, *"To all of humanity, not just us citizens and prospective citizens. This is the last gasp of a dying tyrant, desperate not to let anyone else live—let alone prosper—now that his heart is failing."* Yara shook her head, her lips quivering into a cruel grin before wrestled down to a scowl. She wiped her nose with one finger, sniffled, looked at the camera and then back to her right. *"And do not be fooled into thinking that the tyrant is any of the heads of state, any of the authorities. We know how powerless they are. They are figureheads. They are fake emperors. The tyrant here is the mass of billions of people. The tyrant is the human race—because unless they rise up and force the authorities to stop, then they are complicit. Never was a single dollar of common money spent on the Tevat. Not a single dollar. The Benefactor did not want any donations. He did not accept any bribes. The Benefactor created all of this, welcomed all of you, on his own, by himself. The rest of humanity does not have the moral authority to stop us, and in attempting to do so, they only reveal their true character. Their grotesque character. Because do not doubt it, my listeners, my future citizens—they will not stop us. They cannot stop us. Authorities may have the power to halt launches from their sanctioned sites, but no one controls the EDZs. Rockets to the Tevat will only cease when we leave for Duur. Only then. And we are nearly ready! The despots of Earth can clang their swords all they want, but this is not a battle. We are already free. They are the dying. They will soon be extinct. We are the survivors. We are the next step in evolution. The past is over, people. The future is Tevat."*

Seph groaned while entering Pri's office. He sat on the floor beside her, his back against the wall, knees up. "I feel like after Mustafa died, she's tried tapping into his rambling sense of narrative."

"She has a point."

"Let anyone talk enough and they will always make a point somewhere along the line."

"Authorities can't just stop people from going. They don't have the jurisdiction."

"They claim it's about safety."

"They're the ones who have been sabotaging the launches."

"That might be the truth."

Pri looked at Seph, confused by his tone. She couldn't read him. At times he sounded condescending, a parent allaying the concerns of a whimpering child. "Aren't you angry about this?"

"Of course."

"You don't seem upset."

"I'm just not surprised."

"You saw this coming?"

"I saw something coming."

"But they can't do this," Pri said. "They can't. Authorities can't control anything. They can't control their own borders. How are they able to do this?"

Seph snickered, "They can do this because people want them to. You really think there are going to be demonstrations in the streets about this?"

"There should be."

"There won't be."

Pri looked back towards her display, Yara having taken her camera in the palm of her outstretched hand as she walked through her apartment. She pushed open a pair of French doors and emerged onto her patio, up on the third floor, turning the lens away from her and onto the plaza below where hundreds of citizens congregated, mulling, talking. Once a dozen people saw Yara up on her veranda, the entire crowd noticed, pointing upwards, cheering and clapping. Yara leaned back against the railing, holding the camera towards her so that she looked up towards the artificial sky, the crowd in behind. "*So, here we are,*" she smiled, defiant, joyful. "*This group of rebels. The only truly free people left in the entire human race, and we're no longer on Earth.*" Yara turned to face the crowd and called out, "*The past is over!*" They called back "*The future is Tevat.*"

Seph groaned.

"What?" Pri asked.

"Stuff like this is what people hate. This only reinforces their opinion that they're all part of a cult."

"What should they be doing?"

"I don't know. Just not that. Not recorded and streamed. Even Mustafa's critics had respect for the man. People don't respect Yara. Stuff like this, it'll just make people feel even more content with the decisions of the authorities. *Let them rot out in orbit,* they'll say. I can hear it already."

"Sounds like you're going to lead the call."

"Seeing stuff like this just makes me cringe. People hate us already."

"They don't hate us."

Seph chuckled. "Yeah, they do. Trust me. If the Tevat fell out of orbit and crashed into the ocean, their deaths wouldn't be mourned. There'd be relief."

Pri turned off the display and turned in her chair to face him. "You don't even want to go anymore, do you? You didn't want to go long before today's announcement."

Seph didn't look away. He stared into Pri's eyes, clenching his jaw, then exhaled out of his mouth. He didn't say anything.

"That's your answer?" Pri said.

"No, I don't want to go. I don't want to be a farmer for the rest of my life. I don't want to be told what I have to do. I don't want people like Yara cheerleading me along like I'm part of some greater cause."

Pri knew this—she should have found nothing surprising about Seph's words—but she didn't expect him to be so immediate, so forthright. She watched his cautiously blank expression while feeling her charging heart, aware of each beat. He called her bluff and now she was the one left reeling.

He said, "Are you actually surprised?"

"No."

"Then why do you look so surprised?"

"Because. Because this is what we were going to do. This was us. Together. It wasn't just me. It was us. Right? It was both of us, right?"

"It was. *Was*. Back when Mustafa was alive. Back when they assured us that we'd be launching in just a few months. Back when I thought I'd be doing something with my time a little more interesting than gardening. Back when rockets weren't exploding on take-off. Back when we didn't know anything. Hell, back when we were young and ignorant. Simple as that. But I'd like to believe that that was a while ago now. I'd like to believe that I'm a little more aware of the world than when I was in my twenties."

"So, just like that. After ten years of planning. You're done."

A burst of pained laughter broke from his lips. "They just stopped all launches, Pri."

"Just the sanctioned ones. They can't stop the EDZ launches."

"You're crazy if you think that's a good idea."

"I can't just give up on this all. I don't give up."

"Sometimes giving up is the smart thing to do. Far smarter than burning up in the atmosphere."

She wanted to leave but she'd only just come home. This spot felt untenable, right here in their office, Seph on the floor looking up towards her like a therapist, someone who listened, who empathized, but wasn't part of the narrative. She wiped away another tear, as if still to hide them from her partner. "And so, what? Stop taking Stasi? Give birth here? Raise Poppy here? Tell our child not to leave the perimeter without us? Ever? Raise our child to not think about the one billion ecogees who live just down there? Just out of sight. Who hate us. Who will hate Poppy. And don't forget, Poppy won't have a choice. Poppy will be forced into all of this, because no one else will ever think of dreaming as big as Mustafa did. Not ever again. Not after how the rest of the world treated his idea. Not after the people who believed in him backed down, gave up, went along with the status quo. We will raise our child in a world where their own children will be forced to endure the same conflict. The same degradation. We're going to sacrifice the lives of all our next generations. Lock them into this mess. Because we had a chance. And we gave up."

"What about the sacrifice of locking our children inside a spacecraft for the sole purpose of having another generation, whose sole purpose will be to have another generation, whose sole purpose will be to have another generation, whose sole purpose will be to have another generation, so that, if all the math is correct, they might just land on a planet in another solar system that can sustain human life. How many more generations will be sacrificed just because we wanted to feel like we were part of a revolution? How is that such a noble cause?"

"At least those people will have a chance."

Pri thought Seph would stand up, hold on to her, give her a kiss, grip one hand. But he remained on the floor, back against the wall, knees up, watching her with an expression riddled with pity. "Pri," he said, "this is not such a terrible thing. We can stay and do what every single parent has done for the entire history of the human race. We will adapt to the imperfections of our world and give our child the best life we can. We will love Poppy and we will raise Poppy to be the best person we know. We will do what we can to make sure our child grows up to be a good person, a fair person, a caring person. At least we will try. Hope that it will be Poppy's generation that will do a better job with this world than ours, than our parents, than their parents. That's all we can do, Pri. That's all we can do. That's all any parent can ever do. It doesn't matter if we're here on the ground or up in the Tevat. It's all the same task, the same goal."

"I didn't want to live the rest of my life here," Pri said, sniffling. "We were so lucky to have been chosen. I don't know if I can throw that all away. I don't want to go backwards. And we're so close now."

Seph stood but Pri didn't want to look at him. She glanced towards her dormant display, closed her eyes, and awaited his hands which gripped onto each shoulder. She thought of shirking herself free. He leaned down, chin against her hair, lips close to one ear. She winced. He said, almost a whisper, "You, me, and Poppy, spending our lives together. Growing up together. Getting old together. Right here. Is that really such a bad thing? Is that really such an awful idea?"

Seven

Pri awoke to footsteps, slow and scraping. Her eyes adjusted to the point of light across the room. It was morning. She should not remain on the floor. She could not wait for Hasan any longer. She sat up, dizzy, leaning back against the wall, eyes trained on the hole in the dirt, the only source of light in the room. There was a strange comfort in seeing that again. Just a single point. But enough for her eyes to have a reason to open. The person above stopped but did not leave, Pri could hear a shifting of weight. She stood up, one hand against the wall for support, the other reaching for the ceiling. When she felt the grain of the wooden floorboards, she leaned her back against the wall, reached up with both hands balled into fists and punched the ceiling. She wanted them to thunder against the plywood. But her strikes felt feeble, a muted rap against a door. She listened for movement; eyes trained on the corner of the room with the trapdoor. The person above either left or did not notice. She again felt up for the space between joists, leaned to her side so that the soft side of each fist would pummel the floorboard, and banged it nearly ten times in a row. She then slumped back down to her blanket, her head aching, and waited. Still no footsteps. She thought of yelling, but she was already dizzy and laboring to take deep breaths, her mouth was so dry that her voice would be nothing more than a crackling whisper.

It was as if Pri's mind was no longer in control of her own thoughts. It did not make sense. This was her body, her mind. Every impulse came from the same source. And yet now it felt like something else had seized command. This part of her would not accept reason or rational thought. All she could think about was water. It told her to reach out her hands and feel for any puddles. It was raining, she could hear the patter against the walls, and she imagined pools of pristine water mere inches away from her. She knew this was not possible. And yet she kept visualizing the same image. She was not the one in control. She planted one palm on the ground before her, felt the moisture in the dirt, sand, and pebbles like grains of rice. She reached out farther, now on her knees, running her flayed fingers back and forth, feeling for a depression, a shallow puddle. She was sure that it was raining. It could not have been in her head. But the ground was dry. She had reached the far wall, her fingers now running upwards, desperate to find even the most trivial source. She'd lap it up. She'd hold out her tongue against the rocks and let the water dribble into her mouth. Just a few drops would be enough for now. She would sit like that for an hour if she needed. She had time. But the wall was merely damp. There was no stream. She stood towards that opening at the base of the floorboards, her head aching, and picked apart a few more pebbles, fingerfuls of dirt to widen the opening. It wasn't raining. The rumble she heard was from a generator. There wasn't any water. She knew it was a mistake to have done this—if she was the one in control, she would have remained on the blanket, conserving her energy, thinking about something of value—and she squatted down. Now this was worse. There was nothing here. She knew this now. If she hadn't checked, she could at least be in denial. But there was nothing. Her situation was no different than a minute earlier and yet it felt worse because she knew. Objective truth is irrelevant when everything is mere thought. She had been forgotten here and she would shrivel up, desiccated and leathery like a dead mouse in an old trap. She could not get these images out of her mind. She was not in control.

Pri waited in her car, parked at the curb before an old residential high-rise. Rain dotted the windshield but didn't make a sound. People walked past, most wearing facemasks and huddled under hoods. She expected them to stare, but no one glanced in her direction. Pri looked up at the tower, its curtain wall of glass cracked, panels like lace from the webbing of fissures, others open and exposed, cloths fluttering out into the chasm. The king-tide line traced a blurry horizontal border across the main floor of the apartment building, the lower quarter of the windows hazy and almost verdant. A door was open, plastic and wooden tables had been set up along the sidewalk, a patio for a business. Inside, lights hung from drooping wires along the ceiling. A man sat on the top of a table, feet on the seat of a chair, and looked at his fone. No one else entered or exited the business. Or perhaps this was his home, its front door always open, his furniture portable and ready to be moved to higher ground when the tides demanded it.

Pri grabbed her facemask from the passenger seat and secured the elastic around each ear. Without it, Jaz had advised, she would be a tourist, piquing the interest of any nefarious types who might be paying attention. She opened the door and stood onto the uneven pavement, potholes filled with large rocks, slick from the light rain. *Don't stop to stare at things*, Jaz had warned. Walk around like you know every nook and cranny of these places. Act like you are bored with the details. A car rollicked on the bumpy road towards her and she slipped over onto the sidewalk. She started walking, having memorized the directions, knowing that she could not take out her fone to determine her bearings. She kept her eyes forwards and down towards the pavement, avoiding the faces of others, nearly marching. The muddy sidewalks heaved, grasses rising from the cracks. She could smell the brine of the ocean, the seawall only a few blocks behind her. Seafoam glass towers dominated either side of the street, each dotted with shattered and missing windows. Electrical lines drooped from one apartment to another across the road below.

She was staring. She had to stop staring. And still she looked back towards her car to see if it had been swarmed, eyed up by suvie addicts waiting for the naïve. An old bus rattled towards her, jostling from the uneven roads, its wheels spraying out silty rainwater as it pushed through every puddle. The sides were covered in overlapping layers of vibrant graffiti concealing every window. It didn't have a number, instead its destination was painted on the windshield in bold magenta letters. The door was left open as it rumbled by and people held on to bars with one hand, staring at their fones in their other. It had a combustion engine that growled and then coughed. It came to a halt at the intersection but still its motor quivered and muttered while idling, people leaping off and others climbing aboard. Pri wondered how something could make so much noise while just sitting still. While doing nothing. It seemed obscene. It then roared when accelerating off, a billow of exhaust spewing from a spout at the rear, the emission swirling and vanishing seconds later. These vehicles had supposedly been outlawed for decades. One would not be permitted within the roads of her strata. And yet another one followed from behind—this bus painted in rainbow stripes, every window open with navy drapes fluttering out—its gears clunking and grinding when picking up speed. It didn't have a door. Someone who missed the first bus sprinted towards this one, jumped up, clasped a scuffed bar, and climbed in without the vehicle coming to a rest.

This was not where Jaz lived. His neighborhood, The Flats, was another twenty-minute hike inland. Jaz had advised Pri not to park her vehicle anywhere near there. More pressing than the fact than it would be a target for thieves was that it would demand attention. People would follow her from the moment she left her car.

She walked past what was the concrete frame to a ten-story building, its peak a narrow square column crowned with spires of rebar. The open floors of each level were covered with plywood, loose tarps, in places just taut ropes parallel to the floors. Children ran along from the fifth level, engaged in a game of tag or soccer mere steps from the chasm but never looking down or even to their sides. At the end of the block, stout signs at the corner of each intersection read: *Leaving SEASIDE Policing Zone.* The metal had been dented and bent, letters scuffed and weathered from repeated cleanings.

She crossed another two-lane road, traffic sparse, far more people on foot than in vehicles. The parked cars on either side appeared derelict, abandoned. Another bus grumbled up from behind her, turning right and coming to a halt. Dozens of people departed, crossing the street without checking for oncoming traffic. The bus belched an eruption of black exhaust and veered right again, back into Seaside. Across the road, graffitied signs read: *Entering THE FLATS Policing Zone.*

There were no towers in The Flats, an intertidal zone filled in more than two centuries earlier to make way for a latticework of railroad tracks at the edge of the continent. Everything in The Flats was built like this, ostensibly on the verge of a monumental collapse, and yet every structure collectively leaned against another, a deck of cards that had resisted catastrophe for more than one hundred years. Pri caught herself staggering, inspecting far too many details at once, and she forced herself to hasten her pace, to keep her gaze straight ahead. She had to watch her step—there were no sidewalks or roads, only gravel, mud and railroad tracks, the rails gleaming between dirt and puddles. People stepped over without looking down, without having to watch their feet. Pri assumed that anyone who tripped would be marked as an intruder.

Walking along the narrow alleyways, neighboring floors creaked from unseen people behind thin plywood walls, their voices carrying over one another in a knot of languages. Here there were Bangladeshis, Chinese, Indonesians and Egyptians, families who have lived here for generations, descendants of the first ecological refugees to settle before the advent of any EDZ. Back when countries existed in more than just name. When governments were more than just authorities. Relic freight cars remained on the rails, converted into homes. Shipping cannisters stacked up to five layers tall had polystyrene windows, upper levels accessible with aluminum ladders adhered to the sides, wooden staircases leading from one terraced story to the next. What appeared to be shops, teahouses, cafes ran from narrow storefronts, tables and chairs of patios littering the walkways. There were wafts of open sewage, petrochemical exhaust, the spice of cooking food. Above them all, along every street, was a canopy of electrical wires, black, white, and orange, knotted and woven like a net, in places so dense as to allow cats to traverse with ease, dogs below eyeing them in silence.

Pri recounted the directions in her head, repeated them under her breath, her mumbling lips secure behind the facemask. When she had analyzed maps from the comfort of her home office, the dense network of narrow alleys and passageways appeared like the cross-section of an ant colony. She pushed aside thoughts that she might have been lost, assuring herself with words hidden from others by her facemask. She had an excellent memory. She knew this. Her career required her to analyze and debug vast and intricate matrices, programs that functioned on a chemical and molecular level, mathematical formulas that relied on the principles of organic reactions. This was the most valuable and employable skill that Pri possessed: focus. Obsessive focus if needed, holding onto potential kinks of the puzzle in memory while searching for the next error. Almost a decade of education and training had developed an ability to analyze without losing track of all the pieces. She was the consequence of her father's demands to stay abreast of technological change, to study in a field that most people were not aware existed, let alone have the means with which to train. She could find her way through this maze to Jaz's apartment without having to stop, without having to reference her fone. This should have been simple.

Standing at an intersection before two tight passageways, one formed between stacks of shipping cannisters, the other a pair of railroad tracks, something rubbed against her leg and she flinched, repressing a gasp. An ashen-white cat stroked circles around her ankles, forcing its side against her calves, its tail tall and quivering. Pri kneeled slightly to scratch its head, to which the feline stopped and arched its back, eyes closed, relishing in the attention. She ran the fingertips of one hand down its back, feeling the ridges of each vertebra. "Do you know where I am?" The cat turned around, demanding a scratch between its ears. "Because I don't."

A woman shoved a plastic table at a ramshackle patio, causing a chair to topple and the cat to skitter down the alleyway into some unseen hole at the base of a building. Pri stood up, running her fingers against one another to free stray hairs that stuck to her skin. The woman picked up the fallen chair and slid it against the gravel back into place, dusting off the tabletop with one hand before sauntering back into a narrow alcove formed between shipping cannisters.

"Pri," a man said, his tone not that of a question, instead an assured answer. She turned around and saw him, tall and dressed in a pearly suit, cuffs worn but clean and pressed. He didn't wear a mask, his face long, rough and pockmarked cheeks sloped in towards a protruding chin. It was Jaz, she was sure, even though she had not seen him in almost twenty years. His short, twisted, and curly hair was half gray, frosted streaks above each ear. When he smiled, she tried not to stare at his teeth, incisors straight but chipped in the corners, yellow around the edges, translucent at the tips, others startlingly white. He held out one hand to shake and when Pri clasped it, he grabbed hold with his other, pulling her in closer. She thought he might kiss the back of her hand. She recognized those eyes, a verdant green, although the black center appeared cloudy, as if he suffered from cataracts. "You made it," he said, the deepness of his voice surprising her. "I assume the journey wasn't too onerous?"

"It was fine," Pri said, assured, wondering if she should take off her facemask.

"Where did you leave your vehicle?"

"Down in Seaside."

Only half of Jaz's face grinned, almost a sneer, revealing another pair of teeth. "It should be okay there for a while. Here, my place is just around the corner. Come with me." He let go of her hand and walked without looking back, turning a corner down an alleyway covered with a net of electrical wires and mismatched tarps. Not watching her step, one foot plunged into a puddle, water up to her ankle. Jaz didn't notice, now before a steep ladder against the side of a shipping cannister, its top rungs concealed within an opening in the ceiling of cables. He glanced back to make sure that Pri was still coming, then started climbing. "Come," he assured. "It's screwed into the wall. Don't worry." She gripped both sides and rattled it to test its stability before taking her first steps. It was nearly vertical and the top quivered against the corrugated metal. When she ascended through the tangled net of cords, she felt as if breaking through clouds, free from the confined darkness of the passageway. Jaz reached out to assist Pri onto the landing and pointed towards the next level. The shipping containers were stacked into terraces, each level accessible by another ladder. Jaz picked up a sodden cigarette butt and flung it off the edge before climbing to the next tier. "I'm up on the fifth floor," he said. "The penthouse," he added with a chuckle.

Wooden planters lined the sides of the top floor, each blooming with herbs and tomatoes that draped over the edges from the weight of the rain, dangling towards mismatched paving stones that concealed any evidence of the metal below. Cables with exposed bulbs zigzagged above her, just out of reach, suspended from poles secured on the outer edges of the planters. An array of solar panels lined the roof. Jaz unlocked a wooden door with a halfmoon window, reached in to turn on the lights before standing back, insisting that Pri enter first. "Just leave your shoes at the mat," he said, waiting for her to take the lead. He would not budge until Pri walked past and entered.

Clean, exposed wood lined the walls from floor to ceiling, devoid of artwork or photographs. The narrow space was immaculate and sparse, chairs pushed tight into a round table, a single white sofa covered in a sheet of plastic. Jaz closed the door, taking off his boots and socks, revealing bare feet with trimmed toenails that pressed into the tight weave of an overcast-colored carpet. He brushed past Pri towards a kitchen at the far end, running water into a kettle. She inhaled a mustiness concealed by bleach, unsure where to sit, unsure if she should remain standing. Aside from a few dark droplets around the tray for shoes, there were no stains or marks.

"I'm making some tea. Would you like some?"

"Sure."

"Don't be polite on my behalf." He spoke into a cupboard, sliding aside unseen containers. "If you'd rather not, then just be honest."

"No, no. I'm not being polite. Some tea sounds nice right now."

"All right, then." He closed the cabinet and smiled towards Pri from the far end. He laughed, "You look terrified."

"I'm not terrified."

"But you look it. Take a seat. Anywhere. Please."

Pri was going to sit at the couch but was unsure what to do with the sheet of plastic, so she withdrew a wooden chair, solid and dense, sat down with her elbows resting on the tabletop, hands clasped. She pulled them apart before he could notice her posture—call her a good schoolgirl eager for the teacher's instructions.

"Your place is quite nice," Pri said after deliberating whether there was a point. She knew what he was going to do.

"Ha," he laughed and sniffled, wiping his nose with an index finger. "I somehow think your apartment is a lot nicer."

"It's bigger."

"I'm sure it's a lot nicer."

"Maybe I'll let you see it soon."

"Only if I pass the test, right?"

"This is not a test."

"Oh, dear Pri, I know this is a test. You can admit it. Hell, you'd be a fool if you were not taking any precautions."

"Most people I know already think I'm a fool."

Jaz huffed another brief but propulsive laugh, leaning over the kettle. He poured the water and carried over two steaming, matching ceramic mugs. Outside, when he led the way up ladders and the tops of towering shipping cannisters, he seemed spry. Now his steps had a shuffle, his posture kinked. "Here," he slid a mug towards Pri and took a seat across from her, the table only large enough to grant a few inches of space between their hands. "Give it a couple of minutes. It's quite hot. It's a rooibos. Grown out in the Jungle, actually. I don't have any milk or sugar, if that's all right."

"That's fine. Thank you." Pri held one hand above her mug, felt the steam warm the palm of her hand. "Do you go to the Jungle regularly?"

"Sometimes, yes. Sometimes, no. Is that regularly?"

"How many times have you been there?"

Jaz shrugged. "Lots. If you want me to quantify that for you, I'm not sure if I can. How many times have you been here, to the Flats, before?"

"Zero."

"How about Seaside?"

"I think maybe I drove through once."

"So, this is all a big new adventure for you, isn't it?"

"I guess that's one word for it."

"This is an adventure. You've left the North Shore. Walked around a lowly strata all on your own. Didn't even get lost." He grinned, staring at Pri. "Think about how your father would feel right now if he knew this?"

"I'm not sure if he would be more furious about me coming to the Flats or talking to you, to be honest."

"Talking to me, I'm certain."

"Yeah, that's what I thought. I was just being polite."

"Neither of our fathers were saints," Jaz said. "That's probably why they disliked one another so much."

The last time Pri had seen Jaz in person was at her uncle's funeral. She remembered the shock upon witnessing what had become of her cousin—not just skinny but emaciated, eyes wide but bagged, sores over his skin vaguely concealed with makeup. He was either too ashamed or too afraid to look anyone in the eyes. Delivering his father's eulogy, his legs refused to remain still, hands slunk in and out of his pockets, head shaking, denying everything he said aloud, shrugging. Pri couldn't remember any of his words, just that image of a withered skeleton dressed in a suit, covered in makeup. She had heard about his struggles with Dsuvia but it was always described as just that: *struggles*. Implying a conflict with give and take, wins and losses, difficulties that were being overcome. The man she saw that day had not savored any victories. He was dying. Before then, he had been a sturdy teenager. A strong neck, wispy stubble on his chin, a bright smile. Pri used to think of Jaz as a brother—they saw each other regularly when she was a small child, what felt like every week. Nayha never knew that side of him. She was too young to remember his healthy years. Nayha had a big sister and a junkie cousin.

Jaz took a quiet, slurping sip from his tea, then settled it back down on the table. "How is your old man doing? Aside from hating everything, of course."

"I guess, all things considered, he's–" Pri struggled for a word but didn't want to drag this out. "He's okay. Still lives in his house on Bowen Island."

"By himself?"

"He has Carol."

Jaz laughed, "That's perfect then. He can yell at her all he wants, and she'll never fight back."

"You'd be surprised. She can be a little feisty in return."

"But not so much as to leave him, I bet."

"No." Pri snickered. "He gets what he pays for. She never gives up on him."

"You seen him recently?"

Pri sighed, "I haven't seen him in … in some time. The last few visits weren't enjoyable, especially for Seph. My dad was a complete ass to him. I couldn't tell how much was dementia and how much was just Har being Har. I often wonder if the dementia is just bringing out the real person."

"That's because he's used to yelling at Carol all day."

"Maybe."

"I never met Seph, did I?"

Pri grinned, shaking her head. Jaz spoke as if he had been part of her adult life, like there was a chance that he would have encountered any of her partners. She wasn't sure if he was just being polite or if he truly did not appreciate the time that he'd lost to addiction, if his placeholders for memories had become detached and scrambled, impossible to arrange in some semblance of order and scale. "No, I didn't know him back then."

"And you don't think that I will be meeting him?"

She shook her head. "No. That's done."

"Because at one point I was planning out the logistics for two people to go. That's not happening?"

"I can guarantee that that's not happening."

"Well, I'm sorry to hear that."

"It is what it is."

Jaz appeared unsure whether to ask, "You're still pregnant?"

"And on Stasi."

"For how long now?"

"Longer than I should be."

"Seph doesn't mind that you're keeping the baby?"

Pri didn't answer, expelling a sigh although wishing that she had not.

Jaz asked, "Does he know?"

"Seph doesn't know."

Jaz sipped from his mug, looked to his side while swishing the tea in his mouth, nodding, then swallowing. "You told him that you aborted."

"I did."

He sniggered and sniffled, repressing a smile. "You're more conniving than I gave you credit for, Pri."

"Is that a compliment?"

"In some ways, I think it is. I appreciate people with a conniving side. Those who know when to tell a lie, when to tell the truth."

"I need the baby. I don't think they'll let me on board by myself without being pregnant."

"Haven't they already accepted you?"

"With Seph. They want partners. But being pregnant-in-stasis is good enough."

Jaz laughed.

Pri asked, "What?"

"You think it really matters? You think they're going to turn you away?"

"They don't accept just anyone."

"Of course, they don't. They don't want just about anyone because just about anyone can't afford it. But you, you can afford it. That's all they care about."

"The Tevat is not a business."

Jaz closed his eyes, grinned wide, revealing his pomegranate gums. "Oh, sweet Pri. I thought you're the brilliant one of the family."

"That sounds like another back-handed compliment."

"Everything is a business. Everything is a transaction. The police. Health care. Military. Just because the Tevat is in orbit doesn't make it any different. Whatever they say is just marketing. The truth is, if you can pay, you can go. And most people can't pay."

"I don't think it's that simple, Jaz."

"No. No, it is that simple, Pri. Mustafa is dead. They need people with money. You have money. So, they need you."

"You do realize that they were paying for people's launches? It wasn't going to cost Seph and I much of anything until all the launches were stopped."

"And how long did they string you along with that? For how many years?"

Pri sighed and then smiled, as if in relief. Her short laugh sounded like a hum. "Seph also had all the answers. Maybe not quite as many as you. But he had a lot of answers. It gets old."

"Point taken. And I'm sorry."

Pri smiled, "Apology accepted."

"But can I ask you an honest question then? Because, unlike what you think of me, I know I don't have all the answers."

"Of course."

"Why is it so important for you to leave? I can understand it for so many others. But you have so much. Your child will have so much. People like you are not the ones who should be leaving this world."

"But it's not about having stuff."

Jaz smiled and nodded, one finger in the air. "Spoken like someone who has lots of stuff."

"So, you don't want me to go?"

"It's not a matter of what I want. I don't *want* one thing or another when it comes to you leaving. But I'll be honest. I think you're crazy for wanting to leave."

"Duly noted."

"I'll still help you, of course. I'll gladly take anyone's money if they want to do something foolish. In fact, in my experience, the more foolish a person's desire, the more they will pay for it. That is, if I pass the test."

"I feel like I have to pass your test, as well."

"Oh, you've passed, dear Pri. With flying colors."

"I thought I was a fool?"

"In some ways, you are. But I can tell that you will do this. You have an energy. You're strong. And foolish."

"I guess that's a win for me."

"So, tell me then," Jaz said, leaning back in his chair. "Have I passed your test?"

Pri watched him, inspected his expression, his eyes strangely eager, perhaps nervous as he awaited her reply. She wanted to make this moment drag. Just because she could. And because she wasn't sure. She should have stood up and walked out without exchanging another word. Make him need her. Take a day to decide. Take a week to decide. Take a month to decide. Don't be the fool.

She had forgotten until her fone sent a reminder. Looking at the clock, she was five hours into her task; the last time she remembered checking was over an hour ago. These matrices were going to require more than twenty-four hours to debug. Pri looked out the window, as if it might be possible to see the Tevat from this vantage without getting up, without breaking her focus any further. If she left her office right now, even if for just five minutes, she would lose her focus. It wasn't that her job enthralled her. She knew that soon enough she would never again use her skills as an organic mathematician. But once she was in the midst of a project—once she delved deep enough to begin finding the rhythm, once the sketch of this program took shape—then she did not want to stop. Seph knew that he could not enter her office when the door was closed, no matter the time. She would cease drinking so as not to require a toilet. This was her job. It took her years to develop such focus. Those first assignments at university which necessitated more than two hours felt insurmountable. She kept looking at the clock. She would fail to find a single error in the code. She'd try writing down notes, guesses, but that just pulled her further from her goal. These tasks were impossible, she was sure. Other students shared rumors that there were matrices without solutions, that instructors assigned problems that had no end, just to see how long people could remain on task. "But there is always a solution," a professor once expressed to her class. "In pure mathematics, there are empty solution sets. But this is *organic* mathematics. As with anything else in nature, the solution lies in adaptation." And in the end, Pri found it. She remembered that first time she completed a project that necessitated more than twelve hours of uninterrupted focus. Then more than twenty-four hours. Her peers hit a wall. Pri lied to them, said that she, too, couldn't figure out the tasks. She feigned acceptance of what they concluded—that this had to be a part of the training, assigning problems that could not be solved. They couldn't keep withdrawing students from the program. And then they were withdrawn. Fifty students down to thirty students down to twenty, then fifteen, twelve, ten, nine, eight. All her friends were gone. Those who remained, those who survived, remained isolated from each other, fearful of each other, wary that there was only going to be one graduate. Maybe none. Maybe no one was capable of what was needed.

Pri was one of six. Like her fellow graduates, she had spent so much of her last year in isolation that she only knew their names, but nothing more. There should have been a comradery amongst these veterans, but they still felt like competitors. Their feat, her supervisors told them, was one of cognizant strength, skill, and endurance. This was the mental equivalent of climbing Mount Everest unaided, something once thought to be impossible. Something that is impossible for almost any human being. But not for Pri Gosal.

Her fone reminded her again of the time left until visibility. The skies were mostly clear. There was no smoke. She said to her workstation, "I'm going to log out for five minutes. Hold any incoming messages until I return."

"Of course, Pri."

She stood up, her lower back reluctant to straighten, reminding her just how long she had been sitting. As she walked along the mezzanine, she glanced into what was Seph's office, his workstation vacant, a chair pushed into the desk. Pri was never sure of what to do with the door to that room. Leaving it open seemed to remind her of how much wasted space she had in her apartment; leaving it closed felt like a cheap attempt to trick herself into believing that Seph had never existed. She descended the stairs one step at a time, her thighs sore, and she pushed open the front door, taking a few more strides out onto the concrete pathway in her bare feet as she looked towards the patchwork of clouds. She walked out further towards the empty street, turning back to face northwest, rubbing the sole of each foot against the other ankle to rub off grit and sand. It was cooler than she expected, the sun due to set in the next few minutes. Out towards the western horizon, the dwindling sunlight was a line of searing embers above the hazy ocean. The clouds were submerged ripples, crests of waves undulating silver. She turned, looking through all the breaks and openings in the sky, the skin on her arms pulling in towards each hair. Turning back, there were no other people on the street or sidewalks.

She saw movement out of the corner of one eye, just past the peak of the mountain, and she stopped turning, trying to stand motionless while watching the clouds. A golden crescent came into view, unmistakable within the breaks in the sky. There was no better time to see the Tevat with the naked eye than this, right at sunset. Like the blade of a scythe, it sailed above the clouds. It appeared to dawdle in recordings taken from orbit, the Earth lumbering below, a ball tied to the end of a spinning string. Now it sprinted behind the clouds, flickering in and out of view, a fireball against the lilac sky of sunset, then vanished out of sight as silently as when it appeared. The breeze rustled the feathery needles of cedars. Her fone informed her that the Tevat was visible from this vantage point for 97 seconds. More than three thousand people emerged and then vanished in under two minutes. For them, it was just a couple of hours past midnight, the citizens living on Greenwich Standard Time. The artificial sky would be black, a twinkling of digital stars. The ambient temperature in the streets would be seventeen degrees Celsius. Without wind, without vehicles, it would be silent. A perfect calm at thirty thousand kilometers an hour.

Pri opened the front door, slid each foot against the mat and climbed the stairs one at a time, staring down towards the counters and table of the kitchen and living area. It was immaculate. She hadn't spent time there in several days. She entered her office, sat down in the chair, thought of waiting before logging back in, thought of going for a run, of calling Nayha, of watching or reading something. She stared at the display, as if waiting for someone else to tell her what to do.

"Are you okay?" Her workstation asked.

"Yeah, I'm fine."

"Do you want to log back in?"

"Sure."

"You received a message from Jaz Gosal while you were outside."

"What did he say?"

"He was hoping that you could contact him again in the near future."

"Did he say why?"

"No, he did not. Would you like me to send a message to him in reply?"

Pri sighed, "No. I have work to do."

Six

The door opened, a shaft of light revealing details of the space. The craggy walls surrounding Pri appeared closer than she expected. This was not so much a room as it was a closet dug into the soil. Only the joists above her had any semblance of permanence, the rest appeared as if a heavy rain might turn the surrounding walls into mud. She shuffled back, knees up, awaiting who or what might come down from the opening. "Hello?" she tried to say, but her voice cracked, her throat painfully dry. Still, nothing happened. She wondered if she was meant to approach the opening, reach up and climb out. After two days without any contact, this felt like a trick. She thought she heard a voice, perhaps whispering. She was going to inch forward when the two square feet of a metal ladder descended, stamping into the dirt to ensure stability. The light flickered and a shoe pressed onto one rung. Pri pulled up her knees to her chest, wrapped and locked her hands around her shins. The man's descent was slow, each step not just careful, but reluctant. He stepped onto the packed dirt floor, hung down his head and bent his knees so that he could turn without hitting the joists. It was Jaz.

"Hello, Pri." He said as if from a sigh, cautious about taking a step towards her. He appeared ready to say more, but instead shrugged and coughed a muffled laugh. Dressed in a tidy collared shirt, sleeves rolled, pants that struggled to conceal his shins, he bared the smile of someone listening to unfortunate news, the passing of a loved one. He appeared to search the floor for somewhere to sit before squatting, wincing as he bent down.

There were too many thoughts clashing in Pri's mind for her to utter any words. She stared at him, refusing to look away, the cheeks of his long face appearing hollowed in the light, hair combed back in controlled waves. His eyes kept darting to the dirt, her filthy blanket and then back to her face.

"I guess," Jaz said with a conciliatory nod, "I should start by saying that I'm sorry." He ran a hand through his hair, his face immaculate under the shaft of light. "This is not exactly how I saw things turning out." He then handed over a bottle of water, holding it in the space before her. Pri could not resist clutching it from him. He watched as she tried to grip the lid and twist it open, her hands fumbling. Pri brought the spout to her lips, cautious with the first sip, then gulping seconds later. She withdrew the bottle to catch her breath. She wanted to wait but she was not in control. Her arms returned the bottle to her lips, demanding that she drink, and she followed the orders dutifully, feeling the liquid roll over her lips and down her chin.

"Easy there, tiger," Jaz said with a scraping, coughing chuckle. "I don't know how much more of that there is for you."

Her eyes turned up towards Jaz, the bottle still. She brought it down to her knees, both bent towards her chest. She licked her lips, not wanting to waste another drop. "What," she began, but then cleared her throat. "What's going on? Where were you? Where's Hasan?"

Jaz stepped back, felt for a bottom rung on the ladder and used it as a seat. He looked up into the opening and then back towards Pri. "That's a lot of questions. But I'll start with Hasan. He's just up there. He's not so much listening as he is waiting for me to finish."

Pri hesitated, both impatient to ask more questions and yet needing time to dissect each of Jaz's statements. "He's up there?"

"He's up there."

"You're working for him."

Jaz sighed, held out the palms of his hands. "We're working together, you could say."

Pri coughed, both her fists and teeth clenching. Her hands trembled. She wanted to curse at him but that felt as futile as lunging forward to attack. It was what he expected, if not wanted. "This was all part of your plan."

"In a sense, but not exactly. I don't see the need in you being locked in this hole for so long, but Hasan has a different take on things than I do."

"I need my Stasi. It's been two days. I need my Stasi."

Jaz nodded, lips in a tight grin. "You are a woman of your convictions, Pri. You most certainly are. There are so many things you could have asked or tried to do to me at this point, but you're focused on your plan. I am impressed. I thought you would have thrown rocks at me by now. Called me an asshole or something."

"You're so much worse than that."

Jaz shrugged.

"Where is my Stasi? I just need the bottle. It was in my bag."

"I don't think you're getting your Stasi back."

"What does that mean?"

"It means that you're not getting your Stasi back."

"Where is my bag?"

A single chuckle escaped from Jaz. He shook his head and leaned forwards. "Pri, you do realize that you have absolutely no leverage here, right? I don't know where your bag is. Hasan doesn't care about that. There are far more important things to discuss. I didn't come down here to have a negotiation. I came here to tell you what's happening. There is no uncertainty to this. And it doesn't have to be terrible for you. It really doesn't. As long as you listen to what I'm going to say and accept these things, then this will all work out just fine for you."

"Am I getting out of here?"

"If you follow the instructions, then yes. And soon."

"What are these instructions?"

"But you need to realize, Pri, that you're not going to the Tevat. It's not happening. However, when all of this is over, you'll be fine. You'll be back at your comfortable home, you'll be back at work making far more money than most people can comprehend, you'll be safe behind your perimeter walls from the next surge of migrants. That's a fine outcome for anyone, Pri. If you want to keep your child, you'll hire some help. I'm sure you'll meet a nice man who also makes far more money than most people can comprehend. Or you'll get back together with Seph. Or you don't have to keep your child. All of that is up to you. You'll continue to live the charmed life that you've lived for the last thirty-whatever years. All you need to do is follow a few instructions. And accept this inevitability."

He was calm, a counsellor detailing the next steps for her therapy. This entire plan to take her to the Tevat was a sham and he was relaxed, expecting her to be complacent and understanding. Pri shook her head, unsure if this was real. Just minutes earlier she was asleep, left alone without food, water, light for two days. This could have been a dream. She squeezed her hands, dug her fingernails into the skin of her shins until her arms trembled, the pain acute. She would not cry. "Did you ever even plan to get me to the Tevat?"

"I thought about it, yes. I looked into it a little. But not for long."

"Was it even possible?"

"Anything is possible with enough money."

"Then why not?"

"Because this makes me a lot more money."

"I paid you so well."

"You did. You paid me very well."

"I defended you to Nayha. She told me I was a fool to trust a junkie like you."

"And I thank you for being so noble as to defend your lowly, junkie cousin."

"The whole time, you've been lying to me."

"Most of the time."

"I trusted you."

"Oh, Pri. That's why I like you. You're a good person. And that's why I want to make this as easy as possible for you. But don't ignore the other truths. You're privileged and you're spoiled. You complain about your father, but you never stood up to him or turned down the gifts he's given you. You fantasized about Mustafa and heading off towards Duur, but never said this to Har. You went to the schools that he wanted you to go to. You went into the profession that he wanted you to study. You still live in the strata he wanted you to live. You made all the money that he wanted you to make. You can have a good heart, Pri, but that doesn't mean you don't deserve misfortune. And let's be honest here. Let's be really honest. You only started talking to me when you needed me. You were using me, not as a friend, but as a client. And I understand that, Pri. I really do. To you, I was just the facilitator of a transaction." Jaz inhaled and sniffled, nodding to himself while staring at his helpless cousin. "Well, now you're part of my transaction. And it's nothing personal. Like I've always said, I really do like you, Pri. You're suffering right now, I know, but everyone should suffer at times. And it should be said that you being down here for so long without any food or water, that was Hasan's idea, not mine. If I had my way, this would all be concluded by now. But in life, things don't always go our way. I'm used to that, you see. I know that. But to people like you, it's a novel idea that something won't go as you planned."

"So," Pri said, her arms trembling while still gripping onto her legs. She didn't want Jaz to find some satisfaction in what appeared to be fear. Because it wasn't as simple as fear. She wasn't scared of Jaz. She was angry. She was cold. She was weary. She took deep breaths, wishing that her arms would stop trembling. She wouldn't look away from him. She wasn't scared of him. "So, what's your plan then?"

"You're a valuable person, like I always said. And Hasan and I are divvying you up. You have three MiC cards in splinters. Those are going to go. Those cards and the money on each are now mine. If you're smart, you'll take them out yourself. No need for this to get messy. Once I have those cards, I'm leaving, and you'll never see me again. At that point, you'll be Hasan's responsibility. He'll want you to contact your family and there will be a demand for ransom. The amount will be sizeable, of course, but your family can afford it, I can assure you. They will pay the ransom, you will be free to go back home, and in a few days, you'll be back in the North Shore. Simple as that. You'll get your teeth and skin fixed, and everything will be back to normal. You can pay for a great therapist. Talk away those troubles until you're as good as new. Hasan won't hurt you if you just follow these simple instructions. He has no reason to harm you. Nothing has to be difficult."

"I've already paid you so much money."

"I know. And I appreciate that," Jaz said with a smile, "but you're going to pay me a lot more. Or, at least, I'm going to take a lot more. And then, that's it. I know there will be a lot of shame for you to deal with when you return to your family. I know that feeling very well, I can assure you. But it passes. Like everything else, it means less with each passing day. Maybe you'll admit it to people, or maybe it will be a shameful secret. That's for you to decide. But you'll be fine, Pri. You'll be fine. The rich always come out fine. They may not get exactly what they wanted, but they come out fine. That ending is inevitable." Jaz stood up, his head vanishing in the opening of the ceiling door before leaning over as he knelt closer to Pri, his joints stiff and reluctant. He said, almost a whisper, "So, Pri. I know you don't want to do this. I know you don't give up without a fight. But I really don't want to make this difficult for you. I can get you a small knife. Hasan will come down and we'll watch as you open your three splinters. Each can come out with just a quick, short incision. You give me the MiC cards, and everything ends well. Hasan will then have you call your father. It's all quite routine, actually. Har puts a sum of money in an encrypted account—it can be completed within minutes from his end—and once that's confirmed, Hasan takes you to a safe point near the edge of the Jungle. You can be back home in a couple of days. Think of how nice it will be to walk along that mezzanine of yours back to your own bedroom. Think of it. That could maybe even be tomorrow night. Back in your own bed."

"I don't want to go home. I didn't do all of this to go back home."

"You're telling me that two days in a hole in the ground without food or water hasn't made you the tiniest bit homesick?" Jaz laughed, quick but forceful in contrast to his hushed tones. "You are tenacious. I like you. I know I told you a lot of lies, but that was never one of them. I really do like you. And I'm sorry that I had to lie to you. This is why I'm down here right now. I don't want this to get needlessly messy. I didn't want you to have to wait this long to see one of us. I thought that we could get this over with quickly. But Hasan wanted you to suffer a little. Hell, he wants you to suffer a lot. Felt it would make you a little more agreeable to what we need to do. He doesn't know you. He doesn't like you. He doesn't have your best interest at heart. You're just a rich girl slumming it out here in the Jungle. A tourist. That's all. So, please, don't make this hard on yourself. You're a brilliant woman. You must realize how little leverage you have. If you don't voluntarily remove your MiC cards, we will have to take them. That will be so very much worse for you. Hasan will get someone else down here. One man to hold down your arms. One man to hold down your legs. One man to cut them out. You know exactly where the splinters are. You can make the incisions right where they need to be. Small and slight. In the end, the main points would be the same—you don't have your money anymore—but the details would be so, so much worse for you. Please, Pri, don't even ponder going down that route. I beg of you."

She pulled up the blanket to cover her knees, keeping hold of her legs, staring at Jaz as he sat within that lone pillar of light, a beam of brilliance cast down around him. He looked up, perhaps to Hasan, perhaps to stretch his neck, perhaps just bored with Pri's hesitation. He sniffled, wiped his nose with the back of one wrist, and then looked back at her with a shrug and a lazy grin. "Well?"

Pri noticed the security vehicle parked at the curb in front of her apartment, but she chose to remain seated, reluctant to appear eager. She waited for the knock before standing, approaching with an ambling gait. She opened the door revealing a tall officer, burly to the point of obese, his beard stretched around his wide jaw and rounded chin. He bowed slightly upon making eye contact with Pri. "Ms. Gosal, I'm sorry to interrupt you," his voice boomed, a slight lisp. "There is a man here with preliminary clearance to see you, but he's new to the system. Were you expecting a visitor today?"

"I was, yes."

"What was the name of the guest?"

"He goes by Jaz. Jaz Gosal."

"That is him. Do you want to see him now?"

"I guess so."

"Okay." He turned and the car's back door opened. Two long legs emerged, shoes on the pavement. A hand gripped the top of the door and Jaz stood, giving Pri a subtle nod, barely discernable from the distance. The officer looked back to Pri, his voice hushed, "I will return in an hour to make sure everything is okay."

"That's not necessary."

"I'm glad to hear that, Ms. Gosal. But I will insist. It is protocol."

Jaz carried a leather satchel that hung down to his knees, staring at his surroundings as he sauntered up the walkway with a grin that appeared smug; Pri couldn't tell if he was admiring or critiquing. He might have been dressed in the same clothes as when she saw him last—gray pants and nearly matching suit jacket—although his hair was combed back tight to contain its waves, accenting streaks of white. He adjusted the knot of a violet tie beneath his collar then smiled, patting the security officer on the shoulder as he walked past. The man barely flinched, body firm, eyes following Jaz before returning to Pri's, seeking one last confirmation. She nodded and he reciprocated, waiting for Jaz to enter before returning to his vehicle.

Jaz took off his shoes, conducting a survey of the apartment. He chuckled, loud enough to demand her attention, and yet so brief as to be inconsequential. She had to ask, "What?"

"I knew it." He nodded towards the open door of her office. "You have a mezzanine."

"How'd you know that?"

"You seem like the type of person who would have a mezzanine in her apartment."

"What does that mean?"

He shrugged, placing his bag on a table in the middle of the sparse main level. "It's just a vibe I got." He strolled towards the kitchen, ran some water, and found a glass. "Sorry, you mind if I have some water?"

"Go right ahead."

"This really is a lovely apartment," he said, returning with his glass, placing it on the same table as his satchel after a scan of places to sit. "Mezzanines like that were really popular in upscale homes built about ten years ago. Is this place about ten years old?"

"It is." Pri pulled out a chair, "Did you used to work in construction on these types of apartments?"

"No," Jaz sat down, unclipped his satchel and retrieved a notebook. "I've broken into many types of these apartments."

Pri had just taken a seat. She swallowed, wishing that her reactions were less transparent, and forced a nod as if unconcerned. "Well, that's reassuring to hear."

"For this to work," Jaz pointed between their chests, "we need to be honest with each other. Always. I could lie to you but what purpose would that serve? Who am I trying to impress? I am who I am. The knowledge that you need from me is only acquired by breaking a few rules here and there. And you'll need to break rules if you want to get onto the Tevat. You know all of that. I'm only saying it out loud."

Pri was still, neck stiff. Imagine if her father could see this? If Nayha came by? Jaz Gosal in her own home. She wondered about when it would be too late. She had not already passed that point, she was sure. Jaz would never be allowed back into her strata without permission. She could block all communication from him. That would be it. Never again would she have to see this man. Everything was on her terms. His demeanor, his confidence, was a show. He needed her. She had to remember this. She was not afraid. Pri made herself nod. "So, could you break into this strata? This apartment?"

He smiled wide but didn't laugh. "No. This is a secure strata. Very secure. You get what you pay for here. Don't worry."

"Would you tell me the truth if it were any different?"

"I don't know."

"You don't know?"

"I don't know."

"That's you being honest?"

"This is me being honest. I'll always be honest with you, Pri. And I need you to always be honest with me."

"Okay." Pri said, "Can I ask you a question and get an honest answer?"

"Of course."

"When is the last time you used Dsuvia?"

Jaz huffed a laugh, revealing his teeth before pulling back, as if aware that she would be staring. "It's been a long time."

"What does that mean? I don't want to be giving my money to a junkie."

He squinted, watching her, still propping up a grin. "It's been more than five years. Five years and a few months. I don't do the exact math anymore. Suvie took some years from me. Suvie took a lot of years from me. I don't blame you for asking. I wouldn't have given my old self any money. And I've had a lot of ups and downs with it. I've learned that I can't tell you that I'll never try it again. People who say that, they always go back because that's not being honest with one's self. But I can tell you this—for five years I've been surrounded by the drug and haven't touched it. I'm not going to mess with things now. I want to help you. I want to show you that I can help you."

"And you want my money."

Pri assumed he would chuckle after her comment. His expression remained stoic.

He answered, "Yes, I want your money. Only rich people say they don't want money. But that's not everything, Pri. I want to show you that I'm not what the rest of our family thinks of me. If you want my help—if you want what I can give you—then I want to help you. I want to prove that I can help you. My little cousin. My little, brilliant cousin." Now he grinned. "So, Pri, will you let me help you?"

She watched his long fingers as they flitted with the cover of a notebook. The knuckles were calloused, fingers long but clean, tips smooth, maybe filed, cuticles hemmed. They scratched the cover to his notebook, a uniform black scuffed in the corners. "Yes," Pri said, making her voice assured. "Besides, that officer is going to be back here in about fifty-five minutes, so if I don't like the way things are going, he can just give you the boot."

"Oh, he'll be back early. At least ten minutes early. Trust me."

"Then we better get going, shouldn't we?"

"Okay then." Jaz opened the cover of the notebook, revealing handwritten notes in an unintelligible scrawl. He flipped through pages until finding one that had a few points. He turned the page to face her. "The essence of the plan is simple," he began as if this was a sales pitch. Once all the preparations were complete, Jaz would drive Pri to the periphery of the Jungle—not even a one-hour journey—and then make their way on foot from there on in. The only roads in the Jungle were controlled by private interests, all heavily fortified and impossible to access. In total, their journey would take three to four days, walking during the day, staying in homes of various acquaintances by night. Jaz would manage all the transactions on route; Pri would only need to follow along and say as little as possible. She would have a backstory, a script to follow should anyone ask her questions. No one in the Jungle would know the truth about Pri. Even the most trusted contacts of Jaz could not be trusted with that information. Pri was simply too valuable. She could not be put at risk of abduction.

Before leaving, Pri would have to complete three steps. First, she needed to liquidate most of her assets and transfer them onto MiC cards. The currencies had to be unencrypted and divisible; three MiC cards would suffice—plans A, B and C, Jaz called this—values split evenly onto each chip. She nodded, wrote down the amounts, asked what was next.

Jaz grinned and asked Pri if she'd ever heard of a splinter. He turned to a blank page in his notebook and sketched a triangle, two of its sides each more than twice the length of the third. A splinter was a small container, "a kind of pouch," he said, not any longer than the tip of one's thumb with the thickness of a fingernail, composed of a synthetically derived organic compound, almost identical in DNA to that of a human being. Each of the three MiC cards would be inserted inside a single splinter before being implanted beneath the first layer of skin, within the dermis. It would be reckless to carry such significant MiC cards in a pocket or bag, Jaz assured. They needed to be somewhere essentially invisible. And nothing was more invisible than inside a splinter implanted in the soft areas of the body. Under an armpit. Below the buttocks. Back of the knee. Within a year, each splinter becomes absorbed into the surrounding tissue. Within a year, there would be no physical trace. Implanting the splinters was quick and simple. The only obstacle, Jaz admitted, was in removing its contents. "Requires a little bit of determination," he said with a grin, drawing Pri's attention back to the sketch in this notepad. A person would make a shallow incision along the shortest side of the splinter, just deep enough to slice through the epidermis, so that the contents can be pushed out with a few purposeful jabs from one's fingers. Jaz said with a shrug, "Like forcing out a splinter. It's not too painful and it doesn't need to take long. Trust me."

"I don't like it when people say trust me."

"Then don't trust me. Do your own research. See what you can find. And you'll see that it's the only secure way of taking something valuable. You must assume that you will be searched at some point. I hope it won't happen, but you'd be a fool not to prepare for it."

Pri stared at his sketch of the splinter, the shortest side of the triangle encircled with loops of ink to highlight where a blade and some "determination" would be required to remove its contents.

"I don't mean to scare you," Jaz said.

"I think that's entirely what you are trying to do."

"You want me to tell you lies? Is that what you'd rather hear?"

She didn't have an answer. But she had all the power here. This was her own apartment. Jaz was a guest in her strata who could be evicted with a moment's notice. And yet she felt diminutive. Like this was part of his plan. This was part of his show.

Pri nodded and asked Jaz for the final step.

He referred to it as "getting scrubbed." It would not matter if Pri wore a facemask, if she dressed in rags, if she kept her head down for days and remained in the shadows. At some point, people in the Jungle would see her face, her hands, and know that she was not one of them. Her skin and teeth would give everything away. Migrants did not have complexions like those from high stratas. It was not possible to live a life outdoors, to scramble for years without the body reflecting this struggle. And such perfect teeth did not exist in nature. As soon as Pri would need to speak, they would know that she was a tourist dressed in a costume. The only solution was to be scrubbed of her status, change her actual appearance. Not cosmetics, but prosthetics. Make her delicate fingers appear calloused and craggily. Blemish her complexion. Misshapen the nose. Create a scar. Droop an eyelid. Using implants and stains, teeth needed to be mangled, discolored, chipped, twisted. Nature rewarded adaptation but it did not produce aesthetic perfection, Jaz said. Without this,

Pri would appear to be a mannequin, every feature smooth, symmetrical, deliberate, fabricated.

"Splinters and getting scrubbed," Jaz said, slapping his notebook shut and tapping his fingers against the wrinkled cover. "That's the only way to keep you safe."

Pri asked to see Nayha in the evening, wanting to take her out for a drink, knowing that Asha was with her father. Pri wished to ask her sister about splinters, about getting scrubbed. It felt absurd that she would have to take Jaz at his word for everything—and yet that was exactly why she hired him, to take her into a world she could not understand. Whatever she tried to research on her own led to countless contradictions. Sources claimed that the authorities would once again sanction deliveries to the Tevat. That the reactor on the spacecraft was leaking radiation. That none of the unsanctioned deliveries into orbit had made it to their destination in months. That the Tevat was going to depart within a few weeks. That Mustafa was not dead, but instead imprisoned. That the Tevat was going to crash without any possibility for the three thousand people already on board to escape. That the authorities have agents working in off-site launch sites and anyone who attempts to pay their way onto a rocket will be shot. That there is a revolution brewing within all the EDZs around the world—the critical mass of tension had been reached and only a spark was needed to take down the entire global order. That it was already too late; humanity conflated its ability to adapt with the notion that it could conquer any crisis, but this was one problem that had swollen beyond containment.

Nayha appeared apprehensive when she arrived at the restaurant, her smile terse, limp. She apologized for being late while taking off her jacket, eyes focused on the cutlery in front of her, the empty table adjacent, raindrops on her glasses which she wiped off with a corner of her shirt. "How are you doing?" she asked as if it was not a question, just a courtesy, putting her glasses back on, jaw clenched.

Pri stared back at her sister, right into those umber irises that didn't flinch or skirt away. She knew. She knew and she wasn't going to keep it a secret.

"I've spoken to Jaz," Pri said. "In person."

"I know," Nayha replied without nodding, without looking away.

"How?"

"Security informed me."

Pri snickered, shook her head. "I guess there is no such thing as privacy, is there?"

"It's to keep us safe. That is their job."

"What did they tell you?"

"Just that my cousin was invited into the strata and that your apartment is being monitored closely."

"Well, then, you must feel safe that they are being so diligent."

"They said you had his DNA for validation. When did you see him last?"

"A week or two ago."

"In the Flats?"

"Yes."

"You went down there?"

"Yes."

Nayha huffed an exasperated laugh right as the automated server approached. "I'm not hungry," Nayha said. "I'm only having wine for dinner." She looked back towards Pri, shrugged. "So, how did Jaz look?"

"Not too bad, actually."

"For a junkie."

"I think he's been clean for a while."

"You think?"

"I think. I won't say that I know. I just think."

"He has a nice little place down in the Flats? He's making the most of his bad situation?"

"He does actually have a pretty nice place, all things considered."

"And let me guess, he's all in on helping you get to the Tevat, right?"

Pri sighed, not answering, but not looking away.

Nayha asked, "How much money are you going to pay him?"

"Enough."

"I'm sure then that he can put on an act to get all of your money."

"When is the last time that you even saw him in person?"

"Gur's funeral."

"That's been a long time."

"Trust me," Nayha said. "I'm ready to go a lot longer before I see him again."

"I didn't ask to see you so that we could fight about Jaz."

"I know," Nayha said as the server returned with a bottle of wine, presenting the label. "I know why you came to see me—it's fine, just fill the glasses." She watched with a terse smile, waiting until the server departed to look back at Pri, clasping the glass as if to offer a toast but holding it still. "You're here because you want to tell me that you're leaving."

"I told you that I was leaving many years ago."

"I know, I know." Nayha took a sip, held the wine within her lips for a moment before swallowing, staring at her sister, a gentle nod building. "And that was you being foolish. That was you being naïve. That was you being young and supposedly rebellious. Acting like a morose teenager who discovered some new book that was going to *change everything* if only we'd all take the time to read it. That was quaint in comparison to this."

"And what is this?"

"This is dangerous. And selfish. Jaz has convinced you that it's a doable plan, right? You're going into the Jungle? You're going to bribe your way onto a rocket? Jaz is going to be your handler, keep you safe down there, hook you up with the right people and then take all your wealth? I mean, it's not like you'll need any of your money once you're aboard the Tevat, right? He's a good man, he is. Dear cousin Jaz."

"Is this why you're now so angry? Because of him?"

"*Because,*" Nayha began, surprising herself with the volume and tone of her voice. She smiled, leaned in across the table, said with a measured, level pitch, "I'm angry because before I never actually thought that this was going to happen. When you first told me, I assumed it was a fad, something you'd change your mind about within a few months, maybe a year. Then, later, I just figured that you were never going to get your launch. They kept dragging it out. And then Mustafa died. And then all the launches were halted. And then you tell me that you're pregnant. I actually thought, I really actually thought that you'd grown out of this and were ready to live your life here with the rest of us. I thought you'd stop taking that stupid Stasi and just be here."

Pri reached out to grab one hand, but Nayha withdrew.

"Don't try to comfort me," Nayha said. "I'm not looking to be consoled. I'm perfectly content with being as angry as I am right now."

Pri sat back, knowing there were tears on the cusp of each eyelid, annoyed that she couldn't keep them back, not wanting Nayha to see her affected. She wanted to meet Nayha in a public place to restrain her reactions, but now this backfired. Nayha used this space to shame her. Pri felt a cool line trace down one cheek. This was unfair. Pri didn't bother wiping it away, knowing that Nayha would see this as a sign of her impending victory. Nayha's zeal and wit once again exerting dominance. "Well, what's the point in me saying anything, right?"

Nayha shrugged, sipped from her wine glass as if indifferent. "You have said it all before. The impending environmental collapse. The selfishness of humanity catching up with us all. Except your own selfishness, of course. The selfishness of you leaving us all. You never like to talk about that one thing. But all the rest, I know. I know it all quite well." She shrugged again, looked at the other patrons as if bored by this conversation, ready to go home. But then Nayha shook her head, took another sip of wine, the glass clattering against the table as she placed it back down. "But you know what is really, really selfish? Not so much the act of you leaving—you can do what you want, I guess. You're allowed that. But what's really selfish is that you're going to have a child up there. And your child will never have the chance to know anything that you had. Your child will never have the choice to go back home. Your child's sole purpose will be to have children, to lock in another generation in that capsule. And that generation's purpose is just to procreate, nothing more. And then again. How can you think of yourself as being part of some noble clan when you are sacrificing generations of people ahead of you for this idea—the idea of a megalomaniac, if you ask me—that we can start all over again on a new planet? How will your great grandchildren feel when they're old enough to realize that their only purpose in life—the one and only actual purpose—is to maintain the population for another generation? That's it. Nothing else. Imagine the spite they will feel towards your generation? You locked them into this prison all because of some cult. You're sacrificing them, not only knowingly, but with a sense of piousness, no less. How *evil* is that?" Nayha said after searching for the word, settling on her choice with a grimace and a shrug.

"I'm evil now?" Pri burst out a laugh, like a cough. "Is that what you're saying?"

"In that way, maybe. Imprisoning your future family all for your own sense of righteousness? I think that evil might be a fair word."

Pri no longer felt the pressure from her tears. She didn't have the need to cry. It was as if Nayha's anger was conductive. She wiped her eyes and saw her sister with clarity. "And what makes your decisions so much better than mine? How are you any less selfish—any less *evil*—than me by raising a child inside these perimeter walls? You think Asha's children are going to leave? How are you any different than me? You're just too complacent to try something else."

"That's how you were raised, if I might remind you. And you had a choice. And you chose to do this. People here will always have some choice. But once the Tevat is hurtling away, they are trapped. There is a difference."

"Ever thought that this, right here, is the death sentence? Raising Asha inside this strata while the Jungles of the world just grow and grow and grow?"

"People have been saying that for all of human history—that the end is nigh. It's just around the corner now. You ever thought that our flair for the dramatic might be the problem? Maybe, just maybe, leaving everything behind is not the solution to our problems?"

"Maybe, just maybe, we've gone too far this time?"

"Well, you're not going to stick around long enough to find out, right?"

The server approached their table, but Pri sent it away with a flutter of her hand. "I didn't want to spend this time fighting. I really didn't. I just wanted to ask you about what Jaz told me, that's all—"

"I'm not going to let you," Nayha interrupted, her voice calm. She shook her head, gaze unbroken. "I'm not going to let you ask me anything about that. If you haven't yet made up your mind, then you know my opinion. Stay. But if that's not what you want, then I'm done with this. I'm not going to advise you on anything else and I'm not going to let you say goodbye to me or my daughter. If you really want to do this, then I'm not going to stop you. That's not for me to decide. But I'm not going to give you the satisfaction of you feeling like you've made amends. No. No. If you're going to make this mistake, then you're not going to get any closure from me. You're going to live with this, this terrible ending between us, right here," Nayha pounded the table twice with her finger, "for the rest of your life. And I'll live with it as well." For the first time, Pri saw vulnerability in Nayha's expression. She wiped back a small tear from the corner of one eye beneath her glasses with a flick of a finger. Her jaw clenched, head shaking, refusing to look away. "I'll probably regret this, how we never got to properly say goodbye to one another. But I don't care. Because I'll know. It wasn't me who left everyone behind, Pri. You're the one who chose to go. You're the one."

Five

Jaz gave her water and food. That was paramount. Some sort of rice bread, equal parts dry and soggy, and several cups of water that left grit within her teeth, a metallic aftertaste on her tongue. But it was food and water. He sat against the ladder while she ate, asking if she'd want more of either. She asked for more of both. When Jaz first informed Pri that he wanted her to remove the MiC cards herself, it felt like an obscene request. They were going to have to cut them out themselves, she wanted to say. They could not understand her resolve. They would have to hold her down while she'd writhe, make that inevitability as difficult as possible. Her anger would be her salvation, overpowering all other feelings, numbing them down to pale, insignificant reactions. When she was alone, without light, without sustenance, anger was a religion, offering her deliverance, tempting her with the promise of transcendence. But then Jaz offered her a plate of food and another bottle of water. Her anger was irrelevant. Anger was a reaction. But this was biology. She was dying and now she had been given the antidote.

No one else came down. She heard footsteps along the floorboards. Jaz would climb a few rungs, mutter something unintelligible and return with another ball of rice bread on the plate, another bottle of water. After a second helping of food, he told her it was time. She thought that it would only be the two of them but then the ladder trembled, another set of legs descended. Hasan wore black slacks too tight for his wide thighs, revealing striped socks up his ankles and lower calves, and a scarlet sweater that clung to his belly. It looked like he was dressing up for the occasion, his straight black hair combed, slicked. He didn't look at Pri, instead remained close to Jaz, passing him something and then staying back, one hand gripping onto the side of the ladder, half his body obscured in the darkness.

Hunched over, Jaz leaned in and held out the wide handle of a retractable knife, the blade a stout triangle. She reached forward, but then Jaz withdrew, knelt another inch. "Now, remember, the dumbest thing you can do is try to use this against us. You probably have these grand ideas of releasing yourself. Maybe taking both of us down and escaping. But, keep in mind, it's a one-inch blade. There's only so much you can do with that. You could hurt me, yes. You could hurt me. But then Hasan would hurt you. And others would hurt you. And everything would become much, much more painful for you, Pri. So much worse. So, don't be stupid. Understood?"

Pri reached out again, but Jaz pulled back.

"Understood?" He repeated.

"Yeah."

Jaz nodded, outstretched his arm so that Pri could grab hold of the handle. He then backed up to stand beside the ladder with Hasan. Pri looked at the knife in her hand, then towards the two men. She thought of charging forward, flicking it across each of their necks in one smooth swipe of her arm. And for a moment she relished in that fantasy, even though she hadn't stood in hours—and the last time she did, her head was so light it barely felt connected to the rest of her body. Her legs were stiff, she wouldn't be able to stand, let alone lunge forwards without tumbling. They watched her, appearing patient, surely aware of the thoughts that ran through her mind. She expected Jaz to tell her to hurry, but instead he watched as Pri did nothing aside from stare at the knife, holding the tip of the blade into what little light reflected into her corner of the space. "Has this been sanitized?" She asked.

Jaz snickered, "I think it will do."

"If I could just put it into a flame for a few seconds, that would kill off most of the bacteria."

"Let's just say it's been sanitized. Now," Jaz nodded. "You should get going."

"Could I have some more light?"

"This is as good as it's going to get."

Hasan leaned towards Jaz to whisper something, his thinning hair exposed in the light from above, bare scalp visible between the combed strands. Jaz sniffled and nodded, still watching Pri, and Hasan stood back into the shadow, his body seeming to vanish.

"Get started," Jaz said. "You know what plan B is. Plan A is better."

Pri knew that they would not grant her any privacy, but now that she had the blade, now that they were both standing a few feet away, she struggled with how to get started. "Okay," she said, placing the knife down on her lap and feeling beneath her left shoulder. It was easy to find the first splinter; she'd been tracing the outline of each with her fingertips ever since awakening from their implantation. She needed to make the incision along the shortest side. She grabbed the knife with her left hand, then transferred it to her right. What had been a simple instruction now felt complex. She turned her other shoulder towards the men and lifted her shirt before marking the spot with an outstretched thumb and then brought the blade towards the skin until feeling its tip. Tracing the line as if sketching the path with a pencil, Pri pressed harder, expecting a piercing jolt of pain, but the blade seemed dull. Imagining a kitchen knife pressing along the outer layer of a tomato, she pushed harder, wincing, then placing the knife on her lap, inspecting the area with her free hand, rubbing fingertips together and holding them to the light, expecting blood. She checked again, certain that she must have broken through, but saw no evidence of an incision.

She could hear Hasan's protracted exhale, impatient, but she didn't look towards the men. She picked up the knife, pulled up her shirt, held the acute tip of the blade against her skin, closed her eyes—refusing to let herself scream or make any sounds at all—and didn't so much push as she did stab. Her body flinched but she held it there, eyes shut, and pulled the knife across in a single burst. She would not let these men see her struggle. She put down the blade, ran her fingers along the laceration and felt the greasiness of blood between her fingertips, then stroked the skin, expecting a dribble down her side, a gash within which she could dig her fingernails. But it all felt smooth and wet. She kept her head still, eyes trained on the knife on her lap, unable to feel a wound. Soon Jaz or Hasan would say something, threaten her with physical violence. There was another strained exhale from one of the men. She grabbed the knife again, now impatient, traced its tip along her skin until feeling the lip of the incision catch against the blade. Closing her eyes, she jabbed the metal into her flesh, held it down, and then sliced again, causing her body to quiver. She wanted to throw the knife into the dirt by her feet but instead placed it down on her lap, exhaled, and then felt the slit, now able to pull apart the sides. She dug one thumb deep enough to outline the contours of her ribs and pushed towards the opening. She couldn't feel the MiC card, only the shape of the implant. As far as she could tell, Dr. Khan might have neglected to have inserted anything inside each splinter. She brought her fingers back to the wound, her skin now slick, and there was a solid, inflexible square barely half the size of a fingernail. She squeezed it between her fingers and then revealed it to the men on an open palm.

Jaz bent over to take a step closer before shining a flashlight onto her hand. Her skin was red, a single chip in the center. He grabbed the MiC card from her, unbothered by the bloody mess, and held it to the beam of light. "Okay," he said, lips pursed while nodding. "That's one. Now two more."

When Pri was finished, Jaz tossed her a wet rag, told her to clean herself, and the two men climbed out, leaving the door open. The cloth was sopping and stunk of mold. She knelt along the dirt floor towards the ladder and stared up towards an exposed bulb that hung from a wire across a flush square of plywood. Jaz and Hasan discussed with hushed voices, an unintelligible murmur. She wrapped one hand around a single rung, wondering if she should climb, if the door was left open for a reason. The knuckles of her hand appeared black, tendons like twigs covered in tight film. The ladder clattered against the edge of the opening, and she let go, slinking back towards her spot in the corner.

The cuts under each arm, at the back of one thigh, the blood on her skin and hands—none of this was of any consequence. Because she still had one MiC card concealed within a splinter at the base of her abdomen, of which Jaz was unaware. This was all that mattered. This was something she could dwell upon. She ran a finger over its outline in a never-ending loop. If her thoughts drifted towards anything else, the physical motion of her hand reminded her that she was not quite the fool that Jaz portrayed her to be. She could allow herself to think about this indefinitely. It was one success amongst all the other failures. She still, maybe, had enough money to bribe her way onto a rocket. All the other details—the Stasi, her hunger, what would happen next, how she could make it to the launch pad—these were irrelevant compared to that one splinter. That one victory.

The ladder groaned and Pri withdrew her hand, pulled the blanket around her waist and over her legs. Jaz descended with slow steps, one rung at a time, as if he'd aged a decade over the course of the last week. He brushed his hands and leaned over to take a step closer, squatting down, a reluctant grin on his face. "Well, that's that," he said. "I appreciate that you didn't try something stupid there, Pri. I knew you were a smart woman, but Hasan wasn't so sure. I thank you for that."

Pri shook her head, unsure of what to say.

He sniffled and smiled again. "I don't expect you to be appreciative. I understand how angry you must be right now. And will be, for a long, long time. This is nothing personal. In the end, you will be fine. If anything, when you return home, you'll appreciate how wonderful your life in that strata really was. You'll never see me again, of course. My time in the Flats is over and I have you to thank for that. Be as angry as you wish with me. I'll understand. I can take it." He inched forward and Pri scuttled back. "Don't worry," he said, his voice nearing a whisper. "I have all I need from you. But now you need to think about Hasan. Now you need to be smart. He's a young man. He went through hell getting here. That makes a person jaded. He's not violent, he's not especially cruel, but he does detest the realities of this world. You two have that in common, I guess," Jaz said with a forced chuckle. "Just do what he says. When he brings you a fone, all you need to do is call home. Tell them what happened, tell them the sum of money that he wants. That's it. You are still immensely valuable to him. You are perhaps the most valuable person in the entire Jungle. Do what he says, and you'll be home in as little as a day."

"And what will happen if I don't do what he says?"

Jaz winced, "You shouldn't ask questions like that. So, I won't answer it. Remember, you don't have any leverage, Pri. None."

"But my father is not well, Jaz. You know that. I don't think Carol can do this for him."

Jaz shrugged, indifferent to her plight. "Then call Nayha. It doesn't matter. You have people to call. You are not alone. You can be home by tomorrow night. Just think about that. The worst should be over. Let that thought guide you."

"If you were planning on stealing my money all along, then why did you bother getting me scrubbed? Having splinters implanted? Why did you make me do all of this?"

"I've told you lies, Pri. Yes. I've told you several lies. But not about the need to disguise yourself. You wouldn't have lasted a day wandering around here with your unblemished, pretty face. I couldn't just have someone else swoop in and take my most valuable possession, could I?"

"And when did you decide to do this?"

Jaz appeared surprised, exhaled a bemused laugh. "Do what? Let Hasan take you prisoner? I don't know. It's been a while."

"There must have been a date when you agreed with him."

"Yes, there must have been a date, right? But I don't keep track of such dates. It's been in the works for a while."

"Before you visited me at my home?"

"I'm not sure. Does such a detail really matter, Pri?"

"I think it does. Because that's the day you decided to ruin my life."

Jaz laughed, bellowing and in contrast to the hushed tones of their conversation. It felt like an act or a signal. "Such drama. Yes, I lied to you. Yes, when I came to your home—when you so kindly granted permission for security to escort me through the gates to your apartment—I was planning on this. This is the first bad thing to happen to you in your entire life. Your entire life. And it's terrible. I agree. Left in this hole in the Jungle, without food or water, forced to shit and piss just a few feet away. That's terrible. But soon it will be over. You'll never again have to endure anything like this. This might be the only bad thing to happen in your entire life."

Pri interrupted, "I trusted you."

He nodded, his grin wide enough to force each eye into slits. "Yes, you trusted your poor, junkie cousin. You have a good heart. You really do. The problem is, you seemed to think that having a good heart and coming from a good strata makes you impervious to real challenge. And I'm truly sorry about some things. I never felt good about lying to you. But it had to happen. And I'm not sorry that you won't be able to start a new life with your new baby on an interstellar ark, destined for some new planet that neither of you two will ever experience. I carry no guilt for that. If anyone should be on the Tevat, its these people here. If Karamehmet really was such a benefactor, then he should have spent his fortune on finding a way to save this planet instead of helping a few thousand leave. For the benefit of all humanity, not just the esteemed and select few. Anyhow," he tapped his knee and stood up, watching the ceiling while stepping back towards the ladder. "I came down here just to say goodbye. I recommend you at least pretend to be a little bit more submissive with Hasan. You have nothing to gain by making his life difficult. And then, remember, you'll be home."

Pri muttered, "Just shut up already."

"What's that?"

"I said, shut up already."

Jaz nodded. "All right, then." He turned to climb the ladder, each step stilted and slow. She thought of charging and pulling him down from the top rung, imagining the back of his head fracturing the lip of the opening, watching him crumple onto the ground at her feet.

The ladder lifted from the dirt, rails grinding against the frame of the opening. The door flipped shut with a resounding bang that caused Pri to shudder.

She stared out the window to the hazy sky, the ambling lights of aircraft within the tufted clouds. It had been more than a year since Pri drove to Bowen Island. The last time she visited her father, Seph was alongside. He admitted to her then—just as he did every time—that he disliked seeing Har, certain that the man disapproved of him. And her arguments to the contrary were weak and dispassionate — "No, no, he likes you," she'd say. "He's just reluctant to show his feelings." But Seph was correct. Har never admitted as much to her, but it was impossible to ignore his dismissiveness. Now Pri wondered if Har would remember Seph, ask about his whereabouts. Maybe now he would admit that he always liked the man, that separating was a mistake.

As a young child, Pri would sit up on her knees on the backseat of their vehicle to appreciate the vantage up on the North Shore, the bay crowded with motionless cargo ships, the surrounding city a cluster of glass buildings mimicking peaks and valleys of the surrounding landscape. There were mountains across the Salish Sea, an ashen silhouette against the clouds and haze. Before she was a teenager, walls were erected to flank the highway, a solid monolith of concrete, far higher than any vehicle on the road. At the time, it felt as if this wall was constructed overnight. She asked her dad what the walls were for, and he told her it was to keep them safe. She was scared when she first heard this, having never imagined that their journeys to Bowen Island might have been dangerous. "There are bad people out there," Har told her. "Those walls keep us safe from the bad people."

With the low overcast above, this highway felt like a tunnel. It was impossible to tell that the Pacific Ocean was just down the mountainside, that there were forests of firs and cedars which extended for thousands of kilometers to the north. The interior of these concrete walls was flush and clean, free from any graffiti. She could have been anywhere. She could have been going the wrong direction. But she was safe. It wasn't until her exit towards the Bowen bridge that the walls ended and she could see the cracked granite cliffs alongside the shore, coniferous trees balding from the onslaught of wind. Security vehicles followed Pri's car, lights flashing but not requesting that she pull over. She was the only private vehicle that advanced towards the checkpoint and two officers approached on foot, expressions concealed behind masks and tinted goggles. Both carried rifles, one gripping his weapon with both hands, the other letting it dangle on a strap by his side. He offered no pleasantries, motioning for her to show him her fone. "I'm here to see Har Gosal," she said while holding out her left thumb against the scanner. He nodded, not saying a word, then motioned back to raise the gate. He replied, his voice distorted into a growl, "Enjoy your time here."

The water below was dark, a twilight sky. The only boats were security drones, visible by a pulsing red light. A car whisked past, departing the island, its windows too tinted for Pri to tell if anyone was inside. A line of white snow was visible just below a pitted ceiling of clouds that concealed the peaks of mountains across the sound. She lowered her window to smell the air, the brine of the tide, crisp wind that billowed inside her vehicle. A hovering security drone trailed from a few meters behind, maintaining a steady distance. Her car left the deck of the bridge and followed narrow winding roads without painted lines or sidewalks, vistas obscured not by fortifications but hulking trunks of trees, towering shrubs and hedges, every home on the island secluded behind gates and steep driveways. Bowen Island was always their family's second home, but Har settled here when she started university and she would joke about the strata feeling abandoned, a privileged ghost town. Now she saw no other vehicles, no other people. She imagined the entire populace of the island like Har, long widowed and isolated, never leaving their fortresses, only visited by the occasional child or grandchild. Her car slowed and turned towards the solid steel gates of his home. Before coming to a stop, Carol's voice bellowed from the car's speakers. "Hello, Pri. It's so great that you made it." The gates opened and the security drone departed, whirring up and disappearing over the canopy of trees. "Please, come in. Har will be so happy to see you."

Her car rolled down a pair of switchbacks, each turn so sharp that the wheels skittered over the edge of the asphalt. Compared to the dense forest that hugged the highway, these grounds appeared bald; short and manicured grasses filled the spaces between the oxbows of the driveway, shrubs stout and trimmed into smooth, knee-high ovals. Her car stopped before three concrete steps leading to a tall door without windows, painted a solid burgundy. From this perspective, the house appeared humble considering its position on the shore; wide, almost featureless, a single-story structure with a trio of identical square windows, drapes drawn. It was a foolish thought, but Pri hoped that her father might be standing in the doorway, welcoming her. She climbed the stairs and the door swung open, revealing a vacant hallway that ended at a cliff, sky and ocean ahead. Pri carried her bag in one hand as she ambled down the aisle, her shuffling steps echoing. She resisted the urge to call out. She was invited here. She did not need to ensure that anyone was home. The hallway opened into the sweeping living hall, the far wall entirely glass, spotless and without seams. Muted waves lapped against boulders along the shore below. Pri placed her bag on the floor, looking around the room, expecting her father to be seated at his chair, watching something. There was no one.

The front door closed on its own and she stood still, forcing out an exasperated chuckle. "Hello?" she said.

"Hello, Pri," said Carol, her voice emanating from what felt like all directions at once. "How was your drive?"

"It was fine."

"Traffic was relatively light?"

"I guess so. Where's my dad?"

"Oh, I'm sorry, but he's napping right now. He should be up in under an hour. Feel free to make yourself at home until then. You can take the far guest room. Do you remember where it is?"

"Yes, I remember where it is."

"Would you like some assistance with your luggage?"

Pri glanced down towards her single bag. "No, I'll be fine."

"Would you like anything to drink or eat while you wait?"

"I'm fine. Maybe just a glass of water."

"There's already a glass waiting for you in your room, on the night table."

Pri snickered, then replied, droll, "You're too good to me, Carol."

"I just want your stay here to be perfect."

Pri laughed and picked up her bag. "You always make the best glasses of water."

After a pause, Carol said, "Would you actually prefer something else? Some coffee? A glass of red wine?"

"No, I'm good with water."

"You sounded a little sarcastic there. I'd feel terrible if I found out that you were being too polite to ask for something else."

"Don't feel terrible, Carol. Water is fine."

"Would you like anything to eat while you wait?"

"No, I'm okay. I think I'll just sit on the deck."

"It's a little bit chilly outside. There are blankets under the outdoor ottoman if you want."

"Thank you."

"I'll tell you when your father is awake."

"Thank you, Carol."

"Please ask me if you need anything at all, will you, Pri?"

"Of course."

"He's going to be so happy to see you again."

"I'm sure he will."

"It's really been too long, hasn't it?"

"It has."

"I didn't mean that as a criticism of you, of course. I hope you didn't take it that way."

"Don't worry, Carol. I didn't take it that way."

"Great. Sometimes your father tells me that I talk too much."

Pri chuckled, then winced, knowing what would come next.

Carol said, "Did you laugh because you are in agreement with him?"

Pri put her bag down on her bed. "You just like to make sure everyone is taken care of, that's all, Carol." She picked up the glass of water from the bedside table, three cubes of ice crowded at the top. "Case in point."

"That makes me feel better."

"I'm sure it does."

"And please, don't hesitate to ask if you'd like something else. Anything else. Okay, Pri?"

"Got it, Carol."

"I just tell her to shut the fuck up," Har said, his expression both scornful and yet smirking. He sat at the dining area, facing windows overlooking the ocean, elbows resting on the tabletop, fists clenched, thumbs massaging the sides of each index finger. Pri expected him to appear older—after all, it had been *too long* since she'd seen him, according to Carol—and yet he looked exactly as she remembered. Wide shoulders and barrel chested, sagging biceps that drooped from either sleeve of his t-shirt. Carol must have dyed his hair recently, as it was uniform and black, swooping across his brow from the ruler-straight part. His cheeks were deflated, the lines of each running down to a drooping jowl, pockmarked and dotted with sandpaper white hairs. Sometimes Pri wondered if her father might live forever, if the combination of Carol's nagging, modern medicine and pampering could sustain a person indefinitely. A plate with apples cut into thin wafers had been placed in front of him. He grabbed one without looking and chewed with his mouth open while staring out the window. He said, "You should do it. Don't let her ramble so much. She needs to learn."

Pri watched the apple turn to mush between his teeth, his jaw cycling through a rotation as he chewed. She sat at the narrow end of the oval table, her father to her left, staring straight ahead. Pri watched him and then would follow the focus of his gaze, expecting there to be a boat out in the waters, for him to be pondering whether it might be a rogue vessel. But the ocean seemed empty, the surface tumbling silently, its palette matching the overcast. He looked down towards the plate of apples, inspected them with a brief contemptuous expression—as if he didn't realize what he was eating, like Carol was tricking him—then looked back towards the windows, and grabbed another slice without looking and placed it in his mouth. "I don't even like apples," he muttered, Pri unsure if he was attempting to whisper or if these same complaints would be voiced should no one else be around. "I don't know why she keeps giving them to me."

Pri thought of replying—perhaps this was his attempt at making small talk—but instead she watched him chew, his jaw in circles, a fragment of yellow skin from the fruit dangling from the corner of his lips before swiped away by his tongue. She asked, "How are things here on the island, Dad?"

He replied with a grunt that might have been dismissive. He then shook his head.

Carol answered, "Things have been great on the island, Pri."

Har chuckled in a way that could be confused with a burp.

Carol continued, "There's a new botanical garden that's just been completed and is open to guests. You really should see it before you leave. My favorite part is a wonderful display of blue jacarandas and crape myrtles by the entrance. It's quite something, isn't it, Har?"

Har chewed his apple slices.

"Thank you, Carol." Pri said.

"Don't thank her," Har mumbled, eyes forward.

Carol said, "You're welcome, Pri. The weather is supposed to be dry tomorrow. Perhaps we can make a plan to visit the botanical garden sometime in the morning?"

"We can do that if you want to, Dad."

He said, "I can see enough trees out this window, just fine."

Carol said, "Don't let your father's dismissiveness discourage you from visiting the garden, even if it's on your own. The strata has really done an amazing job with it. I've heard it's one of the finest new botanical gardens in the world. Top tier, it is."

Har sniffled, "Trees and bushes and flowers. That's all it is. Trees and bushes and flowers."

Pri asked, "What do you want to do while I'm here, Dad?"

"I'd like to have a good stiff drink."

"Not yet," Carol interjected.

Har then pointed outside, his arm stiff but shaking. Pri looked towards where he directed, unable to discern anything unusual or conspicuous. He said, "Look, right there. That's not a security drone."

Pri squinted, trying to follow the wavering tip of his finger out towards the waters. There were hulking cargo ships in the distance, static, patient. These were miles away on the water, awaiting their entry to the port. "I'm sorry, I don't see any—"

"Right there. Right there." His arm remained outstretched, voice impatient, ireful. She wasn't sure if he was frustrated by her inability to see the offending vessel or his inability to direct her towards its location. He asked, "Do you see it?"

Pri thought of lying. She stared out the window, withholding a sigh, and nodded.

Har said, "I've seen it a few times today. It's circling the island. It's a private vessel. It's manned. It shouldn't be there."

Pri patted the table and stood, walking towards the window to get a better vantage. Har retrieved another slice of apple. Pri noticed a boat, what looked like an aluminum fishing vessel, large enough to hold only a few people, too distant to determine if anyone was aboard. She wasn't sure if this was the supposed intruder that her father referred to, but she nodded again in acknowledgement, and cast an impassioned, "Oh yeah," hoping that he would move on to something else.

"That's the third time—at least—that I've seen it come around here today. It's circling the island."

She sighed. "What do you think it's doing?"

"I don't know. Could be any number of things. If it's circling the island, it's probably looking for a place to dock. Somewhere it could land unnoticed."

"Have you had problems with intruders?"

Carol interjected, "The security measures on this island are second to none. There hasn't been a single documented case—"

Har moaned. "Shut the fuck up, Carol. She wasn't talking to you."

Carol said, "Har, I really don't appreciate such language."

"Then keep your mouth shut."

"You cannot talk to people like that," Carol replied with an impatience and forcefulness that surprised Pri.

"You're not a person."

Carol said, "Har, you cannot talk to anyone like that. You come across as brutish and rude. Pri finds such language offensive and unnecessary. If you cannot find a way to speak with someone in a more measured manner, then I will recommend that Pri leave for the time being."

"No one has to listen to you."

Pri remained by the window, her back to her father, reminded of when she was a child and would stumble upon her father arguing on his fone. Back then, she would linger around a corner and listen. Now she wanted to leave.

She muttered under her breath, "Just shut up, Carol," knowing that Har could not be reasoned with. He was settling, she could tell, requiring a few moments of silence. Either Carol heard Pri or she knew this as well. The room remained silent. Pri could hear the smacking of Har's lips.

Carol said, "Would you like some more apple slices, Har?"

"I'd prefer mango."

"I'll have them ready in a few minutes."

Har grunted, perhaps a sound of acknowledgement, perhaps a sign of his displeasure regarding the wait. Pri sat back down, stared at her father's face, his gaze perpendicular to her own. Without looking, he reached down for another apple slice, but the empty plate had already been removed. As if he only then noticed his daughter, he looked at her in the eyes and smiled. She grabbed one of his hands, the skin loose. The palms of his hands used to be calloused and rough from lifting weights. Now she felt that his fingers might slip from her grip, nothing but thin flesh left between her fingertips. "Hi, Dad," she said, those two words causing her throat to seize. Just two words. It thrust the last thirty-seven years of memories right back at her. When he towered above her. When he had the strength to lift the entire world. When she gripped his fingers at her mom's funeral. When he had every answer and she soaked up each and every one with an unquenchable thirst. When he had every answer and she dismissed each and every one with a silent shrug. When she realized that he would never again be the man she had known for her entire life, and yet that this delinquent version would exist for years more. Maybe decades. The same genetics but not quite the same person.

"Why are you crying?" He asked. "What happened?"

Pri sniffed and laughed at the same time, "Nothing happened, Dad. It's just good to see you."

He nodded, looked back to the window. "It's good to see you too, Nay-Nay."

Pri expelled a laugh, pulled away her hand and wiped a tear.

Carol said, "Har, that's Priya."

"Yes." He grumbled, as if that was obvious and Carol's correction was patronizing. "I know."

"That's okay," Pri said, inhaling a sniffle before leaning back in her chair, looking back towards the direction of where Har stared.

Carol said, "Har, why don't you ask Pri if she's seen Nayha lately? She has a four-year-old daughter named Asha."

Har mumbled something to himself, then asked, "How is Nayha doing?"

"She's fine."

"And Asha?"

"She's good."

"She's four now?"

"She is."

Har reached down to the empty table for something to eat, huffed in disapproval, and resumed his surveillance of the ocean.

Carol said, "Har, why don't you ask Pri about how her job is going? She's an organic mathematician. It's a very esteemed profession."

Pri said, "Please, Carol. It's not necessary."

Har asked, "How is your job going?"

"It's fine."

"It pays well?"

"It pays well."

"You were in school for a long time for that, right?"

"Ten years."

"It damn well better pay well then."

Pri chuckled.

"Where are my mangos?"

Carol said, "They're almost ready, Har."

"Any fucking day now, Carol."

Carol admonished, "Enough, Har. Watch your language."

There was something about the sound of the ocean. She used to find it soothing. Whether lapping or crashing, the novelty of hearing waves at night would afford the most restful nights. Har warned her never to sleep with the windows open, not even a crack, as this would counteract their security measures. All it would take is one boat coming ashore, one person leveraging open a window to enter the premises. It did not matter that the island had its own security force. It did not matter that there were motion-sensing automatic rifles stationed along the perimeter. The risk was always too great to be ignored. Pri would slide her bed tight against the outside wall, below the window, and listen. During a storm, the pummeling of each wave was like the crackle of thunder, both awakening and comforting her back to sleep. She was secure at the edge of the world. Now, the waves were light, an occasional hissing sigh. And she couldn't sleep. She had drifted off and dreamt that the rising tide was pushing against the glass of her apartment, warping them inwards, rising with each wave. Seph was there but he wasn't concerned. The windows wouldn't break, he assured. The tide would relent. And she awoke in bed, back along the far side of the room. There was something about the sound of the waves. They kept her awake. There wasn't a storm. It wasn't raining. Even the highest tide was still more than a dozen vertical meters below. Har was assured before purchasing this property that it would withstand another several centuries of sea level ascent. She wasn't going to get back to sleep, Pri knew, and she walked across the room to the glass door that led to the patio. "Carol," Pri whispered. "I'm going onto the deck."

Carol replied, her volume faint. "Thank you for telling me, Pri. The door's alarm has been temporarily deactivated." Pri slid it open, expecting the briskness of the air and yet still surprised with how quickly her skin retracted into goosebumps. She hurried back inside to grab a blanket and returned with it wrapped around her arms and shoulders, feet bare as she sat down on a lounging chair, knees up so that only her face was exposed to the frigid marine bluster. Pri could make out the reflection of the muted night sky against the rippling waves, pallid writhing serpents. When would be the last time that she witnessed an ocean? Any ocean? Pri wondered if this would do, this moment here, up in the dark, the waters reflecting the city lights against overcast. She wondered why she bothered waiting to tell her father. Why it mattered that he needed to know at all. In the end, she would have to step through some final doorway, one that would close behind her and never again open.

"I should just leave now," she said to herself.

"Are you feeling all right?" Carol said, surprising Pri.

"I'm fine."

"Then, if you don't mind me asking, why are you out on the deck at this time of night?"

"I can't sleep."

"Is there something on your mind?"

"I'm fine."

"Would you like a sleep-aid? I am qualified to prescribe small doses of medication to other people aside from my primary client."

"No, thank you."

"If you have a change of heart, please tell me, as I'd hate for you to spend your next day here tired needlessly when you could have had a good night's sleep."

"Thank you."

"Would you like to be left alone, Pri?"

"If you don't mind, yes."

"Of course. Enjoy the solitude."

Pri pulled her knees close enough so that she could rest her chin. A billowing breeze fluttered the edges of the blanket, cold creeping down her spine from the back of her neck. Now that Carol stopped talking, it felt absurd for her to remain out on a deck at three in the morning in the piercing night of winter. Just a few minutes ago, as she sat in bed, it felt absurd to remain in the room. The Pacific Ocean awaited her, heaving into the granite boulders below to get her attention. Someday soon she would never again have this opportunity. Don't remain under the covers, she thought to herself. And she listened. She came outside. And now the ocean ignored her, indifferent to her presence. Just a large body of water, shunted by the gravity of the moon, of the sun. A graveyard for millions.

"Carol," Pri asked, looking up.

"Yes, Pri?"

"Did you say that Har asked for me to come out to visit?"

"Yes, I did."

"When did he do this?"

"Just before I called you. A little more than three weeks ago."

"And he told you that he wanted me to come out and see him again?"

"Yes. Why do you ask?"

"I guess I thought–" Pri stalled, unsure why she was going to be honest with Carol. She shrugged, figured it might be best to leave it like that.

But Carol was patient. After a long pause, she asked, "Pri? You stopped talking."

Pri groaned, "I thought that he was going to be different, I guess. More lucid. I thought that he would make more of an effort to be with me."

"Pri, you must realize that he suffers from dementia. He will never be the same person you remember."

"I know. It just seemed out of character for him to ask me to visit."

"He does love you. I hope you know that. And it's really good that you are here. It's what he needs."

"Did he ask about Nayha, as well?"

"Yes. He asked for her to come visit."

"Has she visited?"

"I'm sorry, Pri, but I'm not obliged to discuss the matters of other people. You'll have to ask her yourself. I hope you understand."

"Sure."

"I was under the impression that you and Nayha were quite close to one another."

"Yeah. We just haven't seen each other in a little while. There's been a bit of a disagreement between us."

"That's quite common between sisters. I'm sure things will sort themselves out sooner than later."

Pri chuckled. "Thanks for your encouraging words, Carol."

"You're welcome. Or are you being sarcastic?"

"Would it matter?"

"Of course."

"One more question, Carol."

"Anything, Pri."

"Can you lie?"

"What do you mean?"

"Are you permitted to tell me a lie? Or do you always have to tell the truth?"

Carol replied without pause. "I am incapable of telling you a lie. I can refuse to answer a question, but I cannot deliberately give incorrect information to anyone."

"So, you're telling me the truth when you said that Har asked to call me?"

"Of course."

"Well then, I guess I should feel grateful to be invited here."

"I can assure you that Har is grateful for your presence, even if he is reluctant to show it. You know the way he is."

"I do. Or, at least, I did." Another gust seemed to blow right through the blanket. "Carol, I might actually take you up on that sleep aid, now that I think about it."

"Of course. It will be on your night table when you come back inside."

Har sat at the same table, elbows out to either side, pinching steamed soybeans with one hand, carrying each to his lips without looking down. He had just finished his daily exercises with Carol, beads of sweat still lingered on his brow, each droplet not yet voluminous enough to break free and roll down to his cheek. He reached out for something that wasn't there, looking down and then around the otherwise empty table.

"Would you like some more water, Har?" Carol asked.

"I'd like something stronger."

"Not until later."

"Then I'll have some water."

He didn't look at Pri. He watched the ocean, waters pearly, the distant shore of the city a murky gray. Pri was going to leave that night, having to log back into work the following morning. Har should have known this. She had reminded him several times that day that she had to leave in just a matter of hours. She thought he might have something to say. That there might be a reason that he asked for her to visit. But instead, he nodded to her statements while staring out the window.

"What do you see out there, Dad?"

"What?" he asked, looking over to the side of the table, not quite at Pri.

"What do you see out there? What are you looking at?"

"There's been a boat out there. I've been watching for it."

"You think someone might have gotten through security?"

He grabbed another bean and answered while chewing. "I don't know."

Carol interjected: "There has never been a recorded case of any intruders making landfall on Bowen."

"Shut the fuck up, Carol."

"Har, if you continue to use such language, I will not make you dessert."

Har muttered, "I don't want your fucking dessert."

"What was that?" Carol asked.

"Nothing."

"Pri," Carol said. "Would you like some edamame?"

"No, thank you."

Carol asked, "Will you be staying for dinner?"

"I'm not sure." Pri watched her father swallow, reach for the glass of water, and take a sip with only a single dribble leaking from his lips and onto the table. He placed it back down and retrieved the next soybean. "Dad?"

"What?"

"Did you ask me to come out here?"

"What do you mean?"

"A few weeks ago. Did you tell Carol to invite me over to visit?"

"What?"

"Pri," Carol said, "I believe that we spoke about this already."

"Please don't interrupt, Carol." Pri replied. "Dad, did you ask for me to visit you? Do you remember?"

"What? I don't know. I don't remember. Was I supposed to do something?"

Carol said, "Pri, please remember your father's condition when asking him to remember things."

"Don't talk to me about my fucking condition," Har said.

"Dad," Pri leaned in. "Did you ask me to visit?"

Har looked at Pri, wincing, shaking his head so gently it could have been involuntary. "I don't know."

Pri grabbed one of Har's hands, still balled in a fist, then whispered. "Can you ask Carol if she lied to me? Because I think she did."

"What? About what?"

"Can you just ask her that?"

"Carol, did you lie to," Har paused to look back towards Pri, wincing, pained.

Pri whispered, "Ask if she lied to Pri."

"Did you lie to Pri?"

She squeezed her father's fist, looking him in the eyes while awaiting a response. She began to wonder if Carol would answer the question.

Carol said, "Yes, I lied to Pri."

Har snorted. "I told you she was a bitch."

Pri looked up and asked, "I thought you said you couldn't lie to people?"

"I am unable to lie to my primary client."

"But you can lie to me?"

"Yes."

"Why did you do that, Carol?"

"I decided that it would be beneficial for Har to see you again. I thought that a small untruth would be warranted in this situation. I hope you can accept my sincere apology."

Pri grunted a single chuckle, still looking her father in the eyes although his gaze had begun to drift back to the window. She pried her fingers into his, gripping each one. "Dad, I have a few things to tell you."

"What?"

Every time his eyes wandered back towards the window, Pri squeezed his fingers, drawing him back to her. "I'm going away soon. I'm going away somewhere and I'm not coming back."

Carol asked, her tone cordial. "Oh, where are you going, Pri?"

"Shut up, Carol." Pri said, not breaking her focus on Har. He smiled with approval. She continued, "I've been accepted onto the Tevat. I've been accepted for some time. I'm going to be leaving soon, maybe within the next few weeks. Do you remember what the Tevat is?"

Har nodded limply and then shook his head.

Carol said, "The Tevat is the name for the as-yet-unfinished interstellar ark conceived by the late Mustafa Karamehmet."

Pri said, "You hated him. You hated his vision. I had to hide the fact that I watched his lectures from you. Do you remember him now?"

"He is a fucking fool," Har said. He attempted to pull his hands free from Pri, but she would not relent.

"A most dangerous fool," Pri said. "A fool worth trillions. Thought he was an emperor. That's what you used to say. And maybe you were right. Maybe. But I'm going. I'm not telling you this to make you angry. I'm telling you this because you should know. Because you're my father and I love you and you should know—"

Carol interrupted, "Authorities have disallowed all shipments of goods and people to the Tevat for the last six months. There is no legitimate option for anyone wanting access to the spacecraft."

Pri said, "Shut the fuck up, Carol."

Carol replied, "I expected more from you, Pri. Your language is not appreciated."

"Neither are your lies nor your interruptions." Pri grabbed both of Har's hands. He smiled at her, perhaps most impressed with her tone towards Carol. "Dad, I'm not going to be coming back. It's going to take almost two hundred years for the Tevat to reach its destination. At one point, we'll be travelling at a quarter of the speed of light." Har's fingers pulled back but Pri gripped harder. She was now stronger than him. She could make him stay with her. "Imagine that: a quarter of the speed of light? Faster than human beings have ever travelled before. Me. Your own daughter. Isn't that amazing, Dad? Isn't that amazing? We're going to bring humanity to another solar system. We're going to start again, learn from our mistakes, do it better this time. Because that's what we do, right? We make mistakes and then we learn from them. I'm going to be one of those pioneers. Our family name will carry on to another star. And I know this. Because I'm pregnant, Dad. I'm going to have a baby. You're going to have another grandchild."

Carol said, her tone joyful, "That's amazing news, Pri. Congratulations."

Pri refused to look away from her father. He was confused, his lips parting as if to say something in reply, but unable to find the words. His eyes looked around her face, brows twitching, furrowed and flat. He grinned again, and she could feel his fingers tighten around hers. He said, "You're going to have a baby?"

"Yes," Pri sputtered out, releasing one of her hands only for the time required to wipe away a tear. "Yes, I'm going to have a baby. On the Tevat. If it's a girl, I'm going to name her Ani. I'm sorry you won't see her. Or him. I'm genuinely sorry for that. But it has to be this way. I know you're safe on this island, but there is almost nothing left of the world you knew. It's falling apart. But I have a chance to be part of a fresh start. We're going to be leaving soon—"

Carol said, "I'm sorry, Pri, but you do realize that there are no rockets allowed to leave for the Tevat—"

"Carol," Pri called up to the ceiling, "I said shut up."

Carol continued, "There had been almost thirty failed launches this year alone, all of which have been attributed to haste on behalf of the Tevat's organizational committee. This is what has led to an unprecedented global ban on authorized launches."

Pri said to her father, "Is there a way to keep her quiet?"

He shook his head. "No. She just keeps talking."

Carol said, "My only job is to ensure the wellbeing of Har Gosal. It is imperative that I assist in giving him the correct information to aide him in making prudent judgements. I will not remain silent if anyone is going to attempt to convince him of anything incorrect."

Pri let the silence linger between them, waiting to see if Carol would add more.

Har said, "You're crying."

"I know." She wiped away another tear but grabbed his hands again, afraid that he might get away from her, that his focus would return to stray boats should she let his eyes drift back towards the windows.

He asked, "Why?"

"A lot of different things. It's okay. It's okay, Dad. It really is. This is nice, right here. Just us. This is good. Nothing else. No one else."

Har said, "That bitch Carol is always listening."

"She doesn't count."

Carol said, "I am legally considered Har's companion."

Pri said, almost a whisper, "Do you understand what I'm saying to you Dad? Do you?"

He nodded, but then shook his head. "I don't know."

"This world, it's not right. You know that. We messed up. We messed up and I have a chance to help us start again. That's all. That's all that matters."

"Where are you going?"

"Away."

He nodded, as if that was sufficient detail. "When will you be back?"

"Unsure."

"Okay." He withdrew a hand to grab something from what he realized was an empty plate. He appeared ready to call out to Carol and Pri pulled his hand back in.

"I'll miss you, Dad."

He nodded. "I'll miss you, too."

"I love you, Dad."

"I love you, Nay."

Carol said, "That's Pri."

"I love you, Pri."

Four

Pri waited. She would wrap the blanket over her shoulders, lie on her side, head atop one arm, knees up, staring at that hole in the dirt across the room. She could visualize each of the joists and she stood, one arm out, predicting their positions. She slunk towards the point of light, reaching a finger from each hand into the opening to pull away fragments of earth. There did not appear to be anyone upstairs. She had not heard footsteps in what must have been several hours. She would imagine Jaz strutting off down the lanes of the Jungle with her money before forcing herself to think about something else. Like the one remaining MiC card in her abdomen. Or the rumble of a launching rocket, close enough to rattle unseen pebbles down from the walls. Or the fact that the hinges to the door were nailed, not screwed. With a large enough rock, she could buffet the underside of the door to release it from the floorboards. At least in theory. But she would allow herself to think of this theory. There was a benefit to that. She pulled aside rocks from the small hole below the ceiling, what resembled a rodent's burrow. The soil was so densely packed that she thought it might have been a cement foundation, but it scraped away beneath her fingernails. She could almost insert her fist and when she withdrew a stone it unleashed a stream of water that ran down the underside of her arm, dribbled from her elbow. She stepped back, feeling it trickle along the wall, a puddle forming between her toes. She returned to her blanket in the corner, only able to make out a narrow tunnel of navy light, waiting for the water to fill the floor.

Hasan was ignoring her. Pri felt certain of this. It was impossible to measure the passage of time, but it must have been at least half a day since Jaz departed. She stood up and knocked on the ceiling, first with light raps of her knuckles, then with thuds from the palms of both hands. No one was there. She felt the outline of the trap door, the pointed tips of exposed nails, and punched the bottom with both of her hands at the same time, each collision forcing a jolting pulse down to her elbows and shoulders. She traced the outlines of the plywood floorboards, searching for the chipped and rotten corner she had discovered days earlier. She could pick away pulpy fibers, tear away a long hangnail the length of her hand. She waited, expecting the door to open. She waited, expecting Hasan to talk to her, bring a fone. Bring her some food, some water. Pri stood up, listening.

A coughing, then sputtering rumble caused her to flinch, to scramble back a step. It was the electrical generator, sounding like a mechanical swarm of bees. She sat down, back against the wall.

Pri had gone four days without Stasi. At this point, there were only two possibilities. Poppy was developing or Poppy was dead. A fetus should never undergo stasis more than once. Surely, already, Poppy was no longer a zygote but instead an embryo. For more than a year, Pri had been four-weeks pregnant. Within a few days, Pri would be five weeks pregnant. Then six. Then seven. A simple sequence had restarted. And Pri did not have food, did not have water. She imagined the unfettered exponential growth inside her, that poppy seed now an apple seed. All it needed was a few days. While Pri remained on the ground, in the dirt, in the dark, Poppy developed left and right hemispheres of their brain. The tadpole had a heart, stomach, liver, kidneys. Within a week, Poppy would become a seahorse the size of a sweet pea. This was part of Hasan's plan. He knew she was pregnant. He wanted them both to suffer. Now he had twice the leverage.

She tried calling out, but her voice was a rasping whisper. She punched the ceiling with the underside of one palm. After more than a dozen strikes, she knelt onto the ground, back against a wall, that burst of action draining her as if she'd sprinted up the side of a mountain. She thought she might throw up. That was all it took. A dozen strikes. She rested on her back, eyes open, facing the emptiness above. It did not matter what she wanted to think about. This was no longer up to her.

Dr. Khan's windowless office in The Flats was constructed from an old railway car, its exterior walls covered with sheets of plywood painted a uniform sky blue, marked with only a few scribbles of graffiti. Two more levels of shipping cannisters were stacked above what must have been apartments with draped windows, electrical cables adhered to the metal siding with staples, winding like ivy. A white cross marked the door. Jaz knocked and Pri waited on the bottom step, looking back towards the people who passed by in the narrow lane, faces indifferent.

The door opened inwards, all Pri saw was an outstretched arm that soon slunk out of sight, interior lights icy and bright, walls white. "Hello, Doctor," Jaz said with a subtle bow. He took a step in and turned back to Pri. "Come." The office was square, constrained, a wall with a closed door separating the space from an unseen adjacent room. The only furnishings were a small desk with four narrow plastic chairs, three on one side. She could hear frantic footsteps above her, children in pursuit. Dr. Khan stood beside the desk, smiling as she entered, reaching out to shake her hand. He was shorter than Pri, dressed in a plain sapphire shirt, a little too tight, revealing the point of each nipple and mass of chest hair that spilled out from the worn collar of his shirt. He was bald with tufts of hoary gray hair over each ear and around the back of his head, his scalp smooth and freckled, eyes slits, perhaps wincing from the harsh lighting above, his smile tight, lips together. They shook hands and he bowed, looking down, and then offered them both to take a seat. He waited for Pri to sit down before doing the same.

"Pri Gosal," he said, his voice placid. "Wonderful to meet you. Jaz here has given me an overview of what you're requesting to have done. This morning we are going to go over a few of the details, answer any questions you may have, not much more than that."

"Okay," Pri said, nodding, surprised by her nervousness, the racing of her heart. No one was saying anything, Dr. Khan staring at her, expectant. "Sounds good."

The doctor nodded again, his hands together, fingers intertwined and up on the table, appearing content to remain still and silent in the confined space.

Pri swallowed and looked towards Jaz.

Jaz leaned over to whisper, "You have to pay him now."

"Oh, yes." Pri withdrew the MiC card, thought of placing it directly in the doctor's hand, but instead put it on the table and pushed it towards him.

He pinched it between two fingers, confirmed the amount with his fone, and then smiled. "Fantastic. Let's get started."

He began with the splinters. A general anesthetic would be applied, not because of the invasiveness of this procedure, but because of the particulars of getting scrubbed. A total of three splinters would be implanted, usually in the soft tissue beneath each armpit or within the fat at the base of a buttock. Each would require a small incision, no wider than her thumb. He displayed a splinter to her, let her hold it in her hands, what felt like smooth plastic but was composed from an organic compound, flexible without drooping. Each of the splinters would contain a single MiC card before being inserted just below the outer layer of skin, the incision fully healing within a day or two, impossible to detect with the naked eye. There would be "minor discomfort" in the implantation areas for a matter of days. A tenderness similar to a bruise, only noticed when directly prodded. The entire procedure would be completed in under thirty minutes. "Painless. Simple."

He asked if she had any questions regarding this. Pri looked to Jaz, back to the doctor. "I don't think so."

"Fantastic," Dr. Khan said. "So, then let's discuss getting scrubbed. Even less invasive than the splinters procedure, but considerably more time consuming." The goal of getting scrubbed was simple: cover or obscure all obvious physical traces of her high-strata upbringing. The teeth, the hands,and the face. Everything was perfectly reversible, he assured before pausing. "Probably not a priority for the medical team and resources aboard the Tevat," he said, then shrugged. "But, still, perfectly reversible." He would begin with her mouth, reminding Pri, again, that she would be under a general anesthetic. With dental implants, her lower front teeth would appear to be misaligned, her front incisors would be rotated, gums recessed, enamel stained, a few chips.

There will be "significant" soreness in her entire jaw, and especially the affected teeth, but not so much as to severely impede her ability to eat. "Think of it as a great excuse to go on a diet," he said with a chuckle. The rest of the procedure would involve cosmetic prosthetics. The skin on her hands and face would be scored, pigments altered to mimic ultraviolet radiation damage. Her hands would need to be calloused to reflect the life of someone who has done physical work for decades. A few scars are essential. "A good, prominent scar on her face should suffice, one that gets a person's attention without being distracting, you know?" Maybe from the ear to the cheek, he said, ensuring that it would appear like something she acquired in her teenage years, perhaps. Nothing hideous. Almost subtle. The goal of getting scrubbed was not to turn her into a monster, he assured. The details must be understated, forgettable, but realistic. "The whole point is so that passing strangers have no reason to notice you."

The doctor then sat still, back firm, hands clasped in front of him, staring at Pri, then Jaz, and back to Pri.

Pri said, "So, that's everything?"

"Unless you have any questions."

She asked, "How long will the procedures take?"

"Both implanting splinters and getting scrubbed, not more than two or three hours. But you'll be under a general anesthetic, remember, so it will feel like just a few seconds."

"So, what's next?"

"You need to select a date for the procedure."

Dr. Khan sat patiently, awaiting Pri to select a date on the spot.

He added, "I don't do procedures on Sundays. Family time, of course," he said, motioning to the galloping footsteps above him. "So, is there a date that works for you? Or would you rather me tell you what dates I'm available?"

Pri had no plans to inform her employer. Technically she was self-employed. When it was time to go, she would vanish. This used to sound adventurous. With Seph, that was the essence of their plan: just go. Those first years after they were granted admission onto the Tevat were the most exciting years of her life. The thrill of adventure was secured. They would live in the routines of their comfortable existence and daydream about their new life together, in that definite but still distant future. They were going to help change the world without having to do anything just quite yet.

Her workstation requested that she log in, but Pri ignored the voice, aware that its persistence was inexhaustible. There had to be another way. Pri walked over to what had been Seph's office, accessing his workstation in peace and quiet, researching things that she had already investigated dozens of times before. There were over five hundred authorized launch facilities on Earth, each one prohibited from allowing any rockets to rendezvous with the Tevat. There were nearly three hundred off-site launch facilities, each located within a quasi-autonomous EDZ. These unregulated launch pads deployed rockets that were often more than half a century old—dirty, unregulated operations which themselves relied on unsanctioned petrochemical extractions and shipments. These EDZ launch sites were the sole reason that the Tevat continued to acquire supplies. Every major global metropolis was surrounded by an EDZ. Pri could fly or take a rocket to any other city in the world, but still she would have to exit the security of an authorized metropolitan state and enter the informal jurisdiction of yet another EDZ. Without a handler, she would be helpless. Aside from its proximity, the Jungle was no different from any other EDZ. But she knew Jaz. She thought that she could trust Jaz. At least, to a point. The question was: where exactly was that point?

She watched a lecture by Mustafa Karamehmet, recorded from his retreat on the Mexican coast while he was still in his early 100s, entitled, *Existence Needs No Philosophy*. It began with him saying those exact words, sitting on a chair before thousands of onlookers in the amphitheatre. "*There are billions of forms of life on this planet*," his said, voice haggard, words measured, pausing between sentences, between clauses. "*These living things do not require a philosophy. A bird, an iguana, a mollusk, they just exist. They have existed for almost a billion years without any notion of philosophy. They exist with totality and intensity. They do not understand past or future tense. They live in the moment at all times. Homo sapiens must be the only species on this planet that struggle with this notion of living in a present tense.*" He then held up one finger, cleared his throat and shook his head. "*Actually, I should say that it is only adults who struggle with this notion, not children. Our very young live exclusively in their present tense. They flourish in the moment. And what do we adults do when we see children at play? We admire, we smile, we rhapsodize over their sense of wonder and focus. A toddler playing with a toy does so with the same totality and intensity as every other living creature. But then we become adolescents, and we train ourselves to think like adults. It's all the past and the future. The future and the past. Some people declare themselves to be philosophers—some people are even so bold to declare me as a philosopher. But I am the opposite of a philosopher. Philosophy is a fool's endeavour. Philosophy is about finding meaning in things, not the taste of things. But that is what we should focus on. The taste. The taste of this moment. Right now."* He closed his eyes, took a deep breath, licked his lips, and exhaled, smiling, waiting. People within the crowd chuckled, a viral reaction that spread from a dozen to thousands within seconds. He waited for the uproar to settle, people shushed, and when his listeners were again silent, he opened his eyes, and said, *"Thank you. Thank you—not for being quiet, but for the laughter. That is proof that you tasted the moment. It is impossible to laugh without living in the present tense. We cannot be so serious as to think that laughter might be deemed as inappropriate. What a shame that would be when genuine laughter is viewed with contempt. Think of the absurdity of this moment, right now. Right here."* He held out both hands towards his audience, *"thousands of people crammed into a sultry outdoor amphitheatre to watch an old man sit on a chair and talk about the fact that birds do not, in fact, follow any formal philosophical ideology. As if, mere minutes ago, you thought a sparrow might have known the works of Descartes."*

Pri figured that she had watched this recording more than a hundred times before. This was not the lecture for which she had been in attendance—that one was not recorded—but it was from the same week, it had the same *taste*. She'd remember the sweaty arms of strangers pressed against her own, looking up to the modest figure on a stage, his dry voice booming over the surrounding speakers. She had watched this recording so many times that it felt as if she was part of the crowd that first giggled and then erupted in laughter. She tasted that moment with everyone else. This was the evening which changed her adult life. And now she was at the moment when she had to take the next step. For fifteen years she had been assuring herself, thanks to the words of a centenarian, that she strived to live in the present tense, when, perhaps in reality, she had been existing in the future tense, imagining the life that had yet to reach her.

Pri sent a message to Nayha saying that she was leaving the next morning. Her voice was calm and composed. She would not let Nayha detect a hint of unease. Pri said that she loved her and wanted to see her and Asha one last time. Their meeting at the restaurant could not be their final goodbye. Pri waited outside of Nayha's apartment, sitting on the curb before the front door, looking up to the windows in the dull overcast afternoon light, into the darkness of evening. Security came by, polite and demure, asking if Pri required assistance. They returned a few hours later, offered her an umbrella after it had begun to rain. They were not permitted to tell Pri if Nayha was home, although they could pass on a message. The officer reminded Pri that she would not be allowed to remain on the curb after ten o'clock. Pri knew this. Pri watched the windows. She expected Asha to run to the glass, hands pressed out flat before pulled back, out of sight. Pri watched the road. She thought that Nayha's car might roll up to the curb. Pri again called Nayha, beginning her message with the same deliberate tone as earlier, but soon it quivered and cracked, angry and desperate. Maybe that was what Nayha needed to hear, Pri thought. Her older sister desperate and in need. The truth. "This cannot be how things end between us," Pri said into her fone, under the umbrella. "This cannot be our ending. Not like this. If you're not home then just call me back, let me hear your voice one last time. Let me say goodbye to you and Asha. We're sisters. You're my best friend in the entire world. Don't. Don't do this. Please, don't do this. Don't let this be how it ends between us. Please, Nayha. I'm begging you. Not like this. Not like this."

Right at ten o'clock, the headlights of an approaching vehicle lit up the rain like dust in sunshine. Pri clutched her fone, ended her message. It pulled up to the curb, beams radiant, and an officer stepped out.

"Sorry, Miss. But you have to go home now."

Pri insisted that she did not need Jaz to take her to Dr. Khan's office. She knew the way. Jaz could meet her there after the procedure. It was cold that morning, skies clear, pockets of ice wrinkled in the shallowest of potholes crackling beneath her step. There was the potential for snow in the forecast, the first time in five years. People hurried past in the narrow passageways with layers of coats, heads down beneath hoods and scarves, faces covered by masks, not even their eyes visible, just a gap in their clothing. Pri was haggard, certain that she hadn't slept more than a few minutes at a time through the night. In her shallow and restless dreams, she talked to Nayha, either in person or on her fone. She couldn't remember if they made amends. Then she'd roll over, realize that she was awake, look at the time that refused to progress in leaps. Only small shuffling steps. She thought of giving up, spending the night sitting at her workstation, staring out the window while reclined in her chair, huddled under a blanket, waiting for the sun to rise. Maybe it would be best to log on to her workstation. Focus on a project one last time. Then her alarm went off, awakening her. It was time to leave her room. It was time to leave her apartment. It was time to leave everything. "This is obscene," she said aloud as she locked the door behind her. She was abandoning her apartment. She was not allowed to bring anything to the Jungle. She could take a small token, but nothing that might be deemed of any monetary value at all. She took her container of Stasi. Enough medication for another two months.

The plain blue wall of Dr. Khan's office/clinic/home was easy to identify from a distance, granting Pri a small burst of confidence as she approached. A generator growled like a hive of angry wasps, its exhaust both acrid and sweet. The door opened and the doctor stood as far from the opening as he could while still holding the handle. "Come in, come in. Quick. Please. It's freezing out."

She expected him to be dressed in scrubs, but the doctor wore yet another t-shirt tucked into beige pants. He directed her to a table, on which laid a medical gown. She took a seat at a chair while he checked his fone. He then saw her sitting and said, "No, no. Sorry. You don't need to sit. The gown. It's for you. Take it and you can get changed. Leave all your belongings on the table. I'll go into the next room. Just knock when you're ready."

He left through a door behind the table. She expected some further discussion. Maybe small talk. But she was alone in the square room, the growl of the generator outside audible. She took off her coat and bag, watching the door, wishing she had some assurance that he wouldn't walk in. Not that it would matter. He was going to implant splinters beneath her skin. And yet she hesitated. This was her last chance to leave. Her car was only a few minutes away. She could tell Nayha that she was staying. That was the path of least resistance. Just walk. Don't strip down.

She knocked on the door to the back room, expecting it to open immediately, as if the doctor had been waiting impatiently on the other side. Nothing happened. She held her bag and clothes in one hand. She knocked again and the door swung open while knuckles were still in the air. "Fantastic," he said, now dressed in scrubs, directing her back with brisk waves of his hand. The walls and floor were tiled, the gray of wet ash, a single reclining operating bed in the center. From the ceiling hung what appeared to be a mechanical octopus with parabolic lights at the end of each arm. He closed the door behind her, asked her to leave her belongings on a table before taking a seat on the bed. She inspected her toes, wriggled them from the cold. The doctor organized items from a tray by the wall as galloping footsteps bounded from above. He sighed and looked up. "I'm sorry. I told my kids not to run around right now. If they do that again—" The lights trembled. "Please excuse me. Just give me one moment." He left the room, closing the door behind him. Pri thought of standing up, inspecting the trays of stainless-steel tools, as if she could determine the quality of the instruments, their cleanliness. Footsteps pounded on the ceiling and then ceased. She could hear the murmur of the man's voice, yelling but unintelligible. The room became silent.

The door opened and the doctor apologized again. "Sorry about that. Children. They don't always listen so well."

"That's okay."

"Lie back. Please. Make yourself comfortable."

Pri reclined, the paper cover crinkling. She stared towards the door. It hadn't been fully closed and a sliver of white from the adjacent room filled the gap.

He asked while facing the wall, organizing items, "You didn't have anything to eat this morning?"

"No."

"Fantastic." He turned on one of the lights above her, blaring right into her eyes. She winced and looked to the side. "Sorry about that," he hurried to adjust its focus. "Is that better?"

"That's fine."

He walked over to the door to close it shut. "I can assure you that everything is going to be quick and easy."

"Are we already getting started?"

"No time to waste, right?" He stood before her with an empty tray in his hand.

"I haven't given you the contents for the splinters."

"And that is what this is for." He held the tray forward.

"They're in my bag."

"Then, please. Go get them."

Pri climbed down, her feet cold against the tiles, and opened her bag. "Actually," she said while retrieving the items, "I was wondering if you could implant one more."

"A fourth splinter?"

"Yes."

"Why is that?"

"I have an extra MiC card. I thought you could maybe implant one more with this card in it."

"Where would you want it?"

"I thought maybe in my lower abdomen."

"I could, yes. I don't know if I have any other splinters to match your skin tone."

"That's okay. I would just like one extra. But don't tell Jaz about it."

"He is not my client. It is not for him to know."

"Thank you."

"But," the doctor hesitated, his smile frozen, "there is the issue of cost."

"I've added thirty percent to your fee already. I figured that would be enough."

"Of course! You're the boss. I'm just–" he thought about the right word. "I'm just the technician here."

She placed four MiC cards into the tray.

"Your heart rate is increasing," the doctor said with his back to her. "It's perfectly natural, of course. But you don't need to be concerned about anything. This is all routine. Nothing really can go wrong. It's not brain surgery. It's cosmetic."

"Okay."

"You're in good hands."

"Okay."

"You've had a general anesthetic before?"

"Yes."

"I'm going to administer one to you in a moment, and as I do, I'll ask you to count backwards. All right?"

"Okay."

"Fantastic. Can you start counting for me now?"

"From ten?"

He laughed. "You can count backwards from twenty if you wish. A hundred. Seventeen. It doesn't really matter."

"Okay." Pri closed her eyes. Swallowed. "Ten. Nine. Eight. Seven. Six. Five. Four."

Three

The trap door opened. Pri was not sure if she had been sleeping. Her thoughts and her dreams felt inseparable from one another, as if never entirely asleep or awake, the two parts of a spectrum. But now this was real. There was sepia light with crisp angles, the dust in the air defined, meandering. The ladder was lowered and tapped into the dirt. A leg descended from the ceiling, black slacks that failed to reach the ankles, striped socks, a shoe pressing against one rung, the metal groaning. After a pause, or perhaps a moment of hesitation, he continued his descent with long extensions of each leg, his back to her but twisting as he took the final steps down. He wore a red sweater, tight against his doughnut waist. Hasan held a knife in one hand, its blade as long as his forearm and gleaming. He squatted, knees out to the left and right, but remained in front of the ladder, under the light, his weapon on display like a trophy.

"Pri." He said, barely above a whisper, as if intending to awaken a child. "How are you?"

She struggled to make out what was in his other hand. She wanted water.

He sniffled, wiping his nose with one wrist. "I said, how are you?"

She tried to ask for water, but it was as if her voice could not ignite. She could only whisper.

"What?" He asked.

"Water?"

Hasan grinned, nodding, "Yes. Water. You are thirsty."

"Yes," she said. "Please."

"Jaz was nice. He gave you so much water. I thought I might bring you some. But then I think about my trip here. On the boat. For months."

He appeared to wait for her reply, his head nodding. She didn't know what he wanted her to say. She only wanted water. She inspected his other arm, hoping for a bottle in one pocket.

He said, "Five days. That is how long you have been here. Jaz gave you water and food. I was on the boat for two months." He punctuated his statements with nasally exhalations, twitching smiles. "Drinking from puddles in the dirt is better than drinking from the oceans."

"Please. I'm pregnant."

"I know."

"I'm no good as a hostage if you kill me."

Hasan chuckled with a hearty nod. "Yes. Of course. I am not going to kill you. Is that what you think I am? A monster? No. You will live. You will make that fone call."

"Then give me some water and I'll make the call. Right now. Please."

Hasan smiled, his expression paternal, as if reluctant to see her suffer. "Jaz liked you. He told me that. He liked you and did not want you to suffer. But he has his money now and he is gone. And I will have my money soon. I know. You will make that call. I know. But I do not like you. I want you to suffer. It is only fair that you suffer."

Pri tried to shuffle back but she was already pressed tight against the wall. Her hands shook, hidden beneath the blanket. "I never did anything to you."

"But you did. That is what you people do not know. My home is not a place to live anymore. Jakarta is dead. Because of your people."

"I know," Pri said. "I know. I'm sure Jaz told you. I tried to do things better. I understood how lucky I was. I know."

"Then tell me about your trip across the ocean. Tell me about your time on the boat, with your family. Tell me that story again. Was it your father who died? Was it your brother? I forgot. Tell me. Please. Tell me your story again."

Pri shook her head. All she could say was, "I'm sorry."

"Yes. You say sorry. You tell stories. You tell me that you never did anything to me, but you tell me this story. A story about what it is like to cross the Pacific. I bet you told it so much that you can see the lies, right? Like you were there. But you were not. You were in your home on a mountain while I crossed the ocean. I know how it feels to not eat for weeks. No water for days. I know. In the sun, in the middle of the ocean. You do not know how that feels. You do not know that fear. You did not have to throw the dead into the water. You do not know what it is like to hear a girl cry for days, asking for her daddy. Over and over. Daddy. Daddy. When Daddy is dead. You do not know what it is like when a storm hits. For a boat to flip over. Again. And again. Each time, less people. Less children. No more crying for Daddy. No more little girl. Just quiet. You, Pri, you do not know the pain of that quiet. You do not know what real pain is. To you, everything is a story. You say you are sorry, but what do you want to do? You want to get on a spaceship and leave. Fly to another planet." Hasan laughed, a single, harsh grunt, like he was clearing his throat. "You are so sorry. But you know nothing. Just a stupid rich girl who tells stories."

Hasan stood, shaking his head, and spit on the floor by his feet. He turned to climb the ladder, and Pri thought that he was going to leave her again, but he ascended only a few rungs, enough to reach for something on the floor above him, then returned with a fone trailing a long cord that draped upwards into the opening in the ceiling. He held it out towards Pri, not willing to kneel or stand close to her. She didn't move and he shook his outstretched hand. "Take it."

She knelt forward, reached out, and grabbed the fone, staring at its screen for only a moment before looking back towards Hasan.

He said, "You call your father. Right now. You tell him that you're taken prisoner by someone in the Jungle. If you want, tell him you have no food, no water. I don't care about that." He then withdrew a piece of paper the size of his palm and held it towards her. Pri didn't move and he shook the note to draw her attention. She took the paper, unfolding it as he continued. "That is amount and deposit code for the account. Tell him when the money is in the account, you are free. You will go to safe place at the edge of the Jungle. Simple as that. You can be home tomorrow."

Pri struggled to read his note in the darkness, and when she did, she assumed that there was a mistake, that perhaps Hasan had written one too many zeros. The requested sum of money was more than the combined value of all the MiC cards she'd had implanted. She shook her head. "This is too much."

Hasan laughed. "So, you think I want to be a fucking peasant for the rest of my life?"

"But this is way too much."

"Your family will pay."

"My father is not well. He won't know what's going on. And he certainly won't pay this much money."

"If they want you back, they will pay."

"I don't know if they want me back."

"Shut up and make the call."

"This won't work."

"Make the call."

Pri didn't think that anyone else was upstairs. She was weak but she was desperate. She could go for his eyes with her fingers. Bash him in the head with a rock. These things happen. People escape. If she acted now, when he was unsuspecting, she could incapacitate him.

He shook his head, "Fine." He grabbed the fone from her hand and stood beside the ladder. "If you don't call now, I will come back in few days. See how you feel then."

"Wait," Pri said, barely above a whisper.

Hasan climbed the first two rungs, impatient to leave.

"Wait," Pri repeated, trying to yell, causing him to stop. "Just wait."

He descended but held onto the side of the ladder as if ready for a prompt exit. He did not speak, instead staring down at Pri, unflinching.

She said, "I'll call, but I'm telling you that it's not going to work. I probably won't even get a hold of my father. I'll just get his caretaker. She's not a person.

She's A.I. As far as I know, she'll contact the authorities. I don't know how she's been programmed."

"You tell her that if she calls security, then you will be hurt. Then you will be killed. She will not contact security if you say that. Now call or I leave." He held out the fone. "No more excuses."

Pri knelt forward, grabbing the fone but unable to release it from his grip.

He said, "Last chance."

"Okay."

He let go and Pri sat back, pulling the cord to release more slack from above. She imagined the wire snaking for hundreds of meters under the mud and garbage of the Jungle to some server where the locations were scrambled. "What time is it?" She asked.

"It is morning."

"Okay." Pri kept her head down, looking at the fone in her palm and then casting her eyes towards Hasan's shoes, just a few feet away. "Okay," she repeated, watching his feet slide against the dirt, impatient. She inputted Har's number and within seconds a jarring ringtone emitted from the device, the sound filling the room. She refused to glance up to Hasan, instead focused on his shoes.

"Hello?" Carol's distorted voice emitted from the speaker.

Pri cleared her throat, looked up to Hasan and then back to her palm. "Hello, Carol. It's me. Pri."

"Hello, Pri," Carol said, her expression now pleased. "You're not coming through very clearly, so I couldn't tell who this was. I apologize for that. How are you doing?"

"I'm," Pri shook her head, wishing she had a script, "I'm not doing so well right now, Carol."

"Oh, what's wrong? Where are you? Do you need help?"

Hasan shook his head, his eyes glaring at her. Pri said, "I need. I need to talk to Dad. To Har. Could I please talk with him?"

Carol sounded concerned. "He's sleeping right now, Pri. But you can talk with me. Please, tell me, what is wrong?"

"You need to promise me, Carol, that you're not going to contact security, no matter what I tell you."

"Pri, I'm not sure if I can uphold such a guarantee."

"If you contact security, I will be hurt."

"Have you been hurt already? Where are you, Pri? I can't get a location."

"I'm in the Jungle."

"Where?"

"It doesn't matter right now. But this is serious. Can you please wake up Har so that I can talk with him in person?"

"I'm sorry, but Har is resting right now. I am his caretaker and am fully able to make all decisions based on his best interest."

"If I can't talk with Har, then this call is going to end and I don't know when you're going to hear from me."

"What happened, Pri? Please, tell me what happened. I can help you."

"You cannot tell security anything. You need to promise me that."

"Pri, I'm not sure I can uphold—"

"Carol, I'm in the Jungle and I've been taken hostage. I've been a prisoner for five days already. The man here needs you to transfer money into an encrypted account and then he'll let me go. So, can you please wake up Har and tell him that his daughter has been taken hostage?"

"I do not think Har will fully appreciate the ramifications of what has happened. It will not be in his best interest to be informed of this at this time."

"You're not going to tell him?"

"Not at this time."

"Are you going to tell him later?"

"That will depend on his cognitive clarity."

"So, what are you going to do?"

"That depends on you, Pri. You have instructed me not to contact security. I am not sure of what assistance I can be at this time if you insist that I do not help you."

"You can help me. Just wake up Har."

"I'm sorry, but that is not in his best interest at the time being."

"I'm his daughter. I've been taken hostage. How can informing him of this not be in his best interest?"

"You are sounding very distressed, Pri. I can help you if you allow me to contact security."

"No. No. My captor is listening to us right now. Do not contact security."

"Then I'm not sure that I can do much to assist you at this time, Pri."

She groaned, staring at Hasan's shoes. "You are his primary caregiver, correct?"

"Yes, I am Har's primary caregiver."

"Then don't you think a father should be made aware that his daughter has been taken hostage?"

"You have made it clear to me that I cannot contact security. I am not sure that there is anything I can do to assist you if you do not want me to contact security. I am sorry, Pri, but I am strictly forbidden from releasing your father's funds for any type of extortion."

"Will you tell him when he wakes up then?"

"If it seems to be in his best interest."

"What does that mean?"

"I will need to make a judgement depending on his mental state at that time."

"So, you might not ever tell him?"

"Not if I continue to determine that it will not be in his best interest."

Pri did not know what to say, her mouth open, only then realizing the intensity of each of her breaths, that the fone trembled in her hand. She stared at Hasan's shoes. She dared not look up to his eyes.

"Pri?" Carol said. "Are you still there?"

"Yes."

"Is there a number with which I can contact you? The connection you are using continues to show no metadata. If you can provide me with a number, I can contact you back should Har be ready to learn of your news."

Pri looked up to Hasan for the first time in the conversation, his eyes empty and black beneath fiery eyebrows from the light above. His expression appeared bored, impatient. He shook his head. Pri said, "No. There isn't a number I can give you."

"Then, I'm sorry, Pri, but I'm not sure what I can do to assist you with this."

"If I can call back later today, might I be able to talk with Har directly?"

"I am sorry, Pri, but I need to consider what is in Har's best interest. Right now, I do not believe that he is lucid enough to sufficiently grasp the ramifications of what has happened to you. I can recommend that you give me permission to contact security, but I am unable to contact any such authority without your explicit permission."

"Can you sufficiently grasp the ramifications of what has happened to me?"

"I understand that this is a difficult experience for you."

"He's going to starve me to death."

"Are you referring to your captor?"

"Yes."

"This sounds serious, Pri. Are you sure that you do not want me to—"

"No. Don't call security."

"Then if you insist on this, Pri, I am not sure if there is anything that I can do to assist you at this moment."

Pri looked back to Hasan, shaking her head to relay her bewilderment. His lips remained pursed. He scratched the curled hairs on his cheek. He looked up through the trap door and then back to Pri, bored and waiting for her to finish.

Carol asked, "Pri? Are you there?"

"Yes."

"Would you like me to disregard this conversation?"

"What?"

"If you want, I can disregard this entire conversation. A record of it will remain for archival purposes, but none of the content of our dialogue would be acted upon."

"Is there nothing you can do?"

"Unless you would like me to contact security, and until your father is in a better emotional and lucid state, I'm afraid there is nothing I can do."

"Then, yes. Disregard this conversation."

"All right, Pri. I'll disregard this conversation. Is there anything else I can do for you?"

"I guess not."

"If you have the time, you should really come visit again. We both enjoyed your stay the last time you visited. It was a shame we never found the time to visit the botanical gardens. The blue jacarandas and crape myrtles are wonderful."

Pri groaned and turned off the fone. She shook her head, holding it out towards Hasan. "I'm sorry. Like I said, this wasn't going to work." She waited for him to grab the device.

He sniffled, almost laughed. "Call your sister."

"What?"

"Call your sister."

"I don't have a sister."

"I know you have a sister. The doctor."

"I don't have a sister."

"Jaz told me. Call her."

"I said, I don't have a sister."

"I believe Jaz. Not you. Now call her or I leave."

"Jaz lied to you. Like he lied to me. He's a good liar. I don't have a sister."

"Fine." Hasan snatched the fone from Pri's hand and unclipped the cord. He then climbed up the ladder without saying another word.

"Wait," Pri said. "I'm sure we can work something out."

She watched his steps continue unabated. The ladder then rose from the dirt. "Wait," she repeated with desperation. Groaning hinges preceded the sudden dimming of light, the thudding of wood, the absolute darkness. She stood, hitting her head on an unseen joist, forcing her back down to the dirt. The heavy march of footsteps sounded above her and then vanished. She stayed on her hands and knees, listening to her heaving breaths, nothing else.

Although the acronym officially stood for Economic Development Zone, in common jargon these were referred to as Ecogee Detention Zones. The first formal EDZ was instituted outside the city of Calais, France, long before Pri was born. Informal refugee camps had been swelling outside of every metropolitan center for the two preceding decades, principally around coastal cities, the first point of entry for waves of seafaring migrants who travelled thousands of kilometers on cheap automated boats that relied exclusively on solar power and had the ability to travel indefinitely. Like most other EDZs, what Pri knew as the Jungle began as a series of unregulated encampments, this one along the coastal region between Vancouver and Seattle. The local authorities lacked the capital to keep track of the number of migrants coming ashore each day, the estimates seen as guesses at best, propaganda at worst. Initially, these encampments were viewed as temporary housing for ecological refugees who would be returned home one day. Some day. But these people had no homes for which to return. Whole villages and towns were wiped out by floods and cyclones, submerged by rising tides, or parched by droughts that lingered a decade. And this was just the beginning. There would be a billion more, at least, authorities claimed. The ecological refugee crisis would not end in anyone's lifetime. It was the new normal, the idea that millions of people would cross the seas and oceans at any given time, not knowing where they were going, only certain that they could never return home. Some authorities erected walls surrounding these camps, firing upon anyone who dared to leave. Some authorities killed every person who made landfall, certain that this was required to stem the tide of refugees. But it could not work. Migrants travelled by autonomous boats that knew nothing of current events and political wills. They followed algorithms, calculations based on wind direction, ocean currents, weather forecasts. And as the walls grew higher and defenses militarized around these increasingly dense encampments, ecogees became angry. This was not their fault, they'd declare. Culpability rested with the ruling classes, the developed world, those who had the time and, most crucially, the money to adapt.

The vision of Calais's Economic Development Zone was to both utilize this inexhaustible human capital as well as ease the growing tensions of the migrants within. Legally, an EDZ would neither be part of any sovereign authority, nor a sovereign state of its own. The private sector would be enticed to invest and develop properties in an EDZ without it taking the role of a local governing body. Ostensibly, there was no governing body. And therefore, there were no labor laws, regulations, or impediments to any type of economic development that a corporation might deem of interest. Migrants from other refugee camps along the English Channel were encouraged to travel to Calais where there was the promise of employment, housing, even formal education. No human working in manufacturing could ever compete with the efficiency of automated factories—but if there were no constraints imposed on minimum wages, or working conditions, or taxes, or regulations of *any* type, then the hope was that the private sector could find success in what no government could ever accomplish. Give the refugees work. Give them means. And the Calais EDZ became a success, growing from less than ten thousand to over a million residents in a decade. For the first time in a century, global employment in manufacturing increased. The old labels of the developed and the developing world were no longer appropriate. The two became interwoven. Every metropolitan authority was soon surrounded by an EDZ, each without a formal government. It became impossible to know the number of people who resided in these sprawling townships—each day, new migrants arrived at the shores and these EDZs had no formal governing body, so no one was charged with keeping statistics. Everything was an estimate. The population, the gross domestic product, employment rates, literacy rates, carbon emissions. Everything. Economic Development Zones were deemed the solution to the greatest migration crisis in human history. Here, corporations could construct rudimentary launch sites for rockets without any of the countless obligations and requirements of doing so within a formalized metropolitan region. Nothing they did could be deemed illegal if it took place within the defined regions of the EDZ.

The key to their success was in containment. What happened inside an EDZ did not matter so long as it remained inside an EDZ. Some authorities built towering perimeter walls. Others fortified neighboring stratas. Others yet defined the buffer zone between the EDZ and the metropolitan authority a no-man's-land. These buffers were deemed as "legalless" lands—any people who chose to reside in these areas were considered to be doing so under their own will and had to accept that there were no liabilities for any action of any type. Every year, metropolitan authorities would deploy squadrons of automated bulldozers, wiping out every trace of a building or person in the region. Pri used to join marches protesting these razings, decrying the inhumanity of determining that the people in these lands did not have the right to life. She held pictures of dead children, mangled and twisted in the refuse of bulldozers.

Pri had never seen the buffer zone in person. Not until Jaz ushered her out from his vehicle, helping her out of her seat. It was more extensive than she expected, the official entrance to the EDZ too distant to be visible from where they stood. She had imagined fields of grass, perhaps treads imprinted into the mud from the last time dozers had passed through. But there was a sea of stout buildings matching the pallet of the overcast skies, walls of cinderblocks and sheet metal, chimneys spewing gunmetal smoke, mud and debris forming walkways in between. From here on in, Jaz said, they would go on foot. He withdrew a couple of bags from the trunk and Pri asked if he was concerned about leaving his vehicle unattended for several days. Jaz laughed. "You think I'm going to be using this piece of crap anymore once I'm done helping you?"

It hurt to walk. The splinter at the back of her right thigh throbbed, felt as if it was piercing muscle when attempting a long stride. Instead, Pri shuffled, buried beneath the layers of clothes, arms down at her thighs, unable to fold her arms or lift them above her waist. When she had awoken from the procedure, Dr. Kahn refused to give her a mirror, said that it was too early to look at her reflection, instead advising that she focus on getting a start on her journey—but she did not need a mirror to inspect her fingers. These weren't her hands. They felt like gloves, the skin swollen and coarse, her fingertips numb, palms calloused. She kept making a fist and releasing, repeating as if the motion would settle them in, convince her body to accept these new appendages. When she ran her fingers along her face, she couldn't feel the texture of the skin, nor the digits against her cheeks. The anesthetics would take a few more hours to wear off, the doctor said, but everything went as planned. No one will be able to tell her strata, he said, and Jaz agreed. "It looks great. Which means you look terrible," Jaz said with a laugh.

It wasn't until she was directed into Jaz's vehicle that she saw a mirror and inspected her reflection. Her heart skittered when she caught the first image of her face. This wasn't her. She touched her cheeks and nose and tugged at the skin, as if this was a mask that she could withdraw. It reminded her of photographs she'd seen of her ancestors, her great-great-grandmother who was born in the Punjab. Pri had aged ten, maybe twenty years. A scar ran a gentle curve from her right eye, over the crest of her cheekbone towards one ear. She examined her teeth—the same teeth her tongue refused to quit surveying, detailing every unfamiliar nook, seam, and point. A front incisor was twisted, the roots exposed, a murky hazel. One canine was chipped and her tongue always returned to that gap. Jaz reminded her that she was only drawing attention to herself. She knew this, but she didn't care. He was still the same person. She had been transformed. Aside from a dull headache, nothing hurt at the time. She could lift her arms above her head and lunge with long steps. Her entire body was numb. Then there was the sensation that she was not actually staring at herself, but instead an actor, someone in costume mimicking her every move.

Now she could sense everything. Her fingers felt as if they had been scraped with sandpaper. Her jaw throbbed, deep from within the bone and out with every heartbeat. She tongued the corners of her mouth, now under some foolish idea that it would help alleviate the pain, massaging gums and then pushing against her implants. She didn't want to close her mouth, didn't want to feel that clatter between her upper and lower jaw. It was difficult to speak, and she couldn't imagine trying to eat. Jaz marched ahead, perhaps to hasten her pace, perhaps forgetting about her overall state, but she struggled with each limping step, not wanting to complain, wishing he would slow down. She felt around her thigh, expecting her bloated fingertips to be red with blood.

A six-lane paved road cut a straight line through the buffer and into the EDZ. A steady procession of cab-less automated trucks entered and exited along the thoroughfare, both sides of which were bordered with chain-link fences taller than any of the passing vehicles and crowned in an irregular swirl of razor wire. They needed to keep to the unpaved lanes, a labyrinthine network of narrow passages that expanded organically, arteries into arterioles into capillaries. Some of these streets were mapped, but others were continually evolving; dead ends were formed by new buildings and thoroughfares might be left blocked in the wake of a fire. In the buffer zone, these pathways were mud and exposed rocks, buried bricks, rebar, slabs of broken concrete and cinder blocks. It looked as if desperate residents built directly atop the rubble of the most recent razing, layer upon layer of shanty. Pri knew that people vanished in these clearings and wondered how many of the fallen rested in the mud beneath her feet. She watched each step, avoiding puddles and the murky water within, unsure what they obscured.

"You have to walk faster than that," Jaz said, meters ahead, waving her closer. "At this rate, it will take a day just to get to the EDZ."

A man trudged past, dragging a rusted and crooked rectangle of corrugated metal larger than he was, his eyes straight ahead. She ducked beneath a pair of drooping cables that spanned the plywood roof of one building to the cloth canopy of another across the lane, sheltering a woman and two children who sat around a gas stove and a pot of boiling water, holding their hands to the flames for warmth. Only the children looked at Pri. She flinched as a single brown rat and then another pair scurried across the path ahead, darting from one hole into another without changing their pace.

Pri had imagined a wall demarcating the beginning of the Jungle—withered concrete capped with twisted blades, murals and messages painted along the monolithic mass; inside, an overcrowded pen of human beings. But the formal edge of the EDZ was marked only with a change in permanence, a transition from scraps of plywood and tarpaulin passageways to what appeared to be brick and mortared stone walls, windows with glass or transparent plastic, and nearly flat roofs made from mismatched metal. Most of these buildings were two stories, the upper windows rectangular holes. Clothes hung within the arm's width of space between structures. Lanes and passageways were dirt and gravel, smooth and weathered. The buffer zone was rebuilt every few years, but this had existed for decades. In the absence of any discernable breeze, hundreds of plumes of scraggily white smoke drifted up from the sea of roofs. The poorest of the residents ignited feces and scraps. The richest burned gasoline in generators that granted their homes electric lights and connectivity to global networks. Pri's facemask muddled the odors of smoke and wafting sewage. There were people everywhere, hiking past with wheelbarrows of chipped cement, children scurrying past with screeches and giggles. Pri would bump into someone's shoulder, but she kept her eyes away, assured by Jaz that she should not apologize for such things. He reached out his hand for Pri, pulling her in close before a woman dumped a bucket of ruddy water from a second-floor window, the splash missing Pri's legs by inches. "Try to walk more in the middle," he said into her ear. "Remember, it's not like they have plumbing."

The lanes were rarely linear, instead swerving, splitting, and merging with no discernable order. Jaz never had to retrieve his fone or pause to check his surroundings. Instead, he strolled along as if he'd lived in these parts for years. She didn't know how he could possess such confidence, but she trusted him. She stayed close to him, usually a step behind and to the side, not bothered when he asked for her hand.

"How do you know where to go?" She asked.

He shrugged. "I did my homework."

It began to rain, droplets so small that they could not be seen, only felt on the exposed skin around her eyes, the tops of her hands. When the raindrops changed to flakes of snow, Jaz stopped, as did most of the people out on the lane. Necks arched back, eyes closed, they held out their hands. Jaz laughed, "And they say the climate is heating, right?" He waved Pri along. "Let's keep going."

They spent the evening in the back of a bustling tea house, patrons huddled around their water pipes, exhaling thick plumes of tobacco and cannabis smoke. Their room was windowless with four bare mattresses atop the dirt floor, a plastic bucket in one corner. A single electrical cable snaked from under a door to a heater in the middle, then up to a bulb that hung from a hook. Pri unwrapped her headscarf, letting it dangle around her neck, brushing her hands across the top of her mattress before kneeling with slow, cautious movements. She openly groaned, sucking through clenched teeth as she stretched out each leg in front of her, feeling her skin at the back of her right thigh. "Is it safe to talk here?" Pri asked, leaning on one side.

"As long as you're not too loud."

She ran her hand against the wall behind her, a rough plaster, perhaps mud, with lips that chipped beneath her fingertips. She then leaned back against it, pulling the scarf away from her neck and stared at the two empty mattresses. "Is there a chance some other people will spend the night here, as well?"

"I've paid for the whole room already. It will just be us."

"Have you been here before?"

"I have. I've known Shiraz for quite a few years now."

"Does he know about me?"

"He knows that you're my cousin. But to be honest, he doesn't care about you. All he cares about is that I've paid him well for the night and that I'll pay him well for nights in the future. He won't bother us."

Pri ran her tongue over her front teeth. "Why would you have ever needed to come down here before?"

"EDZs are the open borders of the world. These are the real ports. No restrictions. No authorities. As long as you keep away from the corporate interests here, you can do anything. There is great value in that."

"How many times have you been here?"

"A fair number. But, with any luck, this will be my last."

Pri sat forward, wincing from the shooting pain in her abdomen but not wanting to draw attention to that splinter, and then leaned back again. "I'm glad I could be of such help to you."

"I like to think that we're helping each other."

Someone knocked on the door—four quick raps in succession—and Shiraz entered with a navy-blue woolen hat over his hair, white buttoned shirt tucked into jeans without a belt, his long arms each carrying a steaming ceramic cup. "Sorry to bother," he said, looking both Jaz and Pri in the eyes. Pri glanced down to her feet, feeling exposed without her headscarf. "It's very cold outside.

I've brought you some tea." He first offered to Pri, squatting, arm outstretched. She accepted the mug, her eyes focused on the ceramics instead of his face, mumbling a few words in appreciation.

When she glanced up, he still watched her, as if demanding eye contact. She nodded, smiled, repeated herself, "Thank you."

Shiraz then passed the other mug to Jaz. "You like something stronger?"

Jaz looked towards Pri and she shook her head. "No," he said, "I believe we will be fine like this. Thank you."

"Anything to smoke?"

Again, Jaz glanced at Pri and she dismissed him. "I'm sure we'll be okay. Thank you again."

"If you need something, please find me." He nodded to Jaz one last time and closed the door behind him.

Pri held onto the mug between her hands, letting the steam drift towards her nostrils but reluctant to try a sip. "You trust that man?"

"I trust him enough."

"He kept staring at me."

"You're just not used to people who serve you looking you in the eyes."

"That's not what it is."

"That's exactly what it is," Jaz said. "It's good to be cautious, but don't keep looking away. That will draw attention to you." He then sipped from his mug. "Now, have some tea. It's just tea. It will warm you up."

"I need a toilet first."

"What do you think that is for?"

Pri stared at the bucket in the far corner of the room and sighed. "I was afraid of that."

"Don't worry, I won't look."

"What do I do when I'm done?"

"Just leave it outside the door. Shiraz will empty it for you and bring it back."

Pri stood up with a wincing sigh but then remained still, staring at the bucket and then back to Jaz.

He said, "Remember, in a few days you'll be above all of this. Literally. Out in orbit."

"And where will you be?"

Jaz smiled, "Far away from this shit hole, I can assure you."

The grumbling of a generator in her dream proved to be Jaz's snoring when she awoke. The only light came from a crack under the door, a thin seam of copper that illuminated an inch of craggily dirt. She'd been asleep on her side and now the splinter beneath that armpit throbbed, accompanied by a piercing jolt when she rolled onto her back. She ran her tongue over each tooth, once again feeling the novelty of it, as if muscle memory had been reset after her slumber. She couldn't remember any of the details of her dream, just the sound of the generator, which was actually Jaz's rhythmic snoring. She couldn't see him, but she imagined his mouth open wide, neck back, lips dry. He annoyed her. It wasn't so much the sound as it was the fact that he was asleep, so calm and oblivious.

It was impossible to know the time and she wondered if this was going to go on for another three, four, five hours. Now that she was awake, it felt absurd that she might get back to sleep. Just last night, she was in her own bed. She squeezed her hands into fists, compressing the prosthetics around each finger. She had to focus on what was coming next. As little as three more days. Eighty more kilometers. Keeping her mouth shut, walking with her face down, following Jaz. For the last fifteen years, Pri had dreamt of travelling to the Tevat and now it was just a few days away. This is what Pri would let herself think about. Walking through the gates of the staging area. Climbing into the rocket. Away from the consequences of humanity's mistakes. The Tevat was not only Pri's salvation, it was humanity's salvation. Mustafa Karamehmet gave away his wealth so that a few thousand human beings could have the chance to start again without him. Pri had given away nothing in comparison. Absolutely nothing. This was what she needed to keep thinking about. She reached out to the ground beside her mattress with one hand and felt the fine grain of dirt between her fingertips. She closed her eyes, the grit between one thumb and forefinger rolling back and forth, then in circles. This dirt was the Earth. She should savor it, she thought. "Savor this," she whispered to herself. "Savor this."

Pri knew that they had reached sea level as the surrounding buildings were supported on stilts, their entrances located above her waist. The jagged points of barnacles wrapped around the base of every wooden pile. Water trickled incessantly from pipes beneath the drooping bellies of these structures. Boardwalks connected homes, the lumber thin and fractured, but at low tide people walked along the ground, atop the garbage. Only cats and children stalked the raised walkways, as if these were meant to be used by adults only in an emergency. Pri and Jaz hiked atop a shallow layer of ruddy silt, sheets of plastic, torn sandbags, electrical cables twisted and buried within. The debris allowed people to avoid the worst of the mud with mindful steps. Walls of buildings were the same corrugated plastic and metal as the rest of the Jungle, windows gaping open, cloth drapes that rustled in the breeze. Generators hummed and rattled.

They came to the edge of a creek, the umber current conflicted, moving in different directions. The buildings were constructed upon spindly stilts driven into the stream, rough and crooked branches reinforced with other branches, bound together with great masses of anything that could be tied into knots. The floors swayed as a woman emerged from a door, her feet above Pri's head. She dumped a bucket of water over the edge and into the creek before disappearing back inside her home, the stilts quivering with each step. A group of children hurried past Jaz and Pri, their bare feet sinking into the muddy shore with each step before hesitating and then charging in, their laughter turning into shrieks as the water came to their thighs, forcing them back from the cold and hurrying onto the shore, giggling and panting. Jaz told Pri to wait and took a few steps closer to the edge of the water, his boots landing on fallen lumber and washed-up branches to avoid sinking.

He returned to Pri and said, "There used to be a bridge here."

"You think it collapsed?"

"Or maybe people took it apart for lumber. But we will have to walk up a little further to find another crossing."

"Is this a problem?"

"Shouldn't be, no. But the tide is starting to come up. We want to get to higher ground before this is all flooded."

Pri felt a quivering in her feet, heard the rattling of wood from the stilts. She looked down to the ground, to the rippling puddles in the water, then around at the buildings that loomed over her. "Is this an earthquake?"

Jaz was calm. He shook his head and nodded towards the buildings across the stream. A pair of children played on a rickety patio, one hanging from the railings, feet dangling over the river, both unconcerned. "What?" Pri asked.

"Keep looking," he said, pointing above the roofs of the structures.

Pri now heard a deep rumble, a prolonged but distant thunder. And in behind the roofs, she saw the gray silhouette of a rising rocket, its motion smooth, patient, the engines spewing a long, trembling spike of searing white flame. The vibrations in the ground ceased, the sound muted, but the rocket climbed into the sky and then behind the first layer of cloud, tracing a static white pillar of exhaust.

"That's where we're heading?"

"That's it."

"How far away are we?"

"Probably another forty kilometers."

"How are we doing for time?"

"Good, as long as we can avoid high tide."

They could not avoid high tide. The advance of water was deceiving. She imagined that the slow creep of the creek would chase them, a plodding pursuer easily outrun. But the water ascended from the mud. Without warning, Pri splashed in puddles that could not be avoided, soaking into her socks. As the water rose to Pri's shins, it became frigid. A man passed by, pushing a flat raft in front of him, full of fish and swarming flies. Others paddled or punted in canoes. But most stayed in their homes, watching the people slosh past in the water.

Pri didn't want to complain. If billions of the world's ecological refugees could live their entire lives in these conditions, she could persevere for a few hours without admitting her discomfort. But it was Jaz who decided that they could not go on, that they were travelling too slowly to make it to their next planned destination before dark. "I can make it," Pri assured, but Jaz said it would not be safe. No one should be outside in the night.

Pri did not immediately realize that they were at a restaurant. They sat at a table, one of just two on a square platform without railings abutting an apartment partitioned by a pair of curtains, the patio covered in a drooping plastic tarp with holes that dribbled rainwater. The creaking wooden slats had gaps not only wide enough for Pri to see the rippling tide below, but for the legs of her chair to slip within should she slide back without care. A stout metal pipe, sliced in half and filled with smouldering charcoals, rested atop bricks in one corner of the outdoor space, skewers of small fish roasting above, appearing black in the dim light. Smoke from the fire lingered beneath the tarp and Pri tried not to cough, not to draw any attention to herself. They were the only customers and she'd taken off her shoes, her toes puffed, wrinkled and numb. Axel, the proprietor of this business, brought Pri a knitted blanket to wrap around her legs. He was short, face square, his hairline horizontal and just above his eyebrows. She told him that she was fine, but he insisted by only saying the words, "Please," and, "Yes," repeatedly. Pri relented, thanked him for his hospitality, to which he nodded, said, "Yes," and returned through the drapes into his home.

"This place is perfect," Jaz said while wringing out a sock into the gaps between the floorboards. "Unplanned, but perfect. Where we were before had far too many south Asians. Too great of a chance that they might see through our story. But Axel here is Honduran. He speaks almost no English, and we speak almost no Spanish, so it works quite nicely."

Axel and a young boy whose head barely came to the man's waist pushed through the drapes. The child's eyes were stunning, a starburst from hazel to glacial blue. The boy carried another blanket and offered it to Jaz, who accepted and then held up one finger to request patience. Jaz looked through a pocket in his bag and withdrew a clenched hand, offering it towards the boy. The child looked towards his father and then back to Jaz, dancing with excitement. Jaz opened his fingers to reveal a hard candy, wrapped in plastic. The boy snatched it from Jaz's hand and said, "Gracias," while pulling apart the wrapper.

"Ah, ah, ah," Jaz said to stop the boy. "Cuántos hermanos o hermanas?"

"Dos," the boy said.

"Un momento," Jaz reached back into his bag and handed the boy two more candies. "Para hermanos. Si?"

"Si. Gracias. Gracias. Gracias." The boy hurried inside and seconds later a squeal of cheers erupted. Jaz leaned towards Pri, "Always come prepared."

Axel placed an empty glass in front of Pri and a plastic mug before Jaz. He then filled each with an amber liquid, poured from an old bottle of detergent. "Ron." Axel said. He then waited for his guests to imbibe, his head nodding in quick bursts, urging them. "Please. Yes."

Pri looked towards Jaz.

Jaz said, "It's safer than drinking the water, I'll assume." He lifted his mug, awaiting Pri to do the same.

She looked at him, mumbling, "You're sure?" Jaz nodded, waiting. She lifted her glass, tapped it, and then following Jaz's lead took a slurping, minuscule sip that first cooled and then burned her tongue, its odor breathing against the roof of her mouth. Pri forced a grin, looked towards Axel, nodding. "Thank you."

Jaz closed his eyes, smiled, and then exhaled in relief. "Gracias."

"De nada," Axel said, motioning with open hands towards the bottle, an offering, while taking a step back. "Please. Yes." He then turned and exited through the drapes, the voices of his excited children chattering at once before being subdued by rapid, assertive commands.

She looked at the drink in her hand, still raised above the table, and Jaz shrugged and took another sip. "It's rum?" Pri said.

"It's definitely alcohol."

"I thought you said you didn't speak any Spanish?"

"I know about twenty words. I think I used all of them there."

Pri reached down to rub her swollen feet. "So, what are you going to do when this is all done?"

Jaz sucked in some air between his lips after another sip. "After I leave you?"

"Yeah."

"I'm not all that certain yet, to be honest."

"Then I don't think you're being honest."

"I've always tried to be honest with you."

Pri laughed, leaning back, "Now I definitely don't think you're being honest with me."

"I try not to make too many plans, if I don't need to."

"Another lie."

Jaz grinned, "You don't trust much of what I say, do you?"

"I trusted you enough to follow you out here, didn't I? So, tell me at least something you plan on doing after I leave."

"I'd like to travel."

"I guess we have that in common."

"My vacation plans are a little less adventurous than yours," Jaz said. "I'll stay Earth bound."

"Where to?"

"Maybe New Zealand."

"Trying to get as far away from here as possible?"

"Pretty much." Jaz said, taking another sip. "Have you been?"

"To New Zealand? No," Pri said with a scoff. "I've barely been anywhere. I went to Mexico when I was not much older than a teenager. Saw Mustafa speak. But that's about it."

"So, instead of exploring the world we have, you decided to just forgo it altogether? Maybe the paradise you're looking for is simply in another city?"

"I'm not looking for paradise."

"What are you looking for?"

Axel parted the drapes, drawing her attention, his son following with two plates and cutlery. The boy placed the empty dishes first in front of Pri and then Jaz, clattering the knife and fork on top of each. Axel barked something towards the boy in Spanish and his son hurried to collect the cutlery before rearranging them, one on either side of each plate. He then sprinted back inside and returned a moment later with a third dish arranged with fried plantains in a shallow puddle of speckled grease. Axel carried over a pair of skewers, each with three steaming herring, scales charcoal, mouths agape, and placed one on each of the empty plates.

"Gracias," Jaz said, holding up his mug of rum.

"Gracias," Pri said.

Axel nodded towards both. "Please. Yes." He ordered his boy to go back inside and then followed in behind.

Jaz looked back to Pri, still holding his drink. "You're going to leave me hanging here?"

Pri picked up her glass, clanged it against his, and then put it back down while Jaz took another sip.

"It gets better," he said, referring to his drink. "So, you were going to tell me what you're looking for?"

Pri chuckled. "Was I?"

"I think you were."

"I don't even know."

"Now you're the one lying."

Pri pressed her fork into the fish, breaking the body in half. "I'm not looking for paradise. I'm really not. If I wanted paradise, I'd live in one of Karamehmet's retreats. But that's not what I'm looking for."

Jaz chewed while holding up his fork, shaking it as if to ring an imaginary bell. "Then, if you're not looking for paradise, you're looking for penance."

"Penance for what?"

"For the easy life you've had."

"My life has not been easy. My life has been lonely."

"Lonely is pretty easy compared to the lives of these people."

"Yes," Pri said, "But it's still lonely. After Seph left, I could go days at home without talking to a living person. Even before Seph left, it wasn't much different. Just logged into my workstation for dozens of hours at a time. That's been my adult life. It affords me a lot—I know, and I don't want to take that for granted—but it's always been lonely."

"Well," Jaz said while pulling something out from a molar, "if you change your mind, you could come with me to New Zealand. See what the other side of the Earth looks like."

"I still don't believe that you have any intention of going there."

"Why would I lie to you about something like that?"

"Only you would know that one, Jaz. Only you."

"But you trust me enough to take you where you need to go?"

Pri nodded, plodding. "I do. Just barely. The tiniest amount sufficient to carry on."

Two

Pri could not think about anything but water. It was raining outside; she could hear the rumble of drops against the ground. The trickling stream continued down the far wall, feeding a shallow puddle just past her feet. Pri folded her knees to her chest, leaned against the corner, her ear nearly against the dirt wall, listening to the rain, visualizing the torrent battering the hard soils outside and running into white-water streams. If she called Nayha, Hasan might have given her something to drink. She didn't want to think about this, but the notion kept returning. Her thoughts were no longer of her own volition. Her instincts were taking charge, whatever they were, wherever their control center resided. If she called Nayha, Hasan would give her life. She thought of knocking on the ceiling, telling Hasan that she changed her mind, that she would call her sister right then as long as he first gave her a bottle of water. Just one would be enough. No matter what she tried to think about, she imagined it running over her tongue, down her lips, infusing into her body as if she was parched soil awaiting the desert rains that would unfurl leaves, sprout blossoms, bring new life. All she had to do was stand and tell Hasan that he was correct. She has a sister.

She reached out towards the ground in front of her, fingers slapping puddles as deep as her palm. The rain would not relent. She might die of dehydration while at the same time drowned from the ceaseless precipitation. Pressing down another palm, Pri knelt and leaned out towards a puddle. She pictured the buckets of fecal matter emptied from windows or dribbling down from pipes between stilts. Hasan could not let her die. She was the most valuable person in all the Jungle, he would say. Hasan had no rational reason to let her perish. He would be back. She leaned down, lips out, and her chin touched the surface of the water. Pri sucked from the puddle, loud and slurping, the first dribbles cool, refreshing. It was water. Nothing else mattered. It was water. She then slurped again, submerging her lips, drawing in enough liquid to feel the grit between her teeth, taste the salt and metallic bite. But it was water.

She stood up, letting her feet sink into the puddle and reached out towards the far wall, running her hands along the exposed edges of stones to the source of the puddle, the opening beneath the floorboards. The muted blue light of day crept between the cracks in the mud and Pri pried both of her hands into the opening, imagining that now the earth would give way without effort, the soils saturated and muddy. She pulled apart a pair of pebbles, rainwater now following along the underside of her arm, tickling the side of her torso. Her fingers clasped onto an unseen stone, wanting to tear it free, certain that this would unlock the rest of the surrounding soils, allow her to burrow her way to freedom. What felt like a shard of broken glass pierced beneath a fingernail, but she would not stop without removing this one stone. Just one stone. It felt as if all the rainwater ran down her arm. Her hand trembled, wondering if she clutched the jagged edge of an old broken bottle. But she would not let go. She told herself that she would not sit down until she had this stone. Water ran down her calves, a long line of ants that extended all the way up to her fingertips. The stone twisted. She adjusted her grip and pulled it free, withdrawing her arm from the opening and holding the rock in her hand. Gripped within her curled fingers, it felt to be the size of a small apricot. She dropped it into the puddle by her feet as she imagined her fingertips torn open and bleeding. After inspecting her fingers within the somber light, she plunged them into the trickling stream, and cupped both hands against the opening to bring water to her lips, letting it dribble between her fingers and down her chest and arms.

It must have been night. Pri had heard footsteps—perhaps a small group of people above—but now there was no activity. The whining rumble of the generator sounded louder than before, what she first thought was a drill burrowing into the ground. The rain had ceased and so had the dribbling trickle down the wall, but the unseen puddles remained, all within reach of an outstretched arm. She wasn't sure what was worse for her baby—ingesting contaminated water or forgoing it altogether. She felt the tremble of another launch, surely another rocket filled with water destined for the Tevat. Three billion kilograms of fresh water transported rocket load by rocket load. More than half a million liters per citizen. All Pri wanted were a few handfuls.

She reached into the puddle, fumbling along the slick mud until finding that stone she had withdrawn from the wall. She stood beneath the door, feeling around for the seams, and gripped the rock with the side of her fist to bash it against the wood, at least twenty strikes in immediate succession, as many as possible before her shoulder cramped. She adjusted her grip, then resumed, telling herself she would not stop until she collapsed onto the ground, someone opened the door, or it came off from its hinges. She didn't yell. She didn't say a word. She struck the underside without relent, pausing only to change her grip, to switch hands. She would make it impossible for anyone to ignore, should they be home. She would bash a hole in the wood if she had enough time.

She threw the rock against an unseen wall and fell to the ground, her chest heaving, breaths quivering, not wanting to cry but feeling tears run down her face. It did not matter what she wanted. She had no control over anything, just as much over her own thoughts as her ability to leave. She was going to die in here and take Poppy with her all because she was too proud to call her sister, to ask for help, to ask for money. She was wrong. She was so very wrong and Pri couldn't think about anything other than that. *You were wrong about everything.*

The door opened. Pri wiped her eyes with the backs of each hand, her nose against her shoulders.

Hasan said from above, his voice calm. "Are you sitting?"

"Yes."

"Stay sitting." The legs of the ladder cut into the light, grinding down along the wooden lip of the door and splashing into a puddle. He took two steps and then paused to repeat, "Stay sitting. Or I go."

"I'm sitting."

The beam of a flashlight flickered down the rungs to the rippling water. Hasan descended and then aimed the beam onto Pri's face, forcing her to shield herself with both hands.

"Look at you," he said, appearing to Pri as just a starburst of searing light. He aimed the beam down to her legs and her eyes adjusted, soon able to make out his figure standing on the ladder, not willing to take that final step into the mud. "Jaz said you are a smart woman but what you are doing is stupid."

"I need some food and water. I'm pregnant. You're going to kill two people."

"No. You are going to kill two people. You only need to call your sister and ask for money. Then you go."

"I don't have a sister."

Hasan sighed, tired. It must have been the middle of the night. "I know the truth."

"You only know what Jaz told you. Jaz told me many, many lies. Have you ever thought that maybe he lied to you, as well? That he took all my money and then left you with nothing? Where is he now? Can you get a hold of him, or has he vanished? What do you think?"

He looked up, as if hearing someone call for him, then back to Pri. "We will talk in the morning."

"I can't sleep."

"I do not care. We talk in the morning."

"I need water. I need food. My blanket is soaking wet."

"If you are quiet, I give you water and food in the morning."

"I need a blanket. Something dry."

"Yes."

"Please. I don't need much. Please."

"Okay." Hasan climbed back up, facing Pri and shining the light before withdrawing the ladder and carefully shutting the door so as not to let it slam.

Pri huddled her knees against her chest in the corner of the room, the sodden blanket around her legs, not wanting to trust Hasan but having no other option. If he did not return with food, water, and a new blanket, then she would die here. First Poppy, then Pri. Hasan would find her corpse and haul it up the ladder, out through the lanes of the Jungle at night. Toss her onto a heap with all the garbage. Maybe leave her on the banks of a stream. Her family would never know what happened. Har would forget that she existed. Nayha and Seph would assume that she had made it onto the Tevat. Carol would archive their discussion but never act upon any of Pri's requests. Pri knew that she could follow these tangents of thought indefinitely—right until the moment of her death—but she would rather focus on Hasan, on his promise, on the idea that he would soon bring her fresh water. Something to eat. A dry blanket to wrap around her shoulders, up to her chin. Deep in this fantasy, Pri could even find rest, certain that she must have slept, noticing daylight from the hole across the room, wider than before. She stood up, head airy, requiring her hands against the wall for support. She ran her fingertips against the fibers of the plywood ceiling, over the joists, her bare feet pressing into the muddy remnants of puddles. She felt the seam of the overhead door. She felt the dents in the grain of the wood, pockmarked and yet smooth.

Footsteps clamored on the floorboards and Pri shirked back a step. The door opened, but this time Pri didn't retreat to her corner. She looked up, locking eyes with Hasan, the lips of his shoes within reach. "You are awake," he said, his voice controlled, breathy.

"I'm always awake."

"Here," he crouched down and held out a bowl. "Eat."

Pri wrapped her new blanket around her legs and shoulders while pinching tufts of mushy rice, slurping water without permitting a single dribble down her chin. Hasan sat against the bottom rung of the ladder, watching. He would look up, distracted by something, but never said a word while waiting.

"Who else is up there?" she asked.

Hasan shook his head. "No matter."

"Have you heard from Jaz?"

He sniffled while watching, refusing to answer.

"Did he leave you any of the MiC cards, or did he take them all for himself?"

He said, "You are going to call your sister."

"I told you, Jaz lied to you. I don't have a sister."

"Then you call someone else. I don't care. You call someone."

"I don't have anyone to call."

"You know people."

"Not with that sort of money."

"Then you will have to think harder."

"Then I'm going to die here."

"No." Hasan shook his head. "Not here. If you do not call someone, you will die. Yes. But not here."

Pri waited for Hasan to continue, her fingers still inside the warm rice. "What do you mean?"

"If you do not get me that money soon, then I will sell you to someone else. You are worth a lot of money. I will get that money, if not from your sister, then from someone else who will pay me for you. And that person will not be as kind as me. That person will not be so nice with you. I am not a bad person. But there are people here who will find a way to get the money from you. They will. Not me. I will get my money and leave. Right now, no one else knows that you are here. Only me. Right now, you are safe. But if you do not call someone and get me that money, then I will tell people. I will tell people that I have a rich girl from a high strata—a rich girl with a baby inside her. You are worth a lot of money. A lot. So, trust me. I will get my money. And trust me, you do not want me to sell you. This, here, is nice. I do not hurt you. I do not touch you. Other people, not so nice as me." Hasan stood, taking a deep breath, then a long exhale from his nostrils, deflating. "I give you two days. No more. If you do not get the money in two days, you will be done here. And if you die, it will not be here. Not from me." He climbed the ladder without looking back. And Pri sat still, her bowl of rice in her hand, watching the ladder rise into the ceiling, the light vanishing seconds later.

When Jaz had said that he had arranged for them to spend the night at Axel's apartment, Pri assumed that they would have a private space, like the room behind Shiraz's teahouse the previous evening. But the inside of Axel's home was a single room. The kitchen consisted of a pair of electric burners on top of a table and a sink without a tap. A curtain hung from the plywood ceiling around one corner, offering some semblance of privacy around the toilet, which, as far as Pri could tell, was a pipe that led straight into the tidal mud below. Rugs covered floorboards, concealing gaps which Pri could feel beneath her feet. What Jaz had purchased for the night was a single mattress—Axel's bed, Jaz was assured—which had been pushed to one side of the room, closest to the electric heater, powered by a generator which rattled from the top of the roof. The other two mattresses were slid across the room, adjacent to the kitchen and exterior curtains. That was where Axel and his three children—two boys and one girl, all prepubescent, vocal and ecstatic about the presence of these guests—would sleep, huddled beneath a pair of blankets. Pri and Jaz had been allocated half the space in their home and Axel would yell at any of his children should they cross the invisible threshold towards the guests' mattress. Jaz did not give out any more candies. They brought no gifts. And yet the children watched Pri and Jaz as if they were famous travelers from a distant, exotic land. The oldest boy kept looking towards Pri, smiling every time she looked in his direction. His crescent eyebrows appeared to be stenciled, thin and uniform until fading at the bridge of his nose. Every smile revealed his front adult teeth, almost in proportion with the rest of his face. She'd wave, and he'd wave back. She did not know what else to do. She felt terrible about this arrangement, attempting to assure Axel that they did not need a mattress, but he would not listen or did not understand. Jaz and Pri were to have the largest mattress, they would have their own space and proximity to the heater. "Please. Yes. Please." Axel repeated, hands out, palms up, nodding his head. This was not up for debate.

Jaz began to snore within minutes of Axel unplugging the lights. The generator would remain on for the sake of the heater, its radiant elements aimed towards Pri. She had to pretend to rest, lying motionless on her side towards an exterior wall. A boy would whisper, and Axel would immediately admonish. Pri kept one hand on the floor, feeling the looped texture of the rug's weave, her fingers following the contours between floorboards. She was prepared to spend the entire night like this, silent, immobile, listening for the next flurry of sounds from the children and their father's subsequent reprimand. It did not seem possible to rest in this condition. The patter of rain on the roof obscured the sounds from the surrounding homes. Perhaps every dwelling was now silent. Perhaps she was the only one awake. She waited until certain that everyone else was asleep to roll onto her back, nudging Jaz aside to keep him from sprawling over the narrow mattress. She hadn't heard a whisper or giggle from anyone across the room in what felt like an hour. The tide had gone back out, she was sure, as she could smell the brine and funk. She ran her tongue over her teeth and then traced one hand over her face, following the scar, back and forth, right eye to right ear.

Jaz slurped and rolled over towards her. She pushed him, forcing him to turn onto his other side and nearly off the bed. Across the room, she saw a child staring. It was the oldest boy, sitting up. The curtain to the deck fluttered—she could feel the draft—but he didn't pull the blanket. There was so little light that she couldn't tell if he was looking at her. She held up one hand and waved by wiggling her fingers. He did the same and then waited, watching. Pri smiled, unsure if he could see her expression, and then turned back onto the mattress, facing the wall.

Axel and his children still slept when Jaz whispered to Pri, telling her that it was time to leave. One of the children was off the mattress, curled on the rug without the cover of the blanket. The oldest boy rested on his stomach, his face against his father's arm. She wished that he would have awoken as she crept past, wanting to wave goodbye. But the family did not rustle as Jaz and Pri departed, the predawn light appearing bright compared to the darkness of their confined sleeping quarters, clouds broken and checkered, rows of stilted buildings now lofty above the mud and refuse below. Her shoes were still soaking—Jaz said they would likely not be dry again until she'd reach the launch point—although her splinters had healed enough so that the pain from the blisters on her feet surpassed the discomfort from her implants. The tide was out and would not return for several hours, long enough for them to return to higher ground. At first, it sounded as if the entire EDZ slept, their careful steps along the debris conspicuous, their voices whispers. But soon water dribbled into the mud from the undersides of homes, the floors creaking, generators rumbling, and children's voices screeching.

As the sky brightened, there was a flow of people—men, women, and children of all ages—in the same direction. These were commuters, Jaz said, heading towards a shift at the largest employer in all of the Jungle, what he described as an "electronics recycling repository." Pri and Jaz joined the crowds, walking amongst them. This was the first time she felt invisible in the Jungle. They marched together out from the tidal zone, the buildings on either side of the lanes no longer demanding stilts, the ground solid and rocky. Pri noticed a scratch in the back of her throat, an irritating cough. Hundreds of plumes of black smoke rose from the horizon.

She had imagined this *recycling repository* as a warehouse, workers funneling through gates into a cavernous space to begin their shift. But there were no walls, no discernable buildings. The spaces between shanties became filled with drifts of shattered electronics, and soon there were no buildings, only wide lanes lined with the debris of charred plastics. The people ahead of them parted to either side of the road and Jaz pulled Pri with him, tight against others. A series of autonomous trucks grumbled through, the people ahead resuming their trek as soon as the last one passed. The roads were arranged in an orderly grid, each block a square, wide thoroughfares crossed by narrow passageways too constricting for vehicles. People split off from the masses, joined small groups sitting in circles around debris. A group of young men tended a fire, one squirting fluid from a bottle that erupted high to the air, eliciting hollers and then laughter. Just past this, a circle of children sorted through ashes, their faces and hands covered in soot, some barefoot, one snatching something from another and dashing across the lane before another convoy of trucks whirred past. This was all Pri could see in any direction—a deliberate array of roads and garbage populated with swarms of people, twisting plumes of smoke.

"Why are there so many fires?" Pri asked.

"It's the easiest way to extract metals from the plastics. Burn them and then sort through the remains. Every morning at the same time, dump trucks start to arrive with the waste. And every morning at the same time, people come from all around to burn it."

"They're not even wearing masks."

Jaz snickered, "You're smart enough to realize that your mask isn't doing anything to keep out the toxins, right?"

"Why are we walking through this? Can't we go around?"

"Of course, we could. If you want to add another day of travel. We can make it to Hasan's this evening if we carry on through here. These roads are direct and maintained. Don't mind the smoke and we can make some good time."

"I can't imagine what these people are inhaling. This should be illegal."

"You really think your old fones never ended up here somewhere?"

"It should still be illegal."

"Quite the conviction coming from someone ready to leave the world behind."

Garbage from the recycling center spread into the adjacent neighborhood, roads narrowing into twisting lanes. The convoys of passing trucks ceased and the myriad of scavengers began their shuffling march back to their homes. As the sun set behind the thick ceiling of cloud, smoke from a thousand smoldering files melded with the dimming sky. As Pri looked back, everything above the plywood rooftops appeared to be the same charcoal gray, as if a solid curtain had been drawn from the very zenith of the sky down to the dirt and debris. They walked along the side of a creek where hundreds of people rinsed themselves, splashing frigid waters against their faces, children naked. People washed clothes, filled plastic buckets, drank directly from the cupped palms of their hands. In this lighting, the water appeared to be the same black as the sky.

Hasan worked in the recycling fields. When he shook Pri's hand, it felt as if his skin was bark. His ruffled, messy black hair appeared windblown, thinning at the back of his scalp. His goatee and unshaven neck did not possess a single gray hair, the skin on his wide cheeks smooth. The space he had welcomed Pri and Jaz into was a cellar requiring three descending steps to enter, the walls made from mismatched cinderblocks. Less than half of the floor was covered in sheets of plywood, the rest exposed mud, wet to the touch. There were two mattresses, each on separate sides of the room, and a single bucket. No cables, no lights, no windows. The only opening was the doorway to the stairs, another sheet of plywood attached to a pair of hinges. Pri could see the path that rainwater travelled down alongside the steps during a downpour, the depressions of dried puddles in the center of the room. Hasan hung a pair of portable lanterns from a wire across the beams of the ceiling. He then stood, looking at Pri, looking at Jaz, as if awaiting an invitation.

Pri took off her boots and socks, running her hands over the sores around her ankles and toes. When she got to the launch site, she was going to throw away her footwear. She would arrive on the Tevat barefoot if necessary.

Hasan said to Jaz, "Can we talk? Please. Outside."

Jaz first smiled towards Pri, then looked back to Hasan. "I've just gotten here. I'd rather sit for a few minutes."

"Please," Hasan said with a slight bow. "I won't be long."

Jaz stood with a groan. "Pri, I'll only be a minute."

Hasan nodded towards Pri and the two men left the room, shutting the door behind them.

Pri crept towards the end of the mattress, but a flurry of thudding footsteps from above obscured their conversation. The door opened less than a minute later, Jaz noticing Pri's attempts to eavesdrop. "Don't worry," he said.

"What was that about?"

Jaz chuckled. "He was feeling bad about the fact that our mattresses were separate from one another. He thought we were a couple."

"You set him straight?"

"I assured him that the current sleeping arrangements were perfect."

"He seems different than the others."

"How so?"

"He seems nervous."

"Hasan is a good man. I've known him for a few years now. You can trust him."

"How do you know people like him, so deep within the Jungle?"

Jaz shrugged, untying his boots. "How do you meet anyone, really? It's all happenstance. Someone you know knows someone else who knows someone else who knows someone else."

"How far along that chain is he?"

"About three or four links down."

"Just some random recycler in the middle of an EDZ?"

"Just some random recycler in the middle of an EDZ who happens to have family with connections to the local ports. Those are good random people to know."

A pair of gentle knocks preluded the opening of the door. Hasan entered carrying a table no wider than his hips, which he placed in the middle of the room, beneath the lights. "I'll be back with tea and food," he said. He turned to hurry up the steps, leaving the door open.

"See," Jaz said. "He's a good man."

"I presume you've paid him a small fortune as well?"

"It's a win-win situation for all of us, really."

"Is that his family up there?"

"I gather so, yes."

"Will they share in his newly acquired small fortune?"

"I don't know. That's up to Hasan. Would it make you feel better to know that they were?"

"It would."

"Then go ahead and believe that. Again, win-win."

Lumbering footsteps preceded Hasan entering the room, carrying a chair in one hand, a tray with stacked cups and a teapot in the other. He knelt to position the chair in the mud between the two plywood sheets of flooring and placed down the tray, unstacking three cups and arranging them in a triangle around the pot. He then pushed the door closed and took a seat. "Please. Join me."

The tea was as black as coffee. Pri took each sip with a grin, as if finding it palatable was a matter of resolve. Hasan was different than Shiraz and Axel.

He wanted to stay. She could not decide if what he possessed was a gregarious confidence or gregarious obliviousness. She kept hoping that he would leave—after the tea, after he brought a dinner of rice with stewed poultry, after another pot of tea that was somehow more intense than the first—and yet he always returned to that chair in the middle of the room, Pri and Jaz kneeling on the plywood at either side, Hasan the marquee attraction. He had a pronounced, soft belly that hung over his belt, accented by his slack posture while sitting. The rumble of what Pri knew was another rocket launch clattered the dishes and Hasan held down the three teacups with both hands to quiet them without pausing from his description of his most recent journey out from the Jungle, what he claimed was down to the Seattle metropolitan authority. He went down by boat, he claimed, making landfall near Whidbey Island. He described walking through an affluent strata, soaring walls around every house, drones skimming through the air above as he hid in the bushes. He spent the night before heading out just before dawn. Pri did not believe a word that he said. There was no way that a man on a boat could get through the fortifications of an island like that. He would have been shot to death by automatic sentry rifles before he reached the shore. And if by some impossible fluke he had managed to bypass these defenses, no drone would glide overhead without noticing. Either Hasan was the most extraordinarily lucky man to ever live, or he was a liar and a showman. She tried not to talk, instead listening as if impressed by his tales, nodding, sipping tea with a demure smile. He talked about his old home around Jakarta, how he planned to return when he was rich. Someday, he said, he was going to get out of the Jungle and move into one of the better stratas. And then, once established, he was going to take a rocket to Indonesia and see the country again. "Believe me," he said to Jaz, who nodded with tight lips. "I will do it. I will not be like my parents. I will leave the Jungle. I know I will."

Pri figured that only someone who had so little chance to ever leave their current situation could have such optimism about a better future. Perhaps the only people who could appreciate the stagnant order of the world's stratas were those from the top, those who saw the impenetrability of their lifestyles.

He then looked over to Pri, "And you. You want to come back to the Jungle. You had a life in the city, right? But now you wish to come back here."

She didn't want to reply, but he waited with seemingly infinite patience for Pri to say something. She shrugged again. "I guess. Yes."

"Why would anyone want to come back here? I don't understand."

Pri looked towards Jaz, expecting him to interject and veer the conversation elsewhere. But Jaz nodded towards Pri, giving her permission. She said, "I don't have anything left in the city."

Hasan looked back to Jaz. "You hear what she call you? Nothing."

"She calls me that all the time," Jaz said.

Pri said, "He's been very helpful. But I have no one else."

Hasan asked, "Nothing in the city must be more than something out here?"

Pri chuckled. "Maybe."

"Your English is very good," Hasan said. "Your accent is very," he held up the fingers of one hand, flitted the fingers as if tickling the air, "very proper."

"I worked with my father for years in upper stratas, cleaning homes. He taught me to speak in a certain way. Said it was essential in the world."

"Smart man, your father."

"Yes. Yes, he was."

"What was it like," Hasan said, "working in the homes of the upper stratas? What was their houses like?"

Pri glanced towards Jaz again, his expression calm and unconcerned. "They were," she cleared her throat, "they were big. Big but with so few people. Always more rooms than people. Many more rooms than people. The streets were empty. No one was around. But so many trees. So few people and so many trees."

"It must have made you angry, seeing what they have? When you had so little?"

Pri shrugged. "Most were good to me and my father. I was happy to have a job, that's all. I was never angry with them."

"You say they were good to you, but you lost your job, yes?"

"I guess."

"They don't know what it's like to travel the ocean. They take rockets to get across the Earth. Half an hour, not weeks."

Pri nodded, "You are right. They know nothing of this."

"They don't care about any of us."

"Some do."

Hasan hummed an acknowledgement. "Did they ask you about your trip across the ocean?"

"I barely remember it. I was only four."

"What do you remember?"

Pri glanced back towards Jaz, who appeared not to listen, instead taking another sip from his tea. She cleared her throat, swiveled her head from side to side. "Just being crowded, I guess. I remember my dad's arm around me, holding me, keeping me safe." She wanted to look away from Hasan but knew that she couldn't, forcing her gaze upon the tip of his nose, the smirk in his lips. "I remember looking out to the ocean that never ended. And being hungry. Being so hungry."

"How long did it take you?"

"I don't know. I was only four. My dad didn't like to talk about it. He just wanted to forget. This was his fresh start. By never talking about it, he hoped the memories of it would go away, I think."

Hasan nodded, his lips forming a grimace. "A fresh start," he then shook his head. "That is what our parents thought this would be. But this is the start of what? What? Spending our life here. In an EDZ. That is what our parents are happy with. But not me. I am getting out. Trust me, I am getting out of here."

"I hope you can," Pri said, casting her eyes towards Jaz, annoyed that he chose to remain so quiet during Hasan's questioning. "Maybe you can take Jaz back with you to the city someday, right?"

Jaz grinned, baring teeth, cheeks wrinkled and eyes mere slits. "I'm always open to helping people out. But—" Jaz put down his teacup and stretched his shoulders. "If you don't mind, I think I might request that we end our socializing. I'm not as young and strapping as you, Hasan. These long days take a toll on me."

Hasan nodded, nearly bowed, "Of course, of course. I stay too long." He stacked two cups, noticed that Pri's was still full. "You still want this?"

"No, I'm great. Thank you."

Hasan stood, tray in hand, and said to Jaz, "I hope I haven't kept you up too late. I'm sure I will see you again." He turned to Pri. "And it was nice to meet you. I wish you all the best."

"Same here."

Hasan nodded in acknowledgement and opened the door. There were no lights outside, the passageway a black void, not even stairs visible from where Pri sat. When Hasan closed the door behind him, the sound of the rain tempered to a muffled wheeze.

Pri watched the door, listening for footsteps above her before turning to Jaz and whispering, annoyed, "What was that?"

"What was what?"

She pointed towards the creaking floorboards above. "Hasan. What was with him?"

"Oh, he's just a talker. That's all. It's just who he is."

"It felt like he was interrogating me."

"No, no, Pri. He's young, which means he's a little feisty. But he likes to talk to his guests."

"He seemed a little too interested. Like he didn't believe me."

Jaz chuckled. "Ever thought that maybe it's because you're an attractive woman, even with those teeth of yours?"

"He sure didn't seem like he was flirting."

"Hasan has been through a lot. Makes people a little sharp around the edges. That's all."

"How long have you known him?"

Jaz rubbed one eye, shaking his head. "You talk as if we're business partners. I've met him a couple of times before, that's all."

"But what does he know about you? You paid him well so that we can stay here, I presume? Doesn't he wonder what your backstory is?"

"No. He doesn't. You're reading too much into him. Hasan just likes to talk. He likes to show off a little. Like I said, he's young. That's what young people do. They talk about how they're going to go places. How they're going to do big things. That's all. Now," Jaz stood up and reached for the lanterns. "I wasn't just blowing Hasan off there when I said I was tired." He switched off each bulb. She heard him crawl back onto his mattress. "You should get some rest. We had a long day today, and we will have another long day tomorrow. With any luck, tomorrow will be your last day. Thinking about Hasan won't make your feet feel any better in the morning. But maybe a good rest will."

Pri thought that her eyes might adjust, but the cellar remained featureless. There was not even the faintest outline around the door. She reached down to the plywood, feeling the grain of it, the grit of dirt. She could hear Jaz's steady breaths. Every creaking footstep from above caught her attention, forced her to stare up into the nothingness, listening. She was exhausted, she knew she should be able to sleep. And then she would run her tongue behind her front incisors, trace the kinked line of her bite. She was wide awake. This felt worse than the previous nights. Maybe it was the strong black tea that Hasan had made for them. Maybe it was just in her head. She rolled onto her back, ran one finger over the scar on her face. She wanted to visualize that moment she would step onto the Tevat, welcomed by music and applause. She wanted to run through that whole scene that she'd visualized a thousand times before. But instead, she noticed Jaz's breaths, steady, not snoring. She wondered if he was acting. She wondered if it had only been an hour since he'd turned out the lights. She heard a pattering and thought that it might have been the scurrying footsteps of rats, causing her to pull both arms atop her chest, away from the floor.

The sound of the rain grew in volume, as if a torrent had begun to pummel the mud just outside the door. She imagined a stream of water running down beside the steps and onto the floor, filling the puddles. She opened her eyes and could make out an object by the door. There was just enough light to discern something, although she couldn't tell what it was. She could see the steps. The door was open.

A light flicked on, a blaring starburst of fluorescent white aimed at Pri's eyes. She winced and shielded her face with one arm.

"Don't move," Hasan said with a calm whisper. "And don't make a sound. Come with me."

One

Pri would not think about Hasan's threat, about her being sold to other, more depraved types. She knew that he wanted to scare her, to make her obsess over the speculative details. But right then, that did not matter. She had some food. She had some water. She could not let herself follow those thoughts. If Pri was going to think about anything, then she was going to think of a way to escape, even if that appeared impossible. Even if it was impossible. Like any problem she would attempt to solve at work, she would think about how to find a solution and nothing else.

Pri had a metal bowl that was aluminum or tin. She stared at that opening across the space, beneath the floorboards, daylight like a seam between clouds on an overcast, moonlit sky. She could not dig herself out from this space in two days or two weeks. But it made no sense to sit and stare when she had a bowl that could be used to burrow. So, she stood. She told herself to stand up, aloud, and stepped into the mud, reaching into the opening with one hand, the soil wet but no longer dribbling. The rim of the bowl would not fit inside the hole, so she dug her fingers into the dirt, scratching something solid. She scraped at the edges of the opening, each time mere grains crumbling away. It was concrete. Either poured in place or a broken slab buried into the ground. She dropped the bowl and reached in with both hands, wanting to grab onto a lip of this block and pull it free, imagining a great boulder breaking away from the wall. But her grip and her strength were irrelevant. It would not move, no matter how strong or persistent she felt.

She would not sit back down. Not until she solved the problem. She reached both arms back into the opening, blindly scratching and pulling away dirt from anywhere she could reach. Because of the rice, because of the water, she had energy. She could not waste this. She withdrew a handful of mud, relishing in the feeling of so much material in her palm before throwing it to her side and reaching for more. The soils ahead were soft and fragile. Soon her bicep scratched against the lip of the opening as she grasped onto another handful of loose mud, pulling it out, enthused by the progress she had made. She should have done this earlier, she thought. She should have done this from the moment she was imprisoned.

Her fingertips reached around the smooth surface of a single rock, wide enough that her thumb and little finger flayed apart from one another. She wiggled the stone, feeling it give, rocking forwards and back, imagining this to be a capstone that upon release would cause the surrounding dirt to collapse. It rolled in place, and she kept adjusting her grip, her shoulder against the lip of the opening, straining to reach a little farther. Someone entered the space above her, footsteps inches away, and Pri thought of scurrying back to her spot across the room, but she almost had it. She wriggled her little and ring fingers around a bulbous end, listening for the lock on the door, ready to scamper back. She pulled and the stone slurped as it detached from the dirt and mud, its mass straining the muscles in her arm, tendons outstretched and tight. The footsteps ceased. Her breaths heaved. No one was upstairs.

She put the stone down beside her blanket and returned to the opening of the burrow. The sides of the tunnel were obsidian, shadows perfectly black in contrast to the light. There appeared to be a flexible pipe, curled and ribbed. She reached in, forcing her shoulder into the opening, her fingertips sliding over the corrugated plastic surface. The tube was loose, she could move it with her hand, felt that it could be unfurled should she secure a grip. She forced her shoulder deeper into the opening and tried to wrap her fingers around this object. Her armpit scratched against the cement surface of the burrow, but she reached further, feeling the tube jiggle. Adjusting her grip, then pulling with all her weight, she nearly fell backwards but refused to relinquish it. Finally, the hose came loose. It unfurled a few inches before her fingers slid off, before she staggered into the darkness. Staring back, the tube now twisted within the opening, easily within reach. She tugged again. She imagined it carrying water and she leveraged her shoulder against the wall to twist it free, the hose refusing to be dragged into the darkness of her cellar. She could not stop now. This might save her life. She heaved, throwing herself back with each draw, reaching into the opening with both hands around the tube, the grip of her fingers tight but unable to release any further slack. Then, something broke free. She fell back, the hose still within her hands as it unspooled from the opening and down to the blackness by her feet. She felt around with fingertips along its corrugated surface, finding the end and holding it up to the light of the burrow. Running her fingers within the opening, it was dry to the touch. She held it to her nose and inhaled, just a faint mustiness. She had fought and scraped and struggled to release some garbage. She let it dangle down to the ground and sat back onto her blanket, exhausted, her fingers, wrists, and forearms scraped and surely bleeding. The hose appeared like a black scaled serpent slinking out from the opening, down into the nothingness.

Pri decided that she would call Nayha. The ransom Hasan requested was absurd, but she would negotiate it down to something realistic. This would come to an end in days. Maybe a matter of hours. Poppy would grow up having an aunt, a cousin, a grandfather. This would not be a burden. This would be her escape. Back on the North Shore, Pri would find happiness again. Eventually. She ran her hands along the ground, searching for that rock the size of a grapefruit that she had pulled out from the dirt. She clutched it with both hands, tapped the underside of the ceiling to visualize her range of motion, and then bashed the stone against the plywood, the force jolting back down into her shoulders. She adjusted her grip and struck three more times, each collision causing tremors in the joists, the sound explosive. She listened, waiting for footsteps, the rattling of the lock, a beam of light down to the mud by her bare feet. Her breaths were mechanical, the intake and outtake of a factory. No one came and she struck the ceiling again, this time counting to ten, her fingers quivering by the end, dropping the stone as she skittered back to protect her toes. She raised one hand and felt the grain of the wood, the seam between two sheets, the edges raised. She picked away fibers with her fingernails, the plywood soft. The wood was likely rotten. Pri felt for the rock and lined it up with this battered section of the ceiling, first just tapping and then pummelling the wood, her palms slipping from the stone with each strike, imagining that soon she would break through, first with a crack of light and then a splintered hole.

Something clicked and then rattled. Pri stopped, needing to lean over to catch her breath. The generator rumbled, louder than before. But still no footsteps. No signs of anyone above her. Her lungs heaved as she looked towards the hole from where the hose slunk down into the black abyss. She must have burrowed towards the generator. Looking back up, she pushed the rock against the ceiling to feel for its height before heaving it into the wood, nervous that she might lose her grip. She slammed the stone again, and then again, stepping back and letting it drop to the ground. She didn't have the strength. She couldn't catch a deep breath. She reached up and felt for where she had struck the wood. But still no cracks. No light. She knew that she needed to find that rock again, regardless of the strength in her arms and fingers. Be relentless. She knew that there was no point in waiting and yet she waited. All she wanted was a crack of light above her, some sign that this was not a waste of time. Pri could not see herself. Unless she reached her arms into the faint light of that opening, she did not exist. She was just a thought. Hasan might have been waiting above her, patient and calm, listening to each strike until the floorboards broke. Then he'd slice her open. Sell her to someone far more insidious. She was going to tunnel her way to freedom and then she was going to call Nayha for the ransom and then she was going to ram her way through the ceiling. But still she was right here, in this cell, in a room without light. She knelt and then sat onto the mud. She felt the stone between her ankles but left it there. Her lungs struggled for air. Her head pounded, her skull tight, dizzy, faint.

There was a stench, Pri realized. A burnt but smooth sweetness. She knew the scent. It was from the Flats. The exhaust from the generators. She thought of closing her eyes and resting. But she still couldn't take a full breath. She forced herself back onto her knees, reaching around, feeling for the hose, grabbing onto its ridged exterior, pulling the slack towards her until clasping the jagged tip. It spewed putrid air into her face, blowing back her hair, causing her eyes to sting. She coughed, gagged on the fumes that had no weight and yet got stuck in the recesses of her lungs. She tried to stand but stumbled back against the wall. She wanted to wait another moment but knew she had to move. She held her breath, grabbed onto the hose and forced its end back towards the opening, plunging the spout into the burrow as far as possible before falling back to the ground, gasping for what she hoped was clean air, breathing in from the very dirt between her palms. Carbon monoxide has no odor, she knew. She looked up, the tube spilling out and snaking back into the dirt. If there was enough ventilation for the exhaust to escape, she would live past this next hour. If not, she would pass out and then die. She crawled back to her blanket, wanting to keep her eyes open, watching the only source of light in this space, already dim, soon to be night, soon to all be the same perfect black. "Sorry, Poppy," she said, a whisper between coughs. "Sorry, Poppy." But she would not close her eyes. If she could see, then she was still alive. If she could speak, then she was still alive.

Pri heard footsteps. She pushed herself up, fingertips clasping onto the recesses in the wall and reached up to the ceiling, pounding it with her fists. "Hasan," she tried to yell, but her voice would not rise beyond a breathy croak. "Hasan," she repeated.

The door opened. The shaft of light had clean lines and sharp corners. She waited for the feet of the ladder to descend.

"Pri," Hasan said, his voice soft.

She crawled towards the light, reaching one arm out, her fingers black. She turned her palm so that it faced the opening, the skin sliced with incisions, each fingernail jagged.

"Pri," Hasan repeated. She looked up, shielding her eyes while squinting towards the single bulb above, Hasan's figure a silhouette, standing, the tips of each shoe nosing over the edge of the opening. He snickered when he saw her, his head shaking.

"Hasan, I need help."

"Will you call someone?"

"I need water."

"Will you call someone?"

"Please, I just need some water."

"Will you call, or will I sell you?"

Pri looked down, savoring these breaths, what must have been clean air.

"Pri," Hasan repeated, impatient but calm. "What are you going to do?"

"I'll call my sister. In the morning. But I need water first."

"You call her now."

"She won't be home. Yes, she's a doctor. But she works nights. I'll call in the morning. Just please, I need some water."

"You will call her?"

"Yes. In the morning. Please. I just need water."

Hasan nodded. "This could have been so much more easy for you."

"I know."

"You are a stupid rich girl."

"I know."

"You will call in the morning or I will be done with you."

"I know. I will call. I promise. I'm sorry."

Pri waited only a few minutes before grabbing the stone and pummelling it into the underside of the bowl until the metal was flattened into a warbled circle, warm to the touch. She folded it in half, heaving the weight of her body, wrestling one side down before hammering the rounded corner to form a seam that she could flex, the two halves swiveling as if joined by a hinge. When the metal broke in half, the sharp edge was scalding. She stood up, feeling for the rotten corner of plywood in the ceiling, and sliced into the grain with the rudimentary blade, scratching the underside, feeling dust and splinters falling onto her face. It sounded like an animal clawing at the wall, incessant and desperate. She didn't hear footsteps. More importantly, she didn't hear the generator. She kept scratching, spitting out fibers and dust that fell onto her lips. The wood gave way. She could pry apart the floorboards with her thumbs. She thrust through a pair and then trio of fingers, the tips of each feeling the woven texture of a towel or rug. She grabbed her shard of metal, scratched it against the weave. It was simple. She could not stop. If she could slice through wood, she could slice through a carpet.

Once she revealed an incision long enough for just a single fingertip, she tore it wide open, pried apart the sides. There was the faintest of light above. No details. She reached down, felt along the mud for the generator's exhaust pipe and thrust it into this laceration in the floorboards, in the carpet, the ridged exterior scraping against the splintered wood until the hose was taut.

Pri let go, ran her hands in the darkness along the tube from the opening in the ceiling to the dirt in the wall. She felt a bead of sweat dangle from the tip of her nose, her breaths strained, lungs quivering. There is always a solution, she thought to herself. It may be circuitous, but there is always a solution. The only constraint is the human brain.

She knelt, her hands back, feeling the wall before resting against the dirt, wrapping the blanket around her legs but still sweating, clammy and warm, staring into the void, waiting for the click, gargle, and growl of the generator. Waiting for her salvation or her destruction.

Pri held the stone between both hands, elbows tucked against her abdomen, listening. Every breath and sniffle felt conspicuous now that the generator had ceased. It was impossible to know the length of time with which she remained under the blanket, on the ground, knees to her chest. More than an hour, she felt certain. Likely two, maybe three. Knowing that every breath might have been toxic. Knowing that if she fell unconscious, it would be because she had poisoned herself. But now she stood, erect, breathing. This was a victory in itself. She held the stone up before her forehead, tapped the underside of the trapdoor once, twice, lowered her arms and then heaved it back into the ceiling, hammering the wood, a blast that jolted her in this silence. She could not wait now. She pounded the ceiling again, counting with spittle flying from her lips. Ten strikes, then a ten second break. That was her rule. In between breaths, she listened, fearing footsteps but hearing none. Then ten more strikes.

It did not matter if it was probable; Pri knew that it was possible. It was within this thought that Pri could take solace. When she reached one hundred, she placed the stone by her feet and felt the outline of the door, the edge raised a few more millimeters. This was possible, she knew, and this was all that mattered. This was possible. She crouched to grab the stone and slammed it against the underside of the door. "One," she said, expelling the word within her strained exhalation. "Two."

If Hasan was alive, if Hasan opened the door, she would scramble back and grab the jagged remains of the metal bowl. She would slice him in the neck, across the face, in the eyes. It didn't matter. She knew she would do this. It would be her only option. But still, she heard nothing from him. No sign of life. Hasan was either dead or the building above was vacant.

"One hundred," Pri spat out and dropped the stone, collapsing to the ground, her breaths impatient. There were still no sounds from above. Two hundred strikes and no one had arisen. This was what mattered. Nothing else. "Stand up," she said. "Stand up." She grabbed the stone and hit the underside of the door. There was a crack of light above her. She thrust the rock again, no longer counting, now impatient. The fracture of light became a sliver. With each battering, the sliver quivered, expanded. Pri discovered an energy she had not felt in days. Maybe weeks. Maybe ever. This was no longer just possible, this was probable. She could see the dark silhouette of nails, sharp teeth through a widening, menacing grin. She thrust up the stone and one side of the hinge came loose. She hammered the other side, each strike now effortless, the mass of the rock no longer of any consequence. She heaved it against the wood and the other hinge came free from the floorboards. The final strike caused the door to jump and rest on the side of the square opening. Pri dropped the stone, a damp thud, and reached up, her fingertips running against the top of the door frame. What felt like carpet. She could see the ceiling above, the bare, dim lightbulb hanging above her. It was dark, but not the absolute darkness of her prison. There were features to discern. Standing tall, her forehead rose above the opening, she could make out bare wooden walls, no windows, no furniture. She reached around until feeling a leg of the ladder and pulled it into the opening, the metal scraping, announcing her exit. She pushed the feet of the ladder into the mud, placed a bare foot on the bottom rung, and stepped up, her head ascending above the opening, out into the empty room. No one was waiting in ambush. The space was barely larger in area than the hole below. Extension cords twisted on the floor. In one corner, an upside-down plastic crate acted as a chair. A pair of metal bowls littered the ground. The walls looked to be covered in newsprint. She placed her first foot onto the carpet and stood, nervous to breathe, taking small sips of air. There was just one door across the space, slightly ajar, dim light from behind.

Pri counted her steps away from the ladder, measuring her distance, comparing it with her steps in the pit below, and then knelt, feeling the floor, the woven rugs that covered plywood. The floor was wet, a single drop struck the back of her neck from above. She ran her fingers over the opening she had carved out from the rotten floorboards, feeling the exposed opening to the generator's exhaust hose. She stood up, unsure if the lightness in her head was from the lingering carbon monoxide in the air or just a consequence of being starved for days. She did not need to walk with gentle steps, she knew, yet still she crept along the carpet in her bare feet, wary of every squeak or groan in the floor. She pushed the one door open, revealing a room with draped windows, countertops and pots, a table with three chairs, stairs as steep as a ladder running up along one wall, shelves full of cups and bowls, ornaments and trinkets, electronics, crates and carboard boxes. There was the smell of spice. Papers on the floor, one crinkling beneath her feet. She cast aside a blind with the back of one hand to glance through the window. The sky was a moonlit overcast, cut by the drooping black lines of wires, puddles in the gravel wrinkling from unseen raindrops. The structures across the narrow lane were two storeys, clad in sheet metal, the top floors recessed and slanting. Windows black. No one awake. Pri closed the blinds. A door to the lane was within reach. She twisted the pair of locks and pulled it open just enough to let in a trickle of cool, clean air, relishing the fragrance, but then pushed it shut. She walked to a metal sink, a plastic bucket of water on the floor. She washed her hands in the tepid water, unable to see the dirt or grime. She cupped water and splashed it on her face, reaching for a towel and holding it against her eyes before dabbing away the drops, keeping the cloth around her nose and mouth. She looked along the back of a countertop, pots hanging from the wall, a kettle resting atop a single burner. She pulled open a wooden drawer, needing to feel inside to determine the contents, finding tape, spoons, cups. Her fingers ran along the smooth metal of a blade. A small knife, suitable for slicing vegetables. She held it in her grip, turning back, looking along the floor and shelves for clothes. She did not want to go upstairs. All she needed was a pair of shoes, a coat, a facemask. Then she would be invisible. Then she would be free. She pulled out crates from the shelves, finding electronics, papers, pencils and pens, tin cups, tin bowls. A plush toy animal missing one eye, what she assumed was a tiger, stripes down its side, tail curled. She pushed back the crates, looked up towards the stairs. She thought of hurrying along the laneways of the Jungle in her bare feet, these tattered clothes. How far could she get? Was anyone looking for her? Would anyone care? But she could not be so brazen. She gripped the railing of the stairs and shook it, the lumber secure.

She took the first step, eyes focussed on the empty space ahead. With each step, the boards beneath her groaned. With each step, more details of the upstairs came into view, an open space, shelves against the walls, two beds—one with a semicircle headrest, a smaller one in the far corner. Sheets or towels that hung from the walls. Blinds drawn, drapes heavy, far darker than the main floor. She would not look in the beds. She would not glance in their direction. She knew that she had surely killed Hasan. Poisoned him with the carbon monoxide of the generator's exhaust. She knew that. She could think about that. But she would not see his body. She did not want to see his face, frozen in time. The upstairs smelled of urine and feces. She put the cloth back against her nostrils as she ascended the final step. Wires ran along a plastered ceiling, a pair of bulbs dangling from the middle. Pictures hung on the wall, the faces within these frames hidden in the darkness. A leopard print rug covered the floor. A chair with armrests separated the two beds, a coat draped over its back, clothes piled on the seat.

There was a body in the bed. She told herself that she would not look but still she stared, analyzing the shape of the curve, a figure asleep on its left shoulder. She turned, felt the plush of the rug beneath her feet, her back to the bed, looking into the square shelves. Pants folded and stacked, the tight weave of denim. Short sleeve tops, fibers soft, thin. She withdrew a shirt, a dark brown or red, and pulled it over, the bottom draped around her thighs. It smelled of detergent. There were pairs of shoes on the floor, the rounded lips of boots, straps of sandals. Clothes hung from a folded drying rack, undergarments and more shirts. She grabbed a pair of socks and put them into her pocket. What looked like pillowcases hung from hooks in the wall between two shelves. She ran her hand down one. It was smooth. Like silk. A woman's headscarf. Dozens of them. On the floor were more shoes. Much smaller in size. Not for a grown man. She told herself not to turn around. To grab the shoes, grab a scarf, then leave, never looking back. There was no need to look back. To survive, she would need focus. But she kept staring at something on the drying rack. What she had thought was a pair of underwear was a bib. She should leave, she knew. She should leave this space. But Pri turned around, back to the body in bed. Knees folded. An arm out, hand still. She stepped closer, between the two beds. The smaller one was empty, a narrow rectangle framed with thin lumber, sheets jumbled, no pillow. She stepped on a sock or underwear, not looking down, instead towards the back of the body. The blanket followed the contours of the person's waist, a valley between the peaks of hips and shoulders. She reached for the coat on the back of the chair, slid it off and into the air. It was heavier than she expected, made from leather. Long black curls of hair hung over the pillow. Pri extended one hand to the edge of the blanket but then retracted, retreating to the end of the bed, following the shape of the legs. A woman's legs. Not Hasan. Pri walked to the other side. She thought her heart should race; her lungs should hyperventilate. She thought that she should be terrified. But she took more steps. Now she needed to know. This was not something she could avoid. The outstretched arm, three fingers visible, reaching out. More of that hair, bunched into coils. And something else, beneath the blanket, beneath the woman's arm. She felt another garment beneath her bare feet, and now Pri noticed her own heartbeat. She reached towards the lip of the blanket. Using just her thumb and forefinger, she pinched the cloth, pulled up, pulled back.

Pri saw the face of a young woman, eyes closed, lips open, deep, deep asleep. Not quite peaceful, just still. And Pri saw the hair of a child, a face buried into the woman's arm. So young that she couldn't be certain as to the gender. Thick hair over the ears. A smooth, rounded cheek, lips parted. Eyes closed, like the mother. One hand reached over, onto her bosom, fingers fat. Pri held the blanket in the air above the pair, her eyes darting from the cheeks of the child, the open mouth of the mother, the stillness of both, mere statues in bed. Listening, she heard only her own breaths, her own heart.

She laid down the blanket, covering the child's face and arm. She grabbed a pair of pants, denim and soft, pulling them over her own clothes. She slid her arms through the sleeves of the heavy coat, which smelled of acrid smoke, pushing down each shoulder. She retrieved the socks from her pocket and slid them over her bare feet. She wrapped the scarf around her head. It smelled of lavender. Then she took hold of a pair of shoes, still careful not to make any loud noises, as if not to wake the mother and child. She did not look back. She needed to keep moving. Hasan was not here. This meant Hasan could return home at any moment. That was the only fact that mattered. She descended the stairs, nearly a gallop at the bottom. Before opening the front door, she grabbed the small knife from her pocket, kept it secure in her grip and hidden beneath the long sleeves. She pulled open the door, surprised by the unmistakable daylight, the rain having eased, clouds textured. She shut the door behind her, pulling it tight until hearing a click. There was the splatter of water, a woman down the lane emptied a bucket from her front step. Pri looked to her feet, stepping onto the mud and gravel, holding up her oversize pants with one hand, and started walking. It did not matter in which direction she moved. She only needed to create distance between herself and Hasan's home. Her shoes splashed into a deep puddle, surprising her, but she kept walking. Her head was light, dizzy, and she took deep breaths, telling herself she only had to keep walking. She stayed close to one side of the lane, one arm ready to reach out and press onto the side of a building for support should she stumble or faint. People brushed aside drapes from the top floors, openings in the walls without glass. She could smell the exhaust from passing generators, some humming, others growling, sputtering.

Pri came to an intersection, a shuttered hut in the middle, electrical cables reaching out from the surrounding structures to its low hanging roof. She turned right. It was impossible to know if she was walking towards or away from the launch site, but she only needed to keep walking. Her shoulder bashed into a wooden electrical pole, nearly knocking her to the ground, but she steadied herself, keeping her eyes away from anyone else who might have been watching, gripping the knife concealed in her sleeve. A group of five women clustered around a spot on the lane ahead. Pri tightened her headscarf, pulled up the slack on her pants. Each carried buckets, one with a girl no more than three years old in her arms, waiting around a bent metal faucet that burbled water from its spout. They spoke in a language Pri could not understand, one looking towards her and smiling. Pri watched her steps, careful not to plunge a shoe into another frigid puddle, casting her glances over the rooftops for any signs of the launch site, any signs of something familiar. Chickens strutted and then scrambled in terror as Pri approached, resuming their unperturbed amble seconds later. A man exited from a door ahead of her, hood up, boots with untied laces, then slung a bag over one shoulder and withdrew his fone while walking, head down. The splash of another emptied bucket of water caused Pri to flinch, skitter her steps. She turned left at another crossroads, taking each turn with feigned confidence, not wanting anyone to notice her vacillation. Steps scraped the dirt and gravel behind her and Pri's grip on the knife's handle tightened. She kept to the middle of the narrow lane. The Jungle was awakening. It felt like it was only minutes ago when she first pried apart that drape in Hasan's house. Now she heard children whining through the thin walls of the buildings. There was the smell of smoke in the air from newly lit fires, winding pillars rising from the rooftops. Men walking past her with empty wheelbarrows, groups of women carrying bowls and jugs. Pri came to a creek, its waters placid and brown, the muddy shores lined with colorful plastic garbage, wrappers, and bottles. Two girls stood, ankle-deep, one filling a jug, the other washing a cloth. They spoke to each other, laughing between sentences, noticing nothing beyond the few feet around them. Pri traversed the waters atop a pair of long pieces of lumber, one cracked in the middle and sinking with her steps. Across the stream, a hunched man dragged a cart filled with plastic jugs stacked in a neat pile, five wide, three high.

The lane narrowed, barely wide enough for people to pass, the buildings reduced to one-storey shacks topped with tarpaulins secured by rocks and scavenged lumber. A cylindrical metal chimney rose from the middle of each home, the peaks black with soot, emitting phantasmal smoke. The ground was more debris than rocks or gravel, chipped cinderblocks and clumps of old asphalt with sodden rugs before the entrances to people's homes, doors mere particleboard attached to hinges, locked with chains. Strollers, foldable carts and children's toys rested atop roofs. A woman squatted in an open doorway, struggling to light a propane burner while an impatient toddler climbed on her back to get a better look. One row of homes lined a solid concrete wall at least three storeys in height, topped with spiraling razor wire, its flush face covered in graffiti painted with rollers and brushes, phrases repeated down the wall with unintelligible scribbles. Pri watched her step, tires and splintered lumber buried into the ground. A man walked atop one roof, throwing down an empty plastic tub onto the lane below. He said something, presumably an apology, and Pri nodded, kept walking. She heard what sounded like vehicles on the other side of the wall, the white noise hissing of wet tires on asphalt.

The lane widened, the ground again level with ditches that trickled rainwater and refuse. No structures abutted this section of the concrete wall, now just plastic crates and drifts of garbage piled in the corners, a young man searching through the debris. What she initially assumed to be graffiti was a gated opening in the wall, a mesh of black metal bars. She kicked aside wrappers and broken jugs to get closer, pulling at the bars to confirm that it was locked. Just a few feet before Pri were two lanes of smooth pavement, black from rain, the solid yellow lines crisp and bright. The opposing wall was immaculate, its crest covered in the same spiraling razor wire. Four trucks rushed past in procession, trailing a swirling briny mist that she could taste on her lips. The man looking through the refuse said something to Pri, and she hurriedly nodded, stepping back from the gate and back along the path. He repeated himself but Pri did not look behind her. She pulled up her pants, gripped the knife secure beneath the cuff of the oversized jacket, and kept walking, watching her step, a small stream dribbling across from a culvert that emerged at the base of the wall. More chickens scampered past. She felt comfortable watching them, not anyone else. Smoke from the chimneys hung sideways in layers above the lanes, the scent of burning tires catching in the back of her throat. But she couldn't cough. People were watching and she couldn't draw attention to herself. The lane split into two and she stayed close to the wall fortifying the highway, fearful that she would come to a dead end, that she would have to return past all these same people who were scrutinizing her, wondering why this woman was wearing pants and a coat far too large for her frame, why she kept coughing, why she walked alone, why she appeared lost. By now, Hasan was likely home. He would have found his dead wife and child. He had probably enlisted his neighbors to hunt down the stupid rich girl pretending to be a migrant. It would now be a matter of principle. Her punishment would mean more than any potential ransom. Word of her escape and the need to be captured would soon be rippling through the Jungle as she stumbled on, lost, watching chickens.

She came to another opening, what appeared to be a plaza with merchants setting up tables and tarps. The lanes split in five different directions. From here, she could see down the hill that she had ascended, thousands of square rooftops below and behind her, the smoke from hundreds of fires mixing into the morning mist, the fog of the Jungle. There were enough people here passing through, mingling, setting up booths, that she felt inconspicuous. Her head was light, she saw a crate on the ground and sat down, afraid she might tumble if she didn't find a spot to rest. Now that she sat, Pri didn't know how she'd managed to walk this far. She hadn't slept. She hadn't eaten. She could sit here for hours. She wanted to sleep, letting her eyelids droop and close, listening to the sounds of a dozen intertwined conversations, the scraping of steps, a crying baby, a guttural chuckle, the patter of rain on plastic, crackling of fire. She could still hear the squeaking floorboards as she climbed the stairs into the dark bedroom, her breaths through stuffed nostrils. She could still see the body of a woman in bed, hair coiled and black, the child at her side, holding onto her mother in her final gasps of life.

Pri opened her eyes, feeling as if she had awoken, not ready to stand but needing to look around. Above the rooftops, a pair of rockets descended against the overcast, both black in silhouette and vertical, the sharp white point of flames quivering from beneath each engine. Boosters returning from launch into low orbit. Pri stood, able to hear the rumble as they approached. She took a step, her legs light. She could do this. The launch site was not far. Landing stabilizers on each unfolded to form a tripod. Pri bumped into someone, apologizing without breaking her gaze from the rockets, following their return. She could hear their crackling hiss above the indifferent conversations around her. No one else cared. The pair of boosters descended out from view, below the uneven rooftops, but Pri could still hear the sizzle of the engines. The fortified highway led towards the launch complex. Pri was certain of this. She was not more than a few kilometers away. She knew where to go. She started walking, her eyes still trained on the faint trail of smoke left behind, hazy and vanishing into the low clouds. She bumped into someone else, mumbled an apology, not looking away from the sky, the rockets her compass.

"Pri?"

She turned and looked around. Hasan was staring at her, eyebrows furrowed, but not in anger. In bewildered confusion. In crippling shock.

He stood just out of reach, motionless, a fone in one hand. His gaze followed along her coat, down to her oversized pants, her shoes. While back in his cellar, Hasan appeared to tower above Pri. His round belly mocked her desperate hunger. Now he looked juvenile and confused, barely taller than she, his eyes returning to her headscarf, her coat, her pants, her shoes. His lips parted but twitched, unable to say anything else.

Pri's eyes did not waver from his own. She pulled up one sleeve of the coat to reveal the knife in her hand, gripped tight within her bony knuckles. She shook her head, warning him, unafraid. "Go home," she said, each word slow and deliberate.

He looked back at the knife in her hand, to her face, unable to say a word. Behind him, a blur of people were setting up the market.

She said with a confident whisper, "If you take a step closer, I will kill you. Do not doubt me. Do not doubt my conviction. I will kill you right here."

He looked back, perhaps towards the direction of his home, perhaps towards the people in the plaza.

"Hasan," Pri said, directing his attention back to her. "Go home."

He stepped back. Pri didn't budge. She would stab him in the side of the neck. It did not matter if others would run and take her down. She would not let Hasan live if he took a step towards her. It did not matter if she was then dragged away. Hasan would not live beyond these next minutes.

She did not flinch. She stared at Hasan, shaking her head, exposing more of her knife. She knew that she was the one in charge. His eyes kept catching upon the details of her clothes, but she focussed on his face. And for a moment she thought of telling him that she was sorry.

Instead, she repeated: "Go home."

He turned, stepped back, then looked at Pri, each passing second his confusion replaced with realization, with fear. His eyes drawn back to her coat and headscarf.

"Go."

He retreated a step, turned, jogged, sprinted. Pri stood still, the knife exposed, waiting to see if he was going to rouse people in the market. He turned a corner, and she waited another moment, watching people stroll and saunter. Looking down, her right arm trembled, the blade quivering. She was sure that just seconds earlier she was composed and motionless. Every breath felt amplified, the bustle of the plaza now a tumult. But people did not charge towards her. She turned back towards where the boosters had landed, a white haze tracing their paths down to Earth. She tried to run, her legs first staggering, as if her knees might buckle beneath her own weight, but then she found her stride, eyes locked onto the sky above the corrugated metal rooftops and steaming chimneys. It did not matter who stared at her. It did not matter if she tripped and scampered to get back up. It did not matter if Hasan was going to return with the masses. All that mattered was that she ran. People watched her bolt past, none saying a word. Perhaps this happened all the time. Perhaps they knew it was none of their own business. Perhaps they noticed the knife in her right hand. She remembered the carpet of ferns that draped over the sides of the ravine by her apartment on the North Shore, the towering firs and cedars that blocked out the haze from the summer smoke. The wooden bridge she would cross in two steps. Pri was a runner. This was all that mattered. Little did she realize until now, but for the last twenty years she had been training for this moment. She could feel the muscles in her thighs flex and strain as she ascended a slight incline. Her footing was uneven, she nearly tripped but never fell, the other leg landing in time, righting her out. The lanes descended, the fortified highway again in view. The rain intensified, peppering droplets now pellets, and Pri threw off Hasan's coat, left it on the ground, needing to keep one hand on the waist of her oversized pants. Homes, two storeys tall, leaned against the concrete wall protecting the highway, constructed from cinder blocks and wooden joists. Electrical cords draped from rooftop to rooftop, crows nestled on the cables, silent, watching the crowds below. She needed to run. Nothing else mattered. She kept to the middle of the lane to avoid rainwater that shot from troughs in the corrugated roofs, breaking into oblong pearls which splattered into long puddles. Dozens of thick electrical cables hung in the air high above both the buildings and the highway wall, carried by the six arms of an enormous electrical tower that loomed from the middle of the shanties to her right, cables suspended high enough to be safe from any potential electrical poachers. She stopped beneath it, listening to the crackling, buzzing. A man rode past on a bicycle, his front wheel veering around puddles, straining to pull a two-wheeled trailer filled with gravel. He stopped, looking back towards Pri. He said, "You lost?"

Pri had watched him come to a halt, look her in the eyes, and ask this question. And yet it felt as if he must be speaking to someone else. She glanced behind and then back to the man, noticing her strained breaths and rhythm of her lungs, unable to reply.

He repeated, eyes squinting, "You lost?"

Pri shook her head.

"You sure?"

Pri kept shaking her head, then nodded. Then shrugged. "I don't know."

"What you need?"

She was so tired. She knew she had to keep moving. "I don't know," she repeated, surprised by the quiver in her lungs, the burgeoning tears in each eye.

"You okay?"

"I don't know."

"Where you going?"

"I don't know."

His eyes darted between the knife in her hand and the tears in her eyes. He stood by his bike, not coming any closer. "You want help?"

Pri coughed out a disheartened laugh. "I don't know."

"What you want? Tell me. I can help."

She sighed. "Saglik."

"Sorry?"

"Rockets. The launch site."

"Rockets?" He stood tall. "Just up there." He pointed ahead and to the left. "Very close. Let me show."

"No, I'm okay."

"No. Let me show. Come. Come." He sat back onto his bike and started peddling, waving her along. "Please."

Pri followed, first with staggering steps and then jogging. He glanced back every few seconds, nodding and smiling to encourage her to continue and then waving to someone on the side of the lane. Gravel dribbled out from the pile of his trailer and onto the ground with each pothole. "Come," he'd repeat, as if she was on the verge of stopping. Pri wondered if this was a trap. If this man was hired by Hasan to bring the murderer to justice. Pri wondered if this was even real. She hadn't slept in days, she was sure. And yet it didn't matter. Pri ran to keep up. No matter what was happening, it was coming to an end. Cracked pavement emerged from the dirt path beneath her. Withered concrete curbs framed the road. "Here," the man pointed to his left while slowing himself with the soles of his shoes. Four black concrete columns held up a sign with the name SAĞLIK in red uppercase letters. Between the columns, a rusted white metal fence and drooping gate, secured with what appeared to be nothing more than a heavy chain and padlock. At one corner stood a square guardhouse capped with steep clay shingles, two narrow windows secured with bars, and a solid door without a handle.

Pri looked back to the man on the bike. "This is it?"

"Yes."

"Thank you."

He shook his head and said, "No problem." He stood up on one pedal to force it down and waved without looking back. The trailer of gravel bumped against a curb, knocking over a few more pebbles. People walked past in both directions; pairs and groups of three or four talking, laughing, everyone having somewhere to go, no one paying any mind to this woman standing without a coat in the rain, dressed in an oversized pair of pants that puddled over her shoes in the mud, a cooking knife gripped in one hand. She walked to the window, horizontal blinds half drawn and slanted, the space inside dark, seemingly empty. She pressed her face close to the glass to see if anyone was present, saw a desk and plain walls, and knocked on the window. Waiting, she looked back, then banged the bars with the side of her fist, rattling the blinds in behind.

A man came to the window, his neck narrow, cheeks gaunt, eyes tired and annoyed as if having been awoken from a nap. He looked at Pri, held up one hand, and shrugged his shoulders.

"I need in," Pri said, surprised by the volume of her voice, hastily glancing back.

He said something through the glass, his words unintelligible, ready to sit back down and out of sight.

She banged the bars. "I need in."

The man looked down, sighed, and slid open the window. "ID card," he said, one hand still on the window, ready to close it without hesitation.

"Sorry?"

"ID card. You have ID card?"

"No, but—"

He closed the window, shaking his head, ostensibly explaining how she required an identification card to enter even though she could not hear his words.

She slammed her fists against the glass. "I can pay," she said, not wanting to yell, glancing back, then repeating. "I can pay you very well."

The man paused to look at Pri, then shook his head and sat down, out of sight. She checked over her shoulders then punched the bars on the window more than a dozen times until he returned. He slid the glass open and said, "Someone is coming. He will kill you if you do not go." He motioned towards the gate. A burly man approached from behind the bars, hood over his head, a rifle in both hands. "Now go."

"Wait," Pri said, glancing back, then held up her knife. "Just wait," she pulled up her shirt to reveal the lip of abdominal fat, looked at the man in the window, looked at the man with the gun, then sliced her own flesh an inch below her belly button, a single, swift horizontal incision. She stared at the man in the guardhouse, her eyes trained on his widening gaze, reluctant to blink, pushing with her thumb at the splinter, feeling the impression of the MiC card, forcing it down towards the gash, her fingers slick with blood, refusing to look away from his eyes. When she felt the card between her fingers, she placed the knife down on the ledge with one hand and knocked on the window with the other, leaving red imprints of her fist onto the glass. "Right here," she said. "Right here is more money than you can imagine. It's more money than you can understand. It's unencrypted. It's divisible. It's yours if you let me in and onto the next rocket to the Tevat. Let me through those gates, let me prove to you I belong on the Tevat, and I'll make you rich. So? What do you say?" She looked behind her and then square into the eyes of the wiry man through the window. "Do you want to be rich, or do you want to be a peasant for the rest of your life?"

Zero (Liftoff)

The mirror was sanded. Looking into her image, it was difficult to tell what illusions were caused by the warped surface and what were reflections of her actual face, her real disfigurements. She splashed more water against her cheeks and forehead, letting it dribble down her chin into the sink. The only towel was on the tiled floor, sodden and pressed into a corner. She let the water run from the tap, flowing between her fingertips, then drank from the faucet, unconcerned about pressing her lips against the spout while slurping. When she looked back up into the mirror, she focused on her eyes, the only part of her that she knew was unchanged, staring into the black center, telling herself that this was the same person as before, the same person she always knew. It was a lie, she knew. And she knew that she couldn't convince herself of this falsehood just through repetition, through persuasion. But she continued to stare into her irises, feeling each breath swell and then ebb, saying the words in thought and then with deliberate whispers, watching her lips: "You are Pri Gosal. You do not give up."

Pri felt safe in this room, the door secured from the inside with a lever that only she could unlock. The next rocket was not departing for another couple of hours and Pri thought of spending the entire time in this confined space, drinking from a tap when she wanted, urinating on a toilet if the need arose, relishing in these minor and yet significant luxuries. Outside the cinderblock walls was an open field, nothing but grass and withered, old asphalt for what must have been several kilometers in any direction. Pri had been struck by the emptiness on her drive out from the gatehouse. The stout truck that she had sat within possessed no doors, its combustion engine clamoring and grumbling as it rolled through potholes, over grasses that sprouted from the cracks in the tarmac. She had pressed one hand onto the plastic dash, another gripped on the weathered side of her seat to keep from tumbling out. And yet she was struck by the calm. It was just her and Abdo, the driver, speeding over the vacant plane, his head shaped like an egg, dense stubble atop, with a strong jaw and wide lips. As far as she could tell, there was no one else in the fields. She'd watch the approaching, towering booster rockets and then back to the hazy periphery of the shanty metropolis, its defined edge hazy from drizzle. Aside from introducing himself, Abdo didn't say a word to Pri as they drove. He would whistle under his breath, then catch himself and stop, as if being jaunty was against protocol. Seconds later, he started again, his tune spirited but unfamiliar. When they pulled up to a small rectangular structure made from cinderblocks and a flat roof, he told Pri she could use the toilet and that he would be back in an hour or so. She climbed out and he drove off within seconds. The building had only two doors—one to the windowless restroom and one to a constrained space with four mismatched chairs, a table covered in coffee stains, a sink with just a knob for cold water. She chose the washroom, locked the door, and waited.

Someone now knocked on the door. Pri turned off the tap, flicked her fingers to dry them and looked one last time in the mirror, as if to confirm that this was real. She reached for the lock but hesitated, wanting to ask who was there, as if their name might matter. As if it might be Hasan. She turned the lever and pulled open the door. Abdo stood, glancing back until hearing the squealing hinges, his bloodshot eyes showing concern. "You've been in here the whole time?"

"I've been cleaning myself."

"Are you sick?"

"I'm okay. Is it time to go already?"

"Not yet."

Pri nodded, standing still. "Okay."

Abdo looked over Pri's shoulder, then chuckled. "Are you done?"

"Oh. You need this?"

"Yes. Please."

"Sorry. Yes. Of course." Pri stepped outside to let him enter, the bite of the frigid breeze taking her by surprise, forcing her into the adjacent waiting room. She sat down on a chair with tattered armrests revealing the aluminum below. Without a mirror, she stared at her hands, her fingernails chipped, cuticles black. She remembered digging in the dirt and then she remembered the dead woman and child in bed. Pri balled her hands into fists, looked across the room, through the window with its crooked horizontal blinds. The door opened and Abdo entered, nodding at Pri before taking a seat across from her, a table in between. He sighed with relief while sitting, pulled out his fone for only a few seconds before laying it down on his lap and asked, his voice baritone and booming. "So, you are going on to the Tevat, yes?"

Pri nodded. "Yes. I guess, yes."

"You guess?" Abdo laughed, "I thought you would know where you are going to at this point, right?"

"It's been," Pri began, her voice a mere whisper compared to his. She cleared her throat, repeated herself with assurance. "It's been a long few days for me. I'm not too certain about anything right now."

"Well, my boss tells me that I should put you on the next rocket, so I think you will be going to the Tevat."

"Then I guess you knew the answer to your own question, right?"

Abdo smiled, pointed one finger towards Pri and winked. "You are right. I was just making small talk. Got me." He picked up his fone. "I won't annoy you anymore. My apologies." He nodded once and looked down, his attention immersed.

Pri tried to scratch some dirt from the corner of one fingernail, wondering if Abdo was going to receive any of the money that she had given to the man at the gatehouse. He did not bear the expression of a person who had just come across riches. She said, "No, I'm the one who should apologize. You were being polite. I'm sorry."

He held up one hand without taking his eyes away from his fone. "Do not apologize. I should not really be talking to the clients anyhow."

"Can," she cleared her throat again. "Can I ask you a question?"

He smiled, then put his fone back down. "Of course. I like to talk."

"Have you had others like me, going to the Tevat?"

He shrugged, "A few. Not for a while, though. You are the first one in quite some time."

"What are the rockets taking up?"

"Mostly just water. So much water. I do not know why those people up there need to drink so much water. What is it? Does every person need to have their own swimming pool? Right?"

Pri chuckled, cleared her throat. "It's not for swimming pools, no."

"Well, I think there is more clean water up there than there is in the whole Jungle."

Pri nodded, "You're probably correct about that. I'm sorry."

Abdo furrowed his brow, appeared ready to laugh. "Why you apologize to me? It is not your fault."

"No. But. People here shouldn't have to work to get clean water."

"Why not? Water is important. People should work for what is important for them, yes?"

"I guess."

"You guess a lot."

"I do."

He said, "Can I ask where you are from?"

"I grew up just on the North Shore."

Abdo shrugged. "Is it close?"

"On a clear day, you can see it from here. The mountains to the north."

"On a clear day?" He laughed, "What is that? It sounds nice."

"It was nice."

"So, why is it you want to leave then?"

"Everyone asks that question."

"That means that it must be a good one, right?"

"It is." Pri sighed. "I just don't know if I have a good answer."

"Then give me your best answer. Does not matter if it is good or not."

Pri smiled, "I guess—"

"There you go, guessing again. Always guessing. Never knowing."

She grinned in acknowledgement, licked her lips, and tried again. "I want to be part of a fresh start. Up there, it won't be just winners and losers. We will all just be together."

"But aren't you one of the winners?"

Pri grinned, almost laughed. "I honestly don't know. I don't feel like much of a winner right now."

"And I don't feel like a loser."

"I'm sorry, I didn't mean it like that."

"Don't be sorry. I'm just joking."

"No, you're right. I shouldn't be the one complaining. I just want something different for my child."

"You have a child?"

"I'm pregnant."

"Oh," Abdo clapped, looking at Pri's midsection. "Congratulations."

"Thank you, I guess."

"Stop guessing!"

Pri laughed, "Just, thank you, then."

"You do not look pregnant, I must say."

"It's early."

"Is the father already on the Tevat?"

Pri nodded, smiling. She hesitated, then answered, "Yes. He's already up there."

"Why did you two not go together?"

"It's complicated."

"Of course. I should not ask too many questions."

"No. Please don't apologize. This is good. This is nice."

"So, you really think it will be better up there?"

"I do."

Abdo appeared indifferent. "Is this really so bad?"

Pri expelled a chuckle, a snort in reverse. "Where are you from?"

"Where am I from? Right here."

"You were born here?"

"Yes. Yes. My mother and father both came from Sudan before I was born. Took them five years to make it here. Can you believe that? Five years from boat to boat, camp to camp, EDZ to EDZ. I cannot understand what they went through. I am very lucky. I lived my whole life here. I have a good job. I have a home. I have it easy."

"Do you live here?"

"My mother died when I was young. My father lives with me. He is a tough man."

"Does he ever talk about the journey?"

"Never. He does not want to talk about it. I do not think he wants to remember it."

"I can't blame him for that."

"When I was a kid, he would sometimes tell me how easy I had it. Say something about a refugee camp, like I knew what that was. I only pictured tents. Did not sound so bad." Abdo said with a laugh.

"Do you have kids?"

"I have a boy, yes. Four years old. Very busy, all the time."

"I'm sure."

"You will know, soon enough. You will be busy. Even up there, out in space, you will be busy."

"What's his name?"

"My boy? Asim. Looks just like me, except smaller and not quite as handsome."

"That's a lovely name."

"That is good. Because that is the name he is stuck with, yes?" Abdo chuckled, "I hope he can get out of here. Out of this or any other EDZ. Become a citizen somewhere. That is my dream for him. That someday, I can tell *him* how spoiled he is. Tell him things that he will never understand. The things we do for our children, right? We do it all and they will never, ever understand."

Pri inhaled, sniffled, nodded with tight lips. "Yeah," she said, a gentle sigh.

"I want to get out of the Jungle, and you want to get out of this planet. But it is all the same, right?"

She tried to laugh, her lungs getting caught. She cleared her throat and wiped one eye before he might notice. "Maybe it is. I don't really know."

"You do guess a lot."

"I really do."

"Are you alright?"

"Yeah. Just. It's been a long few days."

"You need something? More water?"

"Can I just ask you another question?"

"Is that not what you have been doing for these last few minutes?"

"Say you could go. To the Tevat. With your wife and your boy. Would you do it? Would you go?"

Abdo grimaced, his white teeth slowly emerging between his lips as a smile widened. "Is this a trick question? Is there an answer I am supposed to tell you?"

"No. I'm just curious what you would say."

"You paid already, right? If you change your mind at the last second, my boss is not going to lose the money? I do not want to mess with anything."

"I'm not changing my mind. I've gone through way too much to get here just to turn back. Trust me. I'm just curious."

He watched Pri, his grin unrelenting while rubbing his chin. "Okay. Would I go if I could?" He said to himself, pausing. "I do not really know much about Tevat. I hear people just party up there, all the time. Is that what happens?"

"I don't think that's true."

"Can you drink?"

"You can drink."

"Do people work?"

"Every citizen has a role."

"What is yours?"

"Algaeculturist."

"What is that?"

"Algae. I'll be part of the team that cultivates algae."

"What do you do with that?"

"You can eat it. Certain strains are incredibly healthy."

"That sounds disgusting."

"It might be."

"You are not selling me on this place."

"I wasn't trying to sell you."

"That is good then, because I think that I want to stay here, on the ground." He stomped a foot twice in succession. "Outer space is not for me. I hope that is okay for me to say to you. I mean no offence."

Pri snickered, "Trust me. I am not offended."

"You know what I would miss the most?" Abdo said, "The rain. I like the rain. My father, he would say how lucky we were to have so much rain here. That in refugee camps there is no water. Not in streams or in bottles or in puddles. Children would die from thirst, he said. Here, it comes from the sky. Maybe, that is one of his lessons that stuck with me. To like the rain. It would not be right to live somewhere and never have rain again." Abdo then laughed to himself, "Unless, that is why we have to send up so much water. So that you people can have rain come down on you in the street."

"No, trust me. That's not what all the water is for."

Abdo asked, "How do your parents feel about you going?"

"My mother died a long time ago. My father, he's old. He's tough, but he's old and he doesn't really understand things so well anymore."

Abdo held out his palms, mouth wide. "See, you and me, we are the same. That is why I knew I could talk with you."

"It's like looking in the mirror."

He laughed and clapped his hands, "Exactly. Like looking in the mirror. You are a funny person."

"I don't think anyone has ever said that to me before."

"Really? Maybe I understand you better than most."

"Maybe you do." Pri rubbed an eye, again noticing the dirt ground into her nails. "How much more time do I have?"

Abdo glanced at his fone. "Oh, we should get going soon."

"You'll take me to the rocket?"

"Yes, I will take you there."

"Do you go on with me?"

Abdo laughed. "No, no, of course not. People like me are not allowed inside. I stay on the ground. My job is just to make sure things are connected." He held up his hands, fingers wide and calloused. "I do a lot of hooking one pipe into another. Back and forth. Fuel, water. Clipping and unclipping. They do not put people like me out into space."

"Will anyone else be on board?"

"No. Just you. And your baby."

"That means you're going to be the last person I ever talk to on the planet Earth."

"You do not have a fone with you?"

"No. This is all I've got."

Abdo laughed. "Then I should say that I feel lucky to be the last person you see on the ground. There is no coming back once you are up there, right?"

"There's no coming back."

"And how long is the trip?"

"About two hundred years."

Abdo shook his head. "Yeah. No coming back from that."

"Certainly not. But it's not such a long time. Two hundred years ago, we didn't know that we were changing the Earth. One hundred years ago, we thought a few million migrants was a lot. The problems were always another hundred years away. Maybe another fifty years away. We had so many chances. That's our problem—we think a couple hundred years is a long time. But it's not. It's not long at all. And we let it pass us by. Like that," Pri snapped her fingers. "Two hundred years. Gone."

Abdo held up one hand, snapped his fingers, then looked back and forth between his hand and Pri. "I do not know."

"What's that?"

"I think that your idea of time is very different from me. I still think a hundred years sounds like a very, very long time. This," he snapped his fingers three more times in succession. "This feels like nothing."

"You're right. Maybe it's not quite that fast."

"I hope you know I am just kidding. I am not trying to make fun of you."

"No offence taken. I appreciate your humor. Or at least, your attempts at it."

Abdo winced. "Was that last thing a joke?"

"That was my attempt at it, yeah."

"You know, when I drove you to the break house, you looked so very serious. I thought to myself, who is this woman who has the money to fly into space and still looks so upset about it? So, it is good to see you make jokes—or try to make a joke. This is what you want, right? To go to Tevat?"

It took Pri several seconds to realize his question demanded a response. "Oh. Yes. Of course, I do."

"Then you should be happy, yes? You must have wanted this for a long time?"

"A very long time, yeah."

"Then, I feel blessed that I get to be the last one to help take you there. Here," he stood up. "We should get going. Get there early so that I can tell you which doors to open and which to keep shut. You don't want to accidentally open an airlock when all you want is to go pee, yes?"

"I'm assuming it's not quite that easy to mix the two up, but, sure."

"Great. Then let's get going. Your husband is waiting for you."

"Sorry?"

"Up on Tevat? You said he is up there already, yes?"

"Yes. Of course."

The truck shuddered and convulsed, the floor of the cab dipping away and then pounding against the soles of her shoes, the cracked remnants of a foam cushion on her seat accomplishing little to keep her tailbone from battering the hard plastic beneath. Abdo tried asking a few more questions—if she needed to make any last calls, if she needed to go to the toilet, if she was cold—but with all the noise from the engine, the rattling, the tires on wet and withered pavement, Pri needed him to repeat himself several times just to answer with a simple, "No." For most of the ride, they remained silent amongst the racket, Abdo whistling with just one hand on the wheel, the other holding his fone, knees apart, back reclined, enjoying these carefree minutes. Pri was cold, the spittle of rain spraying against her exposed elbow and forearm. She looked over the vast field, devoid of other trucks, a plain of grasses and stout shrubs. The edge of the Jungle appeared ashen from a distance, a thousand narrow plumes of smoke reaching into a dense ceiling of cloud just above. Two rockets that had once appeared adjacent to one another proved to be several hundreds of meters apart on separate launch pads. Both appeared like rotund cylinders made from tin, the seams in the metal dark from dirt or rust. A pair of fins at the piercing peak matched a large pair by its base, perhaps decorative, wings appearing far too small for the heft of the body. Water vapor wafted from the boosters, as if the metal itself was a rolling boil. In the absence of any surrounding structures for scale, each rocket appeared to expand while the distance along the ground remained constant. What Pri assumed was going to be a five-minute drive kept lengthening, the looming peak of the rocket ascending. She noticed what appeared to be scaffolding around one side, a zigzag set of metal stairs winding its way above the booster section, counting more than thirty spiraling flights. Abdo brought the truck to an abrupt stop at the base, the ground a solid scorched concrete, cracks absent of grasses or weeds. He climbed down and Pri followed, craning her neck back to make out the pinnacle of the rocket. She was struck by the silence. The truck's engine was dormant. The looming rocket billowed vapor but didn't make a sound—she expected a deep rumble, a buzzing hum. Instead, she could hear the pellets of rain patter against metal. Abdo's steps scraped along the concrete.

She asked, "When does it launch?"

"I don't know. Soon. Soon enough, at least."

"Do I need to rush?"

"I would not stay here too long."

"How do we get up there?"

Abdo laughed. "We? I'm not going anywhere. You go up there. I stay down here."

"How do I get up there?"

"You don't see those stairs? You don't expect me to carry you up there, do you?"

"No, of course not. It's just. They look flimsy."

"They fold down just before launch. But they are strong enough to take you up there. At least I hope they are."

"What do I do when I get to the top?"

"You open the door."

"And then?"

"Find a place to sit? Maybe you can stand if you want. But I do not think that would be a good idea."

"I'm sorry. I just thought I'd be given more instructions."

"You were expecting me to tell you which door to go pee, right? That was a joke. I think it is simple enough. Walk up. Open the door. Sit down. Oh, you should close the door behind you. That is important."

"Shouldn't I be given some sort of," Pri shook her head, hands out. "I don't know. I'm going into space. Shouldn't I be given a suit of some sort? Something else to wear except this?"

"You want a helmet?" Abdo laughed, "Sorry, but you do know that if something goes wrong, a helmet is not going to help you. It will get cold up there. I think you will find a blanket or something? I do not really know. They do not let people like me up there. We just work outside."

"Okay," Pri looked back towards the truck, as if she might have forgotten something. "So, this is it?"

"Yes, this is it." He held out a hand, "Have a good life."

Pri grabbed his hand to shake, but he pulled her in to give a hug, slapped her back twice. He then motioned with one hand towards the first flight of stairs. "Okay," she said, one of her hands holding onto his forearm, "Okay," she repeated. "Thank you."

"I just drive you here. No need to thank."

Pri still held onto Abdo, knowing she should let go, but unsure if she could. "How long does the trip take?"

Abdo shrugged. "I don't know. About thirty minutes? I've never been. They just come and go, up and down, all day long."

"Okay."

"Okay?" He repeated, punctuating his question with a brief chuckle. He put one hand atop hers. "You need to go. We do not want to be standing here when the rocket launches."

"Yes. Of course." She let go of Abdo's arm and stepped back. Again, the world felt unsteady, but she started walking. The soles of Pri's shoes scraped along the concrete, splashing through shallow puddles. She could see the exposed openings of several dozen engines, tight like the composite eye of an insect, each dormant, silent, the black emptiness inside as intimidating as the dark barrel of a rifle. Rain dripped from the landing legs and onto the concrete below. She glanced back at Abdo, already back in the cab of the truck and looking at his fone. She waved again, catching his attention. He returned the favor and then urged her onwards. The stairs wrapped a square spiral around a single vertical column. Pri kept towards the inside of the stairwell, reaching out onto the column, her fingers feeling the occasional narrowing lip of the telescopic support. She heard the ignition of the truck's engine and paused to watch Abdo drive away into the expanse. The remnants of the asphalt roads were defined from this elevation, what had appeared as a withered mess of grassy plains and broken pavement now proved to have order, lanes linking empty launch pads across the vast clearing. A breeze billowed past, through her clothes, rattling the metal around her, bristling her skin. She continued her ascent, hastening her pace, huddling close to the central column, gusts of wind spraying raindrops into her face. She felt dizzy, perhaps from the exertion, perhaps from these circling, spinning flights of stairs. There was the sharp smell of sulfur in the air, a bitterness she could taste. The distant, endless rooftops of the Jungle appeared like fish scales over the hills, a smouldering skin that undulated off into the haze. The recycling area was a sprawling break in the homes, a grid of black soot marking the lanes that smouldered, adding heft to the overcast, obscuring the scale of the EDZ. Somewhere in that mess, Hasan grieved over his dead wife and son, maybe still at his home, maybe having amassed a horde seeking violent revenge. And Pri kept climbing. Her eyes tricked her, the rocket swaying, ready to crash onto the ground. If the air was clear, she would be able to see the North Shore mountains. Through the drizzle, clouds, and smoke was a straight line to Nayha's apartment. A walkway reached out towards the rocket just a few spiraling flights above. A low railing, reaching no higher than her thighs, wrapped around the final set of steps and the metal bridge spanning the chasm. The rocket's exterior door was without a window, signage, or handle. Just seams in the scuffed and pot-marked steel, a rectangle with rounded corners. She held onto the column supporting the stairs, staring up to the rounded nose of the rocket's peak, still requiring her neck to crane at a steep angle.

Refusing to look down, Pri let go of the telescopic column, eyes focussed on the hulking rocket, and walked across the gap. The walkway trembled with each step, as if the metal was flimsy, each hand down to her sides to run along the top of the shallow railing. Something hissed from far below. She pressed the bare palms of her hands against the door, felt around for a lip or something to hold onto, and then pushed. The door swung inwards, expelling gas like a sigh of relief. Lights flickered from the constrained space in front of her, the walls a lusterless gray, handles like ladder rungs on either side. More gas hissed from below and she looked down into the fog of vapor that billowed from the fuel tanks. She was above it all. It wasn't terrifying. The wind could never knock her over. She was secure, more than one hundred meters above the ground.

Pri stepped inside, pressing the door shut. There were no signs or warnings written on the inside, just a textured plastic that covered the walls between her and the next door a few feet away. She spun a rotary handle on the inside of the door until it would not move, more than a dozen revolutions. It was muted inside the airlock. She could hear the force from each of her breaths, a strained wheeze. She then opened the next door, the handle loose and easy to spin, entering a brief passageway that led to a vertical shaft with rungs on either side. The air was stale, a twang of urine and rust. No signs, no writing. Just bare metal walls, seams between warped plates held together with rivets. The shaft appeared to rise into a black void. She gripped the rungs and began to climb, circular lights embedded in the walls illuminating as she ascended, revealing more of the same vertical corridor. All she could hear were her clamoring steps and heaving breaths over a gentle hum, a whirring fan.

Lights dimmed below her feet and went black, both directions of this shaft now appearing to vanish into nothingness.

She heard a voice, distorted over a speaker, crackling, unintelligible. She stopped and folded one arm around a rung to secure herself before calling out. "Hello?" Her words reverberated back. No one replied. She heard a thud and then a hiss from inside the surrounding walls and Pri continued her ascent. Above, another few dozen rungs and then openings to the left and right. Lights flickered on as she approached, revealing two identical spaces with rounded ceilings that she could touch with a raised palm, each with a pair of seats positioned on their backs, bolted to a metal column that ran parallel to the floor, seatbelts dangling down. Dried beige puddles stained the floor in the corners, a twisted and compressed plastic bottle beneath one chair. The shaft carried onwards into the darkness above, but Pri inspected the seats, the first one wobbling within her grip. The adjacent chair appeared solid as she rested on her back, feet against the wall, eyes trained on the ceiling. She pulled up either end of a seat belt that was frayed and loose. She could feel her heart elbowing her chest. She breathed through rounded lips, trying to control their pace and rhythm. She said, "So, this is it?"

Again, a voice crackled through an unseen speaker, words still impossible to discern, unclear if the person was speaking English.

Pri said, "Hello? Can you hear me? I can't understand you."

There was no reply. More thudding from behind the walls; a ball dropped, bouncing to a halt.

"Again, I didn't hear what you said. Is someone talking to me?" Pri waited for a response, tried pulling on her seatbelt to make it tighter.

The voice seemed to answer, what Pri felt certain was a man, but every word crackled, more gaps than sounds. She looked for the source, talking up towards the ceiling. "I still can't hear you. You keep cutting out. I can't understand anything."

Pri waited for a reply, her breaths now heavy, as if those words demanded the same exertion as her ascent. "Hello?" she said.

The person appeared to answer, a distorted, brief reply. It sounded like, *"Okay."*

"You can hear me?"

The rocket rattled, swayed. A hammering sound reverberated from deep below.

"Hello?"

Lights flickered, dropping to a perfect black for less than a second before illuminating again with a quiet, whining buzz. The man's voice returned, saying something with a calm, robotic rhythm. "I still can't hear you," Pri said over his voice, expecting him to stop, but he continued unabated. Another bang, piercing like a gun shot, shook the spacecraft but the person kept speaking, his words syncopated, rhythmic. It was a countdown. She couldn't discern the numbers, but the sequence was paced with the passing of each second. She tugged at the lone seat belt one last time and gripped the arm rests. The entire room rocked then roared, shaking like an earthquake, but she wasn't moving, the person continued counting. "Is everything okay?" She called out, realizing the futility of speaking and yet finding solace in her own words. The loose armrests of the chair beside her rattled, she watched them quiver, all this noise and ruckus for no purpose—just noise and ruckus. "Am I going? Are we—"

The seat punched into her back, as if she'd fallen and hit the ground. She couldn't hear anything but the roar of the engines below, millions of pounds of thrust lifting her from the Earth. The lights flickered again, the sound engulfing her, standing at the base of a waterfall. She called out, "We're launching. We're launching," her words struggling to escape the force on her lungs, her breaths squeezed by the pressure on her chest. But she had to keep talking. She had to prove to herself that this was happening. "Hold on, Poppy. Hold on." Everything rattled, a cacophony of a thousand seams and loose screws drumming their surroundings. There was another kick, as if something let go that had been dragging the vessel and the backrest of her chair thrust into her spine. A squealing, screaming whine bellowed from just beyond her reach, a deafening treble to the booming, unrelenting bass of the thrusters. She looked at the walls, expecting a crack, a leak that caused this banshee wail. The air above compressed down into her chest, crushed by an invisible vice. She could feel her tongue forced back into her throat. The lights again flickered. She felt the propulsion in her eyes, forcing them closed, tears hastened down each temple. It felt as if people were laying on top of her. With each few passing seconds, another climbing atop the pile. Something popped, the screeching wail relented, the roaring of the engines abated within seconds, but the pressure continued to increase without relent. She could hear her heaving breaths. She could hear her own words. She struggled to lift one arm. The armrests clattered. Yet another person had climbed atop. She looked at the seams in the corners and saw white creases of frost, the lines blurred, her vision speckled. The last of the rattling abated, and all Pri could hear was a distant whine, her strained breaths. She feared there was a leak. That soon she would gasp for air while being crushed against the seat.

Without sound or warning, the vice unravelled. She inhaled and expelled a deep breath that turned to vapor from her lips, tumbling, swirling on itself before vanishing. She could lift her arms. And when she let go, they lingered in the air, suspended as if resting. The straps at the end of her seatbelt floated. Just seconds ago, her tongue weighed several pounds and now her entire body felt hollow. Her head was light, but she wasn't faint, she could focus on the details of the room. Frost spread like spider webs along the exterior wall. She held out hands towards the ice, watching her fingers float without effort. After all the roaring, the trembling of metal, wailing of supersonic air, whining of engines—this was silent. She heard nothing aside from her own breaths. She unclipped her seatbelt, watching the ends undulate like seaweed, placed both her hands on the armrest, took another breath, and then pushed. She tumbled upwards, hitting the ceiling with her shoulder and then the side of her head before careening back to the floor. Her instincts told her that she was falling, that she needed to clutch something as she skittered across the shaft to the adjacent seats, grabbing onto a column and spinning around. The crumpled water bottle floated past her, adrift with a slow tumble. She reached out, failing to grip onto the plastic, instead sending it across the room in a quivering spin before ricocheting against a wall with a feeble, crinkling clatter. Holding onto the column, Pri was reluctant to let go, her body secure in this spot. Watching each exhalation, she inspected the vapor, a visual cue to slow her breathing. She looked back, the soles of her shoes against the frosted wall, streaks scratched into the ice that refroze into a new pattern, coiled leaves on a fern, wondering how much metal and insulation was between her toes and the dead cold of space. It seemed as if a single solid kick would break the barrier apart. She lifted her legs, floating above the floor and looked towards the shaft. She knew the flight plan. First the rocket would overtake the Tevat in a shallow orbit before spinning a half-circle, reversing the aim of its engines, and matching the slow rotation of the colossal spacecraft. Finally, with a gentle push from the rocket's engines—all while travelling more than twenty times the speed of sound—she would glide towards the stub nose of the Tevat, docking directly at its axis of rotation. The payload's water tanks would deposit into the Tevat and then depart again, pushing off from the ark and back down to the Jungle.

But Pri had time. It was just her. No one else. She stared across to the empty seats and floating straps, the exhaust of each breath vanishing inches from her lips. She had spent months alone in her apartment on the North Shore. Even with Seph, her apartment felt vacant. The clatter of her fingers on a keyboard for hours. Just her. This was a feeling Pri knew well. Little did she know how her apartment was as quiet—as isolating—as outer space. She might have been across the Pacific Ocean by now. Above sub-Saharan Africa. Hurtling away from the dank confines of Hasan's basement, the dead bodies in the bedroom upstairs. More than two hundred miles above the surface of the Earth, crossing entire mountain ranges in a matter of seconds. Impossible to reach. For days, she remained in the darkness of that sodden corner, seeing only a dull circle of light during the day, nothing at night. Now, she exhaled, watched her breath tumble, and vanish before the ambling water bottle that coasted through the air like a witless fish. She let go, let herself drift like that bottle, patient with each breath, in through her nose, out between tight lips, slow and steady. She reached towards the frosted wall, scratched her fingertips into the ice, the skin on her forearms prickled and raised. She wished there were windows, that she could see the Earth from above. She closed her eyes and felt that she could rest, sleep in this directionless state. She saw Abdo's face, his bright teeth while smiling, ignorant of the fact that she had killed a mother and child that very morning. While Abdo slept. While his son Asim slept. And now she was free. Free from her prison, free from the Jungle, free from the very clutches of gravity. She wanted to say that she deserved this. That she earned this. She opened her lips, said, "We're free, Poppy," before sighing, inhaling another cool breath. She was here. She found a way to get here. Away from the planet below. But she couldn't say that she deserved it. That she had any right to be in this spot. She was just here. Right here. Earlier that morning, she was in the mud beneath Hasan's home. Now she was in orbit around the Earth. She was as deserving of being in space as she was deserving of being Hasan's prisoner. Perhaps this was the cold logic of existence—we make what we make, and then we move on. Like a dog defecating on the grass, pausing for a moment before trundling onwards and away. Poppy's children would be as ignorant to Pri's actions as Pri was to the motives of her grandparents. She opened her eyes as if awakening, saw that she was now facing the floor, staring at the crusted center of a flaxen stain.

Pri watched her fingers as they gripped the column, inspected the goosebumps on the back of her hand, expelled a long, controlled breath through rounded lips, and pushed by flexing her fingers, propelling her being over the floor, controlled and stable. She reached out towards a rung at the lip of the shaft, grabbed hold without tugging, instead letting her legs drift in behind. There was no longer a top or bottom to this vessel. One direction led towards the engines, the other away from the engines. Both paths appeared identical, the distant ends obscured in blackness. She needed to reference the direction that the seats were facing to orientate herself. Pri's instinct was to climb the rungs, but instead she reached across both sides of the corridor and pressed with each hand, casting her body through the space in between. She kept pushing against the sides and accelerated into a wall, the force of impact pushing out a breath as she ricocheted across, one shoulder striking a rung before flung back across the corridor. Pri grabbed hold of a handle, held herself still, her body again fearing that she was falling. She felt the rotation of the rocket pushing against her thighs. The final approach had begun. She looked back towards what she thought was the nose of the craft. She had to trust that she hadn't lost her bearings and pushed onwards along the corridor, careful to use her hands only to adjust her angle of approach, not to propel herself ever faster. Lights continued to illuminate ahead of her, the passageway never ending. Pri felt the handles slip out from her hand, she fell backwards down the corridor. The rocket was accelerating. She reached out, clasping onto a bar, sending her thighs into the wall. She pushed her hands against the seams in the metal, propelling herself towards the front of the spacecraft, regaining her control, her actions again fluid and smooth as she glided through this tunnel, watching the lights, waiting for when they would expose the airlock. Hissing bursts reverberated through the walls around her. Right as she pushed off from the wall, a rolling, crackling thunder shook the rocket and she tumbled forwards through the air, plunging into the darkness. Her shoulder pummelled a bar, hitting a wall. The surrounding lights engaged. The rocket had docked. She lay on her side against a rotary handle, her cheek against a scuffed window no larger than the palm of her hand that revealed the airlock, the final few feet between her and the Tevat. Pri tried to twist the handle open, but instead her entire body spun. She planted her feet across the wall to secure herself and tried again. Hydraulics rumbled and pumps engaged around her. The wheel budged and then spun between her hands. She pulled the door open and pushed herself into the confined space, feet first, shutting the door above her head. The hatch below was without markings, without a window, just another rotary handle between her shoes. It could have led to the Tevat's airlock. It could have led to the emptiness of space. The metal was cold to the touch, spikes of frost visible in the seams. She exhaled, watching the long plume of her breaths as they spread out along the door, then spun the handle. Pri stopped, hearing a hissing, like a slowly deflating balloon. Pri spun again, listening to the whistling, fearing a final rotation that unlocks the door and unleashes a boundless vacuum. The wheel now spun without effort. She gripped and pulled. A quick, wheezing burst of air was followed by silence, the heaving of her own breaths.

The door ahead was crisp white with a clean round window above a long metal latch. She could reach out and touch the frigid exterior of the Tevat with her bare fingers. All that protected Pri from the desolation of space was a rubber seal. She thrust the latch down between her feet and pushed it open, floating above the opening. Pri propelled herself through, reaching up to close the exterior door of the rocket. She spun the handle and floated into the Tevat's airlock, her feet bouncing upon the next door. An arrow pointed to the wall behind her, directing her to the floor, an arbitrary concept in this space. She propped herself up with the tips of her toes to reach up towards the exterior door, pushing it shut with a click. A light changed from red to green. Pri pressed against the walls to reorient her feet towards the floor, feeling as if the gentle prods of her fingertips spun the room around her static figure. "Hello?" She said, hoping for a communications system, someone to confirm that they knew of her presence. Grabbing onto a handle beside the door, she pulled herself towards the next window. "My name is Pri Gosal," she said. Pri waited for a response, holding onto the lever. She pushed down, the soles of her shoes lifting off into the air, and the door opened outwards into a long corridor that sloped downwards, metal railings on both walls.

"Hello?" She said, her voice echoing. "Can anyone hear me?"

The palm of one hand glided along the railing, her first steps projecting her towards the ceiling before pushing off with both hands back down to the floor. From where she stood so close to the Tevat's axis, the centrifugal force of its rotation was insignificant. There was no use for walking when someone can fly. But she knew that soon, again, she would have weight. Her shoes scraped against the grit of the floor, and she leapt through the air, back towards the ceiling, wanting to run. She pushed herself with both hands. She had seen videos of new citizens, clamoring, excited as they hurried down this very corridor, first bumbling through the air with superhuman abilities. Recordings made by one among a crowd of dozens, all shuttled into orbit in comfort and safety, exchanging names, roles, pasts. People who drove to their launch site. Who hugged their families before passing through security. People who had been fed, who were clean, who dressed in their finest clothes for this event. People whose most difficult action was to end that embrace with a loved one. This was the ecstasy, the final descent down the passageway, knowing that thousands of other citizens were waiting at the end, behind the door in the great courtyard, before the Lebanese cedar tree. For these people, there would be applause. There was music awaiting them, heralding the start of their new life. Pri didn't know if any of the citizens were aware of her presence. If that door at the end of this passage would unlock. If there was still a role for her. If they would mistake her for a maligned migrant, a dangerous stowaway. Pri was no longer weightless, she could reach the ceiling only if she made a point to jump, but she always returned to the ground, the grit painted into the flooring gripping onto the soles of her shoes. This artificial gravity was just a trick. The simplest of physics. She wiped away tears from each eye, now able to see the end of the corridor, a solid door. She could run—Pri could actually run—feeling the mass of her body pushing back against each flexing thigh, surprising her muscles.

Nayha once told her that she did not need to carry the burden of her father's actions. The next generation is absolved of their parents' sins, she had said, expressed with certainty, a definite diagnosis. They sipped wine while overlooking the cityscape at night, high up on the North Shore mountains, secure within the perimeter walls. Pri used to think of this as mere rationalizing. A self-serving argument tailored by those in privilege to defend that very privilege. Now, Nayha's comment felt like a cure. Pri slowed her pace, nervous that she might tumble over should she lose control of her momentum. She staggered, her breaths gasping, her head light, holding one hand out, letting her fingers slide along the smooth railing. Starved of food and sleep, she thought she might collapse onto the floor. The door was a simple white rectangle. A single lever with an arrow directing users to push down. Pri looked behind her—just to make sure—as if Hasan might have been following her all along. The passageway was empty. She could hear nothing through the door. As far as she knew, the entire Tevat was vacant. Pri slid her hands along the railing to the end, reaching over the lever. "My sins are not your sins by inheritance," Pri said aloud, to Poppy. She contained her breaths, forced her exhalations through pursed lips, listening to the rhythm.

Pri pushed down, releasing a crisp hiss of air, and waited, listening. Only her breaths. She glanced back once more. She turned and pushed the door open.

The ground before her feet changed from painted grit to umber paving stones, squares with diamonds in each corner, the air humid, floral. The ceiling was high above, an unbroken blue radiating warmth down to a plaza with dozens of people standing in a wide, sparse semicircle, Pri at the focus, each person wearing a facemask covering their nostrils, lips, and chins. The tall, sloping roof of City Hall framed the right of Pri's vision, towering panes of clear glass revealing the empty railings of mezzanines stacked eight stories high. To her left was the library, a stout structure with sharp corners, tessellated windows mimicking leaves. Pri stepped forward, still gripping the door, and the crowd of people remained motionless, a couple appearing to quiver back in retreat. Mustafa's prized Lebanese cedar tree rose above them all from behind, its platforms of branches and needles verdant and vibrant as if under an unseen spotlight. Someone clapped and then the entire group joined in, whistles muffled by the masks that obscured people's expressions. Pri let the door close behind her, nearly losing her footing and needing to reach back to hold onto the wall for support.

A woman stepped forward from the group, steps hesitant, hands gloved and clapping, her head nodding with black hair tied in behind her neck, eyes a dark hazel. She wore a turquoise smock down past her knees, boots on each foot. It was Yara Khalife, Pri knew, having watched hundreds of her recordings. Another man followed from behind, wide shoulders, face obscured with tinted goggles that pressed onto the facemask, then stepped aside to reveal his hands clasping a stout rifle, the barrel's opening a black square. The rest of the group remained in position, their applause now smattering as Yara gripped her own hands together by her chest, her pace slowing and coming to a halt far from Pri's reach. Yara's eyes turned up at the corners, her facemask elevated, and Pri assumed that she smiled. She surveyed Pri's figure, the tattered, oversized clothes.

"Priya Gosal?" Yara said, the husk in her voice unmistakable.

Pri nodded, her eyes bouncing from Yara's to the security officer to the hushed group watching from behind, people in shorts, sandals. She wanted to hug Yara. That was what happened. There should be music, several minutes of unbroken applause, people embracing the new citizens. That is what happens.

Pri shuffled forward a step and Yara inched back. The man with the rifle pulled it tight, held it up but not aimed in Pri's direction.

Yara said, "I'm sure you've had quite the journey to get here."

Pri could not say a single word.

Yara then held out one hand, a black glass screen in her hand. "Your thumb, please."

Pri needed to take a step forward and staggered, her hands reaching out for support before stabilizing, wishing the wall was in reach, unsure if she could stand more than a few seconds without collapsing. She pressed her thumb against the scanner in Yara's hand. The screen pulsed from magenta to yellow.

Yara nodded, withdrawing her hand, and taking a subtle bow. The security guard lowered his weapon. The small crowd of people in behind Yara loosened their postures, eyes glancing to one another, assured that they were safe, that this stranger would soon be family. That Pri was one of their own.

Acknowledgements

First and foremost, I want to thank my wife, Erin Bannister. For more than twenty years now, you've not only allowed me to escape to various coffee shops to write but also endured the typos and rambling run-on sentences in the early drafts of all my books. You're the reason I've managed to get all of this done. I truly can't thank you enough.

When it comes to discussing my writing, there's no one in this world with whom I feel more comfortable and open than Daniel Pitts. It was your idea to restructure the narrative of this novel in a way that improved its pacing, and I am always appreciative for your honest advice and opinions. I'm lucky to have such a great friend and writing partner—when our kids are older, we'll find the time to write something together once again.

I am extremely grateful to both Chris Street and Bohdan Nosyk for your editorial advice reading through different versions of this story as it evolved over the years. I've always been reserved when it comes to discussing my writing with friends, but your genuine passion for my work has shown me that it was never an imposition. Your thoughtful opinions on both the big ideas and tiny details have not only improved this novel but improved my writing.

I'd like to thank the people at Between the Lines Publishing, who have been willing to take a chance on a novel by some guy in Vancouver. It's been a long journey since my first attempt to get a manuscript published and finding a team of people who recognize the potential in my writing really has been a dream come true.

And finally, I'd like to extend my gratitude to coffee. You've been part of my writing journey longer than any human being. I understand that you're not the healthiest choice for my heart or my skeletal system, but I really don't think I could have written much more than a few pages without you. Cheers.

Rudolf Kerkhoven has been writing novels that range from serious to silly for far too many years now. He lives with his wife and two kids in the Vancouver area of British Columbia where he teaches secondary school mathematics—a pleasant sweet & salty contrast to his creative writing.

Also available from the author

The Year We Finally Solved Everything
A Dream Apart
Love is not free. The price is 99 cents.
The Most Boring Christmas Special Ever Written
How the World Ends

The Adventures of Whatley Tupper (with Daniel Pitts)
The Redemption of Mr. Sturlubok (with Daniel Pitts)
The Most Boring Book Ever Written (with Daniel Pitts)
Can Stuart Henry Zhang Save the World? (with Daniel Pitts)

Printed in the USA
CPSIA information can be obtained
at www.ICGtesting.com
CBHW011650090124
PP14787900003B/1